INSIDE THE FIRE

A NOVEL

By Bill Morris

Inside the Fire

First Edition

ISBN#: 978-0-692-25311-3

Author: Bill Morris

Edited by: Amanda Carter, Ann Eames

Cover Art: Tian Mulholand

Author Photograph: Brian Durban

Acknowledgements

This book has been many years in the making, and in that I have gained many debts to various people. Here are only some.

On the Fire Side: Rob Otto, Mike Powell, Neil Meyers (Engine 72!) Derek Casbon, Patrick Morgan, Chris Marks, Michael Boomer, Brit Rosso, and all of the 1998 Arrowhead Hotshots. And many others from whom I learned valuable skills for effectiveness, survival, and story.

On the Writing Side: Tree Kilpatrick, Jeff Rowe, Steve Howell, Natalie Pacholl, Jack and Amanda Carter, Mark Poe, Ann Price, Stella D'Oro, Grant Gerald Miller, Julie Wisdom, Tian Mulholand, Ann Eames, Bill and Betty Sue Morris.

The following is a work of fiction—any resemblance to persons or situations that exist or have existed in the past is purely coincidental.

INSIDE THE FIRE

Chapter One

April 7th, 2014

In July of 1998 I participated in the suppression effort of one of the worst tragedy fires in Western American history. I was there by luck, accident, and happenstance, and survived for very much the same reasons.

Since this event and the permanent changes it brought, I have struggled to make sense of what happened. Of course I know the general unfolding. But my dreams and memories concerning the entire incident simply became more and more aggressive as time went on. *Why and how* often haunt those who know the most. Eventually, after so many night terrors, I sought therapy. One suggestion I received was to keep a dream journal. This I did, and soon it led to me trying to pen all I remembered—in hopes that if I contained it on the page, I might also contain it within myself. I also assumed that I learned a lesson through the experience that I should share. I soon wanted to find details beyond my memory and perspective, and went to the fellow survivors, forming friendships that led to long nights of drinking and eventually inquiry about what they remembered as well as insights into the internal dynamics of hotshot crews and wildland firefighting in general.

The following is a reconstruction of the event. Much of the dialogue is exact, some comes from the general idea and an attempt of my own to piece together a cohesive narrative from slightly differing accounts. It comes from my own account, long discussions with the other survivors, and research I have done using archived information and formal government reports.

One final note: every summer thousands of young men and women risk life, limb, and skin to suppress the many forest fires of the west. Each of them may come to certain judgments regarding crew and individual behavior at the time before, during, and after the initial devastation. Even if you have never seen so much as a fireplace, you may form your own opinion. I simply ask that, whatever your verdict, be it culpable or exonerated, the sentence be light; thirst and tragedy cause confused decisions.

Thank you for reading *Inside The Fire*.

    --Jonathan Samuels

July 7th, 1998
12:10 AM

Skip Slammer hit his alarm clock several times before realizing the mechanical wail came from somewhere else. He sat up straight in bed for a moment as the siren died down, then turned on the light and got out of bed. He was going to a fire.

He quickly located a pair of green pants, slid into them, and put on a blue t-shirt that had a small emblem of an American buffalo and the words "Bison Hotshots" embroidered on the left side. A can of tobacco lay on the nightstand, and he grabbed a pinch from it before lacing up his boots. He was not in a rush. After ten years on a hotshot crew, he understood that fighting a large forest fire was not battle but war; endurance and pacing were much more important than speed. Besides, for the next hour and a half his duties would be strictly administrative.

He picked up his hard hat and looked at the small label in front stating his name and position: S. Slammer—Foreman. After one month, it was still a thrill to see the title next to his name.

He held the hard hat under his arm and placed the can of tobacco in his pocket. Browsing over the set of books in his small cabin, he spotted the book he wanted to read during all the inevitable downtime: *Zen and the Art of Motorcycle Maintenance*. Book in hand, he walked through the forest of ancient sequoia trees toward the office to find out where the crew was being dispatched. Since they were based in California, it was most likely a Southern California brush fire, but it could easily be a pinion and juniper pine fire in Arizona, a timber fire in the Northwest, a tundra fire in Alaska, or even a lava fire in Hawaii. Wherever it was, the crew had to convene at the base and be on its way within two hours, which concerned Skip. It was Friday night. Most of the boys were down in the city getting drunk.

There was an agreement between all hotshot crews and the National Interagency Fire Center—the agency located in Boise that was responsible for coordinating and dispatching all national firefighting resources—that hotshots could be on their way to anywhere in the country within two hours notice, twenty-four hours a day, seven days a week. There was no compensation for this on-call demand, however, so other than the eight hours a day spent doing project work like building fences, chopping wood, trail upkeep, and equipment maintenance, crewmembers could do anything they wanted—just as long as it was done within two hours of their base.

Skip opened the door to the small office and saw the crew superintendent leaning against his desk while talking on the phone. Bruce Martinson looked the part of a leader: he was in his late thirties, with a square face, cropped black hair showing its first signs of gray, thick arms, and broad shoulders. Yet he had a strange slouch for a man with such a commanding physical presence.

Bruce turned to Skip. "Looks like we got a good one," he said, as he handed Skip a piece of paper that had the fire location on it.

Skip nodded. Not bad.

Skip went back outside and looked at the whiteboard that listed everyone's name and location. Twelve crewmembers were in the city; seven were in station.

A group of men straggled through the darkness to Skip, wearing their green pants and crew sweatshirts. They looked tired.

"What's the deal, Skip?" asked Marcus Hellman, an eight-year veteran of the crew. His eyes were bleary, but they still carried the intensity that his rather round face could not temper. The expression underneath the slightly chubby cheeks was determined as stone, and the lines on his skin creased knowingly around this underlying hardness.

"We'll be heading out in two hours—or as soon as we get everyone back. Just plan on being at the rigs in an hour and a half, and be ready in your cabins in case everyone gets here sooner," said Skip.

"Well, where are we going?" the veteran demanded. His large size, experience, and reputation could often override typical crew protocol, which called for regular crewmembers to not mine overhead for too much information.

"Washington."

"We flying?" asked a rookie, his excitement also overcoming crew etiquette.

"Tell you more as we know it," said Skip.

"Well, um, Richardson's real sick—I don't think he'll make it," the rookie said diffidently, not wanting to break bad news.

"What?" Skip asked.

"That fever he had today during work has just gotten worse. He went right to bed after dinner. Didn't say a word. He looks real bad."

Skip shook his head. The crew suffered colds and flu as a unit. Their constant proximity always ensured another victim. This one had been creeping from member to member for almost three weeks. He walked off to see the man.

12:25 AM

"There's no way Richardson's going to make it," Skip said to Bruce as he walked back into the office. "His temperature is 103. In fact, we should probably get Leslie up here to watch over him after we leave," he said, referring to the crew cook.

"Yeah, all right. That puts us down to eighteen. We can still accept the dispatch if we get everyone else back. But I have bad news. Looks like we're going to a tragedy fire."

"Who?"

"Don't know. Local Washington DNR guys. Two of them. Boys, eighteen and nineteen. Got caught in the grass. Boise didn't have any more details."

Skip visualized a wave of fire moving quickly through the grass, as it often does if there is drought and wind. The boys struggling to get away...

There would be more cameras, more press, more politics. The stark reminder of their occupational hazards might make everyone more safety conscious, but emotions would run high; the younger firefighters might feel they had a vendetta. The situation was becoming more dangerous.

"Boise is going to fly us there," Bruce finally said. "We'll meet up with three other shot crews at the airport in four hours. Two hours to get there, so we need everyone in the rigs in an hour and a half."

"The page went out twenty minutes ago," Bruce continued. "Here's a crew roster. I put a check by everyone who called in and is on their way up."

Skip took the list from the Superintendent's hand and looked at it. There were three names without checks by them: Edgar Rollingson, Steve Andersen, and Michael Miller. Skip looked at the last name.

"Shit, Mike is in town."

1:00 AM

Sipping his sixth whiskey and soda, Edgar Rollingson sat on a bar stool and wondered what the hell he was doing in a place called The Wooden Pecker. The women wore too much makeup and clearly wanted men who drove big trucks and talked football. His beat-up Volvo would never suffice and neither would his ideas on current world events or literature. Even his wiry build didn't fit in—apparently you needed to carry forty extra pounds in either your stomach, your chest, or your mullet just to get through the door and enjoy the smell of urinal pucks and yesterday's beer.

He scanned the bar, taking note of all the promotional mirrors with beer logos etched in them, which covered the walls, and the peanut shells that covered the cement floor. Eventually his eyes caught Steve Andersen, a fellow crewmember, talking to a cute twenty-something girl in tight jeans and a cowboy hat. Steve was smoking a cigarette, and by his wild gestures he was apparently bragging about something. Edgar noted the way the girl's tank top hugged her perky body and the glimmer of interest that ornamented her otherwise vacant eyes. He wished for a moment that he could display the same shameless bravado as his fellow crewmember.

He turned his attention to Mike, who was chatting up strangers and taking a shot of whiskey. It appeared that he was trying to gain access to a mixed group of friends in order to talk with one of the women. With his blunt nose and broad face, Mike's looks were not an asset, and his advances were often rebuffed. But this did not inhibit him. He went after women like he went after his work. He brushed difficulty and hardship aside, always landed on his feet, and moved forward until he found success. Because of this, he enjoyed the company of many women.

Above the clanging sound of the band and the talk of the crowd, Edgar thought he heard a high-pitched ring. It was probably feedback generated by the lousy guitar, but he reluctantly pulled out his beeper for the fifth time that night to check if it was ringing. This time it was an actual fire call. The other men had left their pagers in the car, so he waved down Steve and showed him the pager, giving him a thumbs-up. Steve clenched his fist in a display of excitement and gave his toothy grin. Edgar motioned that he was going to get Mike. He'd meet Steve by the car.

As Edgar walked toward the table to get his crewmember and saw partner, Mike swung his fist into a man's face and knocked him to the ground.

Shit.

Edgar bolted across the bar as Mike's entire table erupted into a fight, which soon spread through the whole bar. A fist grazed Edgar's brow. Moving so quickly he surprised himself, he grabbed the offender by the collar with one hand and swung his elbow towards the man's face. As he came around, the man's devious grin melted into shock and fear, and Edgar stopped his elbow before it hit the bridge of the man's nose. The man was short and pudgy, wearing a bandana and an ill-fitting cowboy shirt. Edgar shoved him out of site. He pushed his way to his drunken partner and dragged him out of the bar, dodging punches along the way.

When Edgar and Mike arrived at the car, Steve was getting the girl's number. He boldly moved toward her, gave her a kiss, and slid his hand along the side of her breast. She giggled, told him to call when he got back from saving the world, then slipped away and returned to the bar.

"Ah, you dumb asses should learn about that kind of goddamn bar," Edgar said, rubbing the sore spot over his eye where the fat man's punch had grazed him.

"What are you talking about?" Steve asked. "I think you dumb asses should learn that you get laid by talking with chicks, not by fighting with dudes."

"Point taken," Edgar said. "Now explain that to him," he said pointing to Mike, who leaned against the car looking at the pavement and grinning aloofly. He cradled his hand.

10

"You okay?" Edgar asked.

"Yeah, yeah, I'm fine," Mike said.

"What the hell was that all about?" Edgar asked.

"Ah, it was just a Chevy versus Ford thing."

"Great," Edgar said.

A security guard ran out of the building, apparently looking for whoever had started the brawl.

"Let's get out here," Edgar whispered.

The men crawled into Edgar's car and drove off.

Edgar looked closely at the pager under the cabin light of his car and realized that it was not the first page, but the second—the men had already lost forty-five minutes of the two hours they had to get back to base. The drive back usually took just under two hours.

The men stopped at a payphone so Edgar could call the dispatcher and tell her three men were on their way, but didn't mention from what location. He noticed that he had to focus on every syllable in order to speak straight.

"So where's it at?" Steve asked from the back seat when Edgar returned.

"I don't know, she didn't tell me. But if we don't hurry up and get our asses there it's all over."

11

"Montana was burning this morning on CNN!" Steve said.

"Yeah, right. We'll be going back to the LP, I promise. And why not? I still haven't gotten rid of my poison oak, so why not get another dose," Edgar said, scratching his arms before turning the key.

"Ah, we're due for an out-of-state dispatch. You watch," Steve said.

The yellow line kept blurring and doubling as Edgar drove down the city streets, and he became self-conscious about the time it took to move his foot from the brake to the accelerator when a red light turned green. The men in the car wouldn't let him concentrate. They continued to speculate about where they were going. Then Mike started mumbling about giving the man another punch while Steve stuck his head in between the two front seats and waxed on about some sexual adventure. It had been some festival in Colima, Mexico. She had been hot, of course, and Mexican of course. She had on one of those Mexican blouses, white, that are shoulderless and ride the bosom just so, and a long colorful skirt. Her hair was up. He had ended up behind some church. Kissing her. Pulled up her skirt. "Own me now, Guapo" she had said in broken English. And he did, right against the church wall. That is until her husband came out with a machete.

Finally they were out of the city, the road opened up into the surrounding farmland, and Steve's story ended with him getting away with all but a terrible case of blue balls. The muggy air and dank smell of agriculture surrounding Fresno gave way to the crisper air of higher elevation. Edgar turned up the music, accelerated to eighty miles an hour, and felt the familiar thrill that had drawn him back to this job over the last three years. They were off to almost anywhere—what scenery, what state, what town, what plane, what hotel or what tent was all a mystery. It was more intoxicating than the alcohol coursing through his veins. When he smelled chinquapin he knew he was only twenty minutes from the station.

A police car suddenly began to tail him, its headlights flooding the compartment.

He slowed down.

"Shit, a cop," Edgar said.

"Be cool!" Steve said.

Edgar became concerned with his driving again. He focused as hard as he could to keep the car in between the white line on the shoulder and the yellow line in the middle, but his car swayed despite his effort. He became more and more nervous, and he thought of just pulling over in hope that the cop car would pass by, or at least to get the confrontation over with. He figured he might get away with a stick of gum and a story about a fire dispatch, but he remembered the beer Steve had spilled on the way down. It still stood half full in the cup holder in the seat, and the cop would certainly smell it if not see it.

The police car nudged closer behind him, then backed off before the blue and red lights began swirling.

1:45 AM

Skip sat in the truck next to the superintendent and counted the minutes. They would need to leave in a quarter hour to make their ETA at the airport. Bruce couldn't leave without the men, but if they couldn't make their ETA, he would have to call Boise and explain the situation, which would embarrass the entire crew. Boise would likely say disregard the dispatch—they'd find someone who could get there on time. Skip could feel Bruce's rising anger as he thought about this possibility—a piece of the crew's reputation was on the line.

Skip got out of the truck and went over to the rigs where the crewmembers had gathered. Even though he knew everything that could be done was done, he wanted to tell the squad bosses to make sure everything was completely ready.

The crewmembers were gathered around the rigs sharing their contempt for the men currently jeopardizing their fire call. They kept looking at their watches.

"Aren't they wearing their fucking pagers?"

"What are they, deaf?"

"Maybe they weren't even in the city. Maybe they were somewhere farther away, out of the two hour range."

"Wouldn't surprise me."

"What time is it?"

"1:50."

"Shit, ten more minutes."

"Okay, give me a stick of your gum. I'll take care of this," Steve said to Edgar while they were waiting for the officer to come up to the car.

"Fuck that, we're in enough trouble as it is," Edgar said.

Steve stretched up to the dashboard and grabbed a piece of gum from the pack; then he was out the door.

"Fuck, what are you doing you idiot, come back—fuck!" Edgar said as Steve shut the door and approached the police car.

A voice through the police car speaker immediately told him to get back in his vehicle. Steve raised his hands in the air and continued walking toward the officer's car. The officer got out of the car and started to yell, but soon the two men were conversing.

Steve shook hands with the man and came back to Edgar's car, his drunken sway visible in his silhouette.

"Looks like I just got us a police escort! Let's go!"

"What the hell did you tell him?"

"Oh just some bullshit about us going to a CDF fire that was about to burn some houses down at Quail Run. And what a hit! Turns out his cousin lives in that suburb." Steve let out his signature high-pitched laugh.

"Dumb luck. I can't decide whether I want to hit you or kiss you," Edgar said.

"I get that a lot."

1:58 AM

The men all turned and looked in the direction of the oncoming clank of an old car. Two headlights appeared around the bend of the small mountain road that led to the crew's compound. Skip confirmed that it was indeed Edgar's car, but his relief was squelched by the blue and red lights behind it. He was sure that he was going to watch the men get a DUI right in front of everyone, but as Edgar's car slowed into a parking space, the police car simply continued to loop around. The blue and red lights ceased, and the patrol car drove off.

Steve Anderson shot out of the car, hooting and saying he was the man. The crewmembers gathered at the back of the rigs started to yell at the men to hurry up and get in their Nomex, but Steve stumbled around in a disjointed victory dance and continued to yell out words of self-adoration.

Bruce got out of the truck.

"We're going to Washington in five minutes. If you gentlemen would care to join us, we'd appreciate it if you'd hurry the fuck up!"

The yell of their usually cool superintendent sobered the men, and they ran up the hill towards their cabins to change.

The three men returned to the crew carriers within five minutes. A crewman started giving Mike a bad time for not having his crew t-shirt tucked in. Someone pointed out that his pants weren't fully zipped up either.

"What the fuck is wrong with your hand?" asked Grump, one of the two squad bosses.

"Nothing, nothing," Mike said, shielding his hand.

"It's not nothing! Look at it," demanded Grump. He pointed to the large swollen lump protruding from the top of Mike's hand. "Your hand is broken and you're too goddamn drunk and stubborn to admit it. Fuck!"

"I can still work," Mike replied.

"How are you going to run saw when you can't even zip up your goddamn pants?" Grump roared.

"Duct tape?" Mike suggested.

Sick of the wit, Grump laid down the verdict. "There's no way you can go to this fire!"

Everyone looked at Skip.

"Goddamn it, Mike," Skip whispered. He ran back to the superintendent's truck, informed Bruce, and then ran up to office to call the park's main office for a fill in.

"What the fuck happened, Edgar?" the squad boss demanded.

"Hey, I didn't do a goddamn thing – don't look at me. I'm not his babysitter," Edgar said.

"Fuck. Get in the rigs," Grump said.

"What if the Park can't find us a scab?" one of the rookies asked.

"Get in the rig!" Grump demanded.

A few minutes later, as the men waited in the rigs, Skip came back out of the office. He circled his hand in the air to indicate they were about to roll.

"So we're getting a detailer?" Edgar asked.

"Yes," Grump said, obviously frustrated.

A young rookie stared at Edgar, his eyes wide open after hearing the man's slurred speech and redundant question.

"Jesus, you're really drunk."

"Fuck off," Edgar said.

Edgar closed his eyes and told himself not to worry about what the others were thinking. He had made it back to base, hadn't he? The young rookie had no idea how things worked. Edgar was a third-year veteran; he knew. They were going to Washington, and they might have been told to be at the airport in two hours, but that sure as hell didn't mean the plane was going to be there in two hours. He was a veteran—three years; he knew. They would go to the airport, shiver in the night air until it turned morning, and no plane would come. They'd sit out on the tarmac and sweat as the sun rose. Hydrate and dehydrate—still no plane would come. And the sun would get higher and higher, hotter and hotter. A rumor would start: the plane wasn't coming; they were already being released. People would speculate, gossip, play hacky sack, and spit tobacco. And just as it seemed they were doomed to return to the station and the doldrums of project work, the rumble of a plane engine would grumble through the air. Bruce would command them to line up, and finally they'd be on their way—drinking warm lemonade on some sweltering Boise-Cascade 767 with no air-conditioning. He was a veteran—three years; he knew.

The rig started lumbering down the winding mountain road.

2:15 AM

I threw the covers over me and off me for the thirteenth time in so many minutes. I opened my eyes again, stared up at the wall and then at the clock. Five more hours until I had to go to work. Five years of a lackadaisical college schedule studying botany had left me unprepared for the unjust and cruel demands of a regular job, particularly the early mornings. Every time the seven o'clock alarm rang, a sense of outrage and hatred surged through me, and it wasn't long until it wreaked havoc on my sleeping schedule.

However, I suffered not from a lack of sleep, but a glut of it. After sneaking in naps during extended lunch hours and going to bed right after dinner, I typically woke up at two and awaited seven with dread. I used this "insomnia" as an excuse for chronically arriving late to work.

I reached for the lamp and clicked it off, happy to see the collage of unclean clothes on the floor disappear into darkness.

Just as it seemed a dream would overtake me, there was a knock on the door.

"Open up, Jonathan. We got a fire call for you!"

"Fire!" I yelled as I jumped out of bed.

"It's me, Stewart," said the voice on the other side of the door. "You got a fire call."

It was my boss, Stewart Jackson. I crossed the room, tripped over the clothes, and then opened the door. The realization of what was probably happening made my heart pound faster.

During a hot summer, there can be over fifty large-area fires burning throughout the country at once. One twenty-five thousand acre fire can require more than one thousand people to extinguish. In order to deal with this massive need for people, agencies responsible for controlling wildfire, such as the Forest Service, Park Service, and Bureau of Land Management, train a large percentage of their workforce to fight fire. These employees, whether they are foresters, computer technicians, administrators, or botanists, are then called to the fire line when needed.

At the start of the summer, Stewart had asked me to take the one-week basic fire-training course that would give me my "red card." This would allow me to work on fires in the simplest capacity— swinging a shovel and taking orders on a Type II crew. This sounded glamorous, and I gladly accepted. I knew there was money to be made from the massive overtime fires offered. I also knew that Type II crews were rarely put in dangerous circumstances. Many veterans of the Park Service seemed to see it as a paid vacation. I also figured it might help my dating resume.

At fire school I managed to keep my sleep schedule intact. I slept through most of the morning lectures, daydreamed through the afternoon, and focused most of my mental energy on a cute, dark-skinned hippie brunette to whom I never gathered the courage to speak more than a few awkward words.

I had chosen botany because I had an excellent short-term memory and could quickly remember plant names. I utilized this talent for the fire-training tests and passed without understanding the concepts whatsoever.

I turned on the light and let Stewart in the door. I was mildly embarrassed about the state of my small cabin, but Stewart's appearance was hardly an example of discipline: green park pants and a pajama shirt, thinning hair twisting in all directions. Besides, in the three weeks I had worked at the Park, I quickly realized that Stewart and I had a certain mutual understanding about the world, namely that it was all bullshit, including one's self-image.

"Ready to fight some fire?" Stewart asked.

"Heck yeah!"

"Well, we got one hell of an assignment for you."

"What is it?"

"Normally we would never do this, but see, the Park resources are spread real thin. All of our normal fire folks are committed to fires already."

"Yeah..."

"Well, the hotshots are a man short, and they just got an assignment. If they want to take it, they're going to have to pick up a fill-in—a detailer—to meet the eighteen-man requirement."

"Yeah."

"Well, you're the one! If you accept the assignment, that is."

"No way! The hotshots?"

Since Type II crews were often comprised of people whose primary jobs were not fire, they were usually assigned to less active fires that posed little threat to anyone.

The hotshots, on the other hand, were a specialized crew of professionals. They were put in the hardest parts of the biggest fires. At fire training the instructors referred to the hotshots or "shot" crews as if they were some mythical elite force of invulnerable heroes with an unquenchable work ethic.

The park where I worked housed one of the finest hotshot crews, but they didn't spend much time there—they were almost always traveling across the nation from one fire to the next. I did catch a glimpse of them during the first week of the summer, though, while they were in training.

I was taking one of my "breaks," sleeping next to a tree, when I heard the commotion of their group. I looked up through the trees and the fog and saw them running in a line up the trail through the forest. All in their blue crew t-shirts and sunglasses, they looked like some special paramilitary force. They ran smoothly in pace with one another up the hill that I hadn't been able to walk up without taking numerous breaks. As they drew near, I saw their determined sneers, the stoic expression of men with something important to do. Beads of sweat formed on their brows as they plowed up the hill with a rugged grace, breathing deeply but not desperately. I shrank, embarrassed to be doing nothing.

However, by the end of fire school and all of the talk about the glorious "hotshots," I was beginning to develop a chip on my shoulder against them. This turned to open resentment when, at the end of the week, the cute hippie girl was picked up by a hotshot with a charming smile who absconded with her in his truck.

Probably just a lot of hype, I thought to myself, as I saw them drive off. I could hang if I put my mind to it.

"Well?" Stewart said, waiting for an answer. I thought about how the hotshots had moved up the grade, each of them running steadily, with only pedestrian signs of exertion. I was out of shape.

"What about Jamey? She's got a red card and has lots of fire experience," I said.

"Jamey doesn't want to go out onto the fire line now that she has a baby," Stewart replied. "There's no way we'll get her to go. You're the one, buddy!"

You're the one. I liked the sound of it. And I'd be a fool to turn down the opportunity—and the money. Besides, what a thing to tell people I did...

"All right, I'll do it!"

"Okay, good to hear. Now there's lots of stuff burning out there, so you'll probably be out for twenty-one days before they bring you guys back for a rest," Stewart said.

"Three weeks, huh?"

"Yep. You get dressed, and I'll go tell them you're coming down. They're waiting in their rigs down at the parking lot right now."

"They're here now?" I nervously scanned my messy room. My red bag was suppose to have my fire-resistant Nomex shirt and pants ready to go as well as all other necessities for three weeks away from home. My stomach sank as I spotted the bag lying on the floor with its contents strewn amongst the mess of dirty and wrinkled clothes that covered the floor. I had dug through it for a clean t-shirt two days earlier.

"Yep! And they got a plane to Washington to catch, so you better hurry.

"These boys are hard workers, Jonathan," Stewart continued. "Most of them have years of experience in fire. I want you to show them that the folks in botany have a work ethic, too. Show them what you can do. Show them that we can be as tough as any hotshot!"

"You got it, Stewart!" I said, trying to sound more confident than I felt.

"All right, I'll go tell them you'll be out in a just a minute," Stewart said as he turned to go. He exited the door in a march, pepped up by his own speech.

I turned and looked in the mirror across the room. I puffed out my chest, and for a moment my belly disappeared and my shoulders looked almost broad. But my round, seamless, shaven face still looked too untouched to play the part. I patted down my sandy brown hair and started to pack.

"Yeah, I'm going to work like hell, hike like hell," I said to myself. "I'm going to show these boys what I can do!"

But my superficial confidence was soon displaced by worry as I fumbled through the ground cover of clothes. I couldn't find my Nomex shirt.

"Come on! Come on!" I said to the room, as I grew more desperate.

I started to envision the stoic men growing impatient and asking things like, "Why the hell is he taking so long! Is he packing his make-up and hairdryer?"

Socks, pants, shorts, and t-shirts went flying into the air as I dug spastically through the dirty clothes hamper. I gave up for a moment and fixed on other items, grabbing a toothbrush, deodorant, dental floss, and an inflatable pillow. I returned to looking for the shirt but found nothing. Still hearing a litany of phantom insults from the waiting crew, I decided to bank on them having a spare shirt. I zipped up the bag in a rush, and a pair of underwear caught deeply in the zipper.

"Fucking great!" I yelled out. I tugged on the zipper so hard I broke a sweat. Then I gave up and ran out of the cabin with the underwear still hanging from my bag.

In the parking lot I saw the white four-by-four Chevy truck marked with a "Superintendent A" decal. Behind it were two green crew carriers, which looked similar to moving trucks with tinted windows along the side. As I ran down the dirt path, I caught an exposed root and sailed into the air. The bag flew out of my hand and, and as I skidded to a stop, it landed on my head. Laughter burst from the rigs.

I got up, dusted myself off, and walked slowly towards the superintendent's truck, where I was then told to go to the rig marked A-1.

"Hey, I'm Ben, your squad boss," said the man in the front passenger's seat as he rolled down the front window and stuck out his arm. It was the guy I had seen drive off with the girl from fire school. Now he was my boss.

"You can call me Grump," he said. "Go ahead and put your stuff up top so we can get out of here."

"Up top?"

"Yeah, the rigs have compartments up top, where we keep all our red bags. You might want to get that underwear out of the zipper, though. Doesn't look too good," he said with a wink.

More laughter from inside the rigs.

I climbed up the ladder connected to the truck and shimmied along the rail that made the upper compartments accessible. I found the latch and pulled on it but it wouldn't budge. I've always had bad luck with latches, zippers, or anything that was suppose to *work* for that matter.

"What the hell is going on up there?" I heard from inside the rig.

I tugged harder and harder, but still nothing. With one final effort the latch gave way at once, causing my hand to smack the side of the compartment. I yelped in pain.

"God, this guy must be the biggest tool ever!" said the same angry voice. "Why is it whenever we get a Taylor, he ends up being a total tool?"

"Give the guy a break, Nobsac. Maybe he'll turn out all right," said another voice.

I stuffed the bag in the compartment and climbed down the rig. I found the door to the seats in the back and opened it to meet the most menacing group of faces I'd ever seen. There were six of them—five men and one woman, all in their mid-to-late twenties. They stared at me silently.

The woman pointed to an empty seat for me to sit.

"Thanks, I'm Jonathan," I said, trying to be friendly.

She smiled sympathetically. "Nice to meet you, Taylor. I'm Cynthia," she said.

"Um...Jonathan." I said, thinking she had misheard my name.

"I heard you, Taylor. Your hard hat is up above you on the rack," she said.

"Thanks," I said, confused as to why she called me Taylor twice. I sensed she wanted me to look at the hard hat, so I pulled it down from the rack and examined its blue plastic shell. Just above the rim, where the name of the firefighter was placed was a tag that read, "D. Taylor."

So that would be my name for the next three weeks...

The door slammed shut and someone yelled "Chalks Up!" The rig jolted forward, driving off with me, D. Taylor, feeling the great unease of a new prisoner.

Chapter Two

July 9th, 1998
2:21 PM

I stood up straight from the crouched position I
had to take to swing my tool and stretched my
aching back, hoping to relieve the spasm I had
developed after working sixteen hours the day
before and sleeping on the ground that night. I
took off a glove and examined my hand; the palm
was covered with blisters. It looked like scabbed
squid skin taken straight from the deep.

I looked up the spine of the ridge and watched the
line of six men and two women who were working
ahead of me. They moved in unison, building an
eighteen-inch trail of mineral soil using shovels
and Pulaskis. (A Pulaski is a hybrid tool with an axe
blade on one side and a hoe end on the other.) The
clank of steel against rock and the occasional grunt
rising above their breath reminded me of a
southern chain gang. They all wore green Nomex

pants and filthy yellow Nomex shirts with the sleeves rolled up to their elbows. Whether men or women, stocky or skinny, daily manual labor and physical conditioning gave them all powerful forearms and lateral muscles that flared down the sides of their torsos from under their shirts. I had rolled up my sleeves and loosened my tucked in shirt in hopes of hiding my gut and emulating this brawny look, but it was futile. Hours spent in front of the TV while eating potato chips could not be undone so easily.

In front of the scrapers, the sawyers cut a twenty-foot wide swath through the juvenile trees. The rest of the crew dug line through the cleared area. I couldn't see all eight sawyers because they were too deep in the brush, but I could hear their saw engines whine and growl, breaking all the serenity typically associated with working outside. They worked in teams of two: one cut the trees and shrubs while the other "swamped" by moving the cut vegetation off of the developing line. They intermittently switched roles so each got equal time cutting.

I looked to the south, past the large valley below me. The far slope was covered with mature timber, and there was a high butte towards its top that formed what looked to be a granite plateau. Behind this slope smoke rose slowly, like a series of lingering ghosts. This was the closest I had come to seeing actual flames over the last two days. Mainly I had seen dirt. I was coming to think that these men should be referred to as "dirtmen," instead of firemen. It wasn't fire, or even water, but dirt that was their most cherished element. They slept in it, covered themselves in it, and dug for it feverishly, through timber, brush, grass, or weed.

They had even christened me with it.

On the morning of my first day on the fire line, while I watched crewmembers unpack their chainsaws, shovels, and fuel from the rigs, a man carrying a saw over his shoulder ambled up to me, coming confrontationally close. The sawyer's face was round and covered with stubble, and his lower lip bulged with a tremendous wad of tobacco, making his mouth look herniated. He looked me over without a word. Then he picked up a handful of dirt from the logging road, studied me like a painter about to attack a canvas, and rubbed dirt all over my shirt as I stood dumbfounded. He even put a pat of it on my hard hat, which ran down over the hard plastic and underneath my collar.

He stepped back and critically evaluated his work.

"It's a start, I guess," the man said. He spit on my boot, turned, and joined the forming line of men.

I recovered and started to dust off my shirt, annoyed. But then I looked up and noted the man's shirt; dirt and grease coated almost all of the original yellow fabric. The few remaining patches of color were decorated with salt stain mosaics, left from heavy sweating. I noticed that all of the sawyers' shirts were in such states, and the scrapers' shirts fared little better. I realized that the sawyer had done me, in his eyes, a favor. My bright neon yellow shirt screamed "new guy."

"Taylor! Get back to work!" Rob barked behind me.

Rob had been appointed my partner after his regular buddy had been shifted on to saw to fill Mike's spot. Rob was none too happy about what he clearly felt was a baby-sitting gig. And he let his anger be known—to me and everyone else. He was six foot one and all muscle, so I didn't protest.

"And don't just swing your tool blindly—use it to move stuff!" he continued.

"Okay..." I said, and started to pay more attention to the way I swung and dragged my tool.

"Hey, can I ask you something?" I asked.

"What."

"Well, if the fire is on the other side of the ridge, why are we digging line way over here? Why don't we go fight it where it is?"

"Didn't you go to fire school?" Rob demanded, while continuing to work on his dig.

"Well, I did, but..." I remembered the constant looks I would sneak at the hippy girl while the lecturer yammered on. "I guess I forgot that part."

"It's pretty basic to what we do, Taylor," Rob said, still scratching at the ground with his tool.

"Yeah, sorry..."

Rob grumbled. "You should know this," he blurted, more to himself than to me, then stood up and mustered the patience to explain.

"The fire is on the other side of the ridge, right?" he asked.

"Right," I said.

"Okay. Well today we're expecting an east wind and low humidity, which means we can expect the fire is going to be active. It's also burning in timber, where fuel loads are high. So do you think since we have dry conditions, plenty of wind, and plenty of fuel, this fire going to have big flames or small ones?" Rob asked.

"Big, I guess."

"Right. So I bet you and I can agree that working next to flames that could be twenty-plus feet high might be kind of...unhealthy, right?"

"Yeah."

"So what we've done is pulled back an entire ridgeline and put our line in here," he said, motioning to the line we were digging.

"I see."

"Now we're on the top of a ridgeline, so when the fire comes at us, what direction is it going to be coming from?"

"Well, coming up the valley, I guess," I said.

"That's right. It'll burn over that ridge, down into this valley here, and then up the hill towards our line. Then our line—as is—will stop it, right?"

"Uh, I guess," I said.

"No, Jesus! Did you sleep through fire school or what?" he said, kicking his foot in the ground, almost as if stomping in protest.

I did, but I wasn't about to admit it.

"Unless wind is a factor, fire moves faster uphill," Rob said. "You think an eighteen-inch-wide line of mineral soil surrounded by a twenty-foot-wide saw cut would stop flames that could likely be twenty feet long? Not to mention all the hot embers that could start spot fires out in front of them?" Rob yelled.

"No, I guess not."

He took a deep breath and went on. "That's right, so this line isn't made to stop the wildfire; it's made to stop our backburn. See, after we get this in, we'll start burning strips off of it. That'll remove the fuel next to our line and, in effect, make our line wider. Once we have the line widened to our liking, they might even bring in a terra torch—

which is this flame-thrower like thing that's attached to a helicopter—and burn out this whole valley. It's called 'indirect line.'"

"Ah, yeah. I remember that."

"At least that's the idea," Rob continued. "The fire moved faster last night than Incident Command expected when they made up the plan. When we got out here and Bruce saw exactly how close it was to us, and considered the predicted weather, he figured we had about a twenty-percent chance of getting it all done in time. We'll be lucky if we get it today. Probably this line is going to get blown over by the fire before we can safely get the burn done, and we'll be fighting this flank of the fire somewhere else."

"You mean we're doing all this work for nothing? Why don't they change the plans? Why waste our energy?" I complained.

"The gears of bureaucracy don't move that fast. We've got our objectives, and we do the best we can. That's our job. That's what it's all about. Besides, twenty-percent chance isn't bad. There're houses in the draw north of here. If we don't stop this thing today, the fire will get in striking range of them in no time. So we're going to do all we can to stop it now and keep those houses safe. If the winds don't get too severe, we might just get the backfiring operation done in time. If we don't, well then we'll have to let her go and hike on out of here. Could be worse. Wait till you work all night putting in line only to see it bulldozed over in the morning."

"How will we know when its time to hike out if we can't get the line and backfire done?" I asked.

"That's the foreman's and superintendent's job," Rob said curtly. "So, now that you got all that, get back to work."

I went back to dragging my tool across the ground.

Soon after, the man I knew as the saw boss walked down the line we were cutting. He was compact in stature, and his handlebar mustache, weathered face, and beady eyes reminded me of a nineteenth-century logger. He also appeared to be a decade or so older than most of the men. His short legs moved over the newly plowed dirt with a sort of busy intention. He carefully avoided the scrapers and their work, but his eyes continually looked nervously past us, to something farther away.

Eventually he passed us and arrived at the object on his mind. It was a large dead tree. The diameter of the tree compared to its height indicated that it had lost much of its top and many of its limbs. Its needles had long since fallen, and so had the bark, so the tree was smooth and pale, looking almost naked. A thick, fifteen-foot-long branch appearing to weigh at least one hundred pounds had broken off from the trunk and now hung in the few remaining limbs.

The saw boss looked the tree up and down while circling its trunk, sizing it up as if it were an adversary. He took out a small hand axe from his backpack and knocked the blunt end against the tree, watching the dead branch shake slightly. He placed his ear near the trunk and whacked the blunt end against the wood several more times. He shook his head. He then walked farther down the line, until he was twenty feet away from the tree, turned, and looked it up and down again. Finally he walked back up the line until Grump met up with him a few feet away from me.

"What do you say, Eric?" Grump asked.

"Ah, she's a bitch of a snag. Rotten through the middle, hollow as pipe, and that widow-maker up there's just waiting for someone's head."

"Do we drop it?"

"If I had my druthers I'd blow the bitch to kingdom come."

"Well, you know we can get a dynamiter ..."

"The fire will be to Canada by then."

"True."

"But she's got to come down, or fire will climb right up her. She'll send out more embers than a cheap roman candle."

"Well, you're the guy that's got to drop it. It's a C class tree for sure." referring to the largest and typically most dangerous type of tree.

The sawyer walked back to the tree and pounded his axe against it again. He shook his head, then paused in thought.

"It's not a C class, It's a D class."

"D class?"

"D as in Dumb to Even Try,"

"Ah. Or D as in Dumb Joke."

The saw boss looked blankly at Grump for a minute, absorbing the oblique chide.

"It's not nice to make fun of a guy who is about to die," he finally said, spitting some tobacco laden saliva on the ground.

"You're right, I'm sorry."

"All right," he finally yelled to Grump. "I'll get Blast up here and we'll take her down."

A few minutes later a short, muscular man came marching down the line with a saw thrown over his shoulder. Blast moved efficiently and precisely, like an Olympic gymnast—as if every step of the foot and sway of the arm were drenched with purpose. His mere presence made scrapers scatter from their work as he marched through the line with minimal acknowledgment of their efforts. I was struck by a vision of him breaking my neck without enough effort to sweat.

Blast talked briefly with the saw boss and Grump. Then after a nod between them all, Blast produced a particularly long saw blade from his backpack, sat on the ground, and replaced the smaller brush blade. Soon we were told to stop working, clear the line, and to get out of the way.

The saw boss yelled, "Coming on!" and pulled the start chord to his saw. It grumbled at idle as he approached the dead tree. Blast came up right behind the saw boss, placed his hand on the sawyer's back and bent his neck so that he could look straight up at the large dead branch pointing at him. The grumble of the engine whined into a scream, and small woodchips whizzed from the saw blade as it cut the tree.

The sawyer moved the blade in slowly, making sure the first cut was straight. Once the saw was a third of the way through the diameter of the tree, he pulled out the blade. He eyed the tree and the first cut, trying to see how to angle his saw and began setting up for his second cut. He angled his saw so that the second cut, or "top cut," would be diagonal to his first and intersect at the end of it, making a wedge or "pie cut." When he believed his aim was true, he revved the saw and began to cut again.

The hanging branch—or "widow maker" – trembled, and crewmembers around me all started to shift their weight nervously, whispering cusses and shaking their heads.

The chips spraying off the saw blade turned to dust as the top cut intersected with the bottom. The saw boss took his finger off the throttle. He twisted the saw so that the pie-shaped piece popped out from the tree. Blast patted him on the back gently, then moved towards the tree and removed the piece of wood, showing it to his partner. Instead of a half-circle, the cut came out looking like a crescent because the center had rotted away. After making sure the sawyer saw it, Blast threw the pie cut down the hill, as if in disgust, and quickly fanned his hand through the cut in the tree, brushing out handfuls of powder.

"Should've just blown that damn thing out of here," a crewmember whispered as the saw boss and his partner positioned themselves on the other side of the tree, preparing to make the final cut that would bring it down.

"Too late now," another said.

"Back cut!" The saw boss yelled out over the idling saw.

"Well, here comes the moment of truth," Rob said.

The saw boss revved his saw and dug it into the opposite side of the pie cut, throttling aggressively.

With the low crackle and whine of twisting wood, the tree started to fall in the intended direction downhill. But as it did, the lower half of the tree buckled, as if it were crushed from the weight of the top. The force of compression caused splinters of bark to stab out around the two men. Then with a tremendous snap, the top half of the tree broke free from the bottom half. Over two tons of wood fell straight towards the two sawyers.

Instantly, Blast swung the saw boss out of harm's way using his own body as an axis and leaving himself in peril. Seeing that the treetop was on course to crush his partner, the saw boss clung to the arm swinging him and wrenched it around in a similar circular motion, so that for a split second it looked as if the men were in some sort of playground fight. At almost the same moment, the saw boss realized his saw was still stuck in the tree. Using the starter chord that was yet in his hand, he yanked the saw out of its cut, just as the three large pieces of timber crashed to the ground. A cloud of dust and rotten wood burst upwards, obscuring the fate of the men from us as a boom echoed through the valley.

A few crewmembers charged into the cloud calling the men's names. They searched frantically between the large pieces of shattered wood strewn along the ground.

"Look Blast, next time you want to dance, just ask," the saw boss said as he stood up and dusted himself off.

"You just looked so pretty, I couldn't wait," said his partner as he rolled onto his belly and came to his feet.

"Must be the new perfume," the saw boss said.

The watching scrapers broke into cusses and applause.

"What about Gladiator?" Blast hollered.

"Shit, where is he!" the saw boss said, looking around on the ground, covered in tree shards. "Stop clapping and help us!" the saw boss demanded, as he began to throw the wood chunks everywhere, searching desperately.

"I didn't spend two hours a day getting that saw in tip top shape to lose it to some snaggletooth."

The scrappers went to removing the debris and looking for the missing saw.

"Well, look at it this way—if it's smashed you guys can spend the rest of the fire scraping dirt with us!" one of the scrapers said.

"Bite your tongue," the saw boss demanded.

"We're tarred and feathered, Eric!" Blast said as he chucked a branch of wood down the hill.

"It'll make it a stupid decision!" the saw boss said as he frantically searched for his instrument.

"We can't lose him; he's the best!" Blast said.

He then leapt at the ground as if to catch prey. He bolted to his feet, thrust the saw over his head like a trophy and yelled, "Found him!" He pulled on the start chord and it fired right up. "That's right! Gladiator! Gladiator!" he said repeating the saw's name and revving it in victory.

"All right, let's get this shit off of the trail!" Grump hollered. "And let's not mention all this to Skip or Bruce," he added quietly.

"Copy that," the saw boss said and the crew quickly disposed of the tree's remains. In the commotion, I looked up to see the saw boss sitting on a rock, wiping a handkerchief across his brow with trembling hands and looking out into a blank distance.

"Two more years...got to make it just two more years," he repeated to himself.

3:00 PM

I stopped scraping at roots and grass when I noticed another crew coming up the line. They were an odd looking bunch. Instead of wearing the green Nomex pants and yellow shirts—the standard garb of all national foresters on the fire line—this crew was dressed in blue jeans, bright red shirts, and hard hats. Many of the men's shirts hung slovenly over their waists. They walked in a scattered single-file line, with large, uneven gaps between the individuals. The older man walking in front did wear the standard green and yellow, and the man directly behind him wore a blue Washington State Department of Natural Resources work shirt and had a large sidearm hanging from his waist. This was a convict crew.

I had never seen convicts or prisoners before, except on TV.

"Don't gawk, Taylor, just work," Rob said.

I did as I was told for a few minutes, until ...

"Hey, young fella!" the older man who had been leading the crew said, demanding my attention. He was in his fifties, about my height at five foot nine, and, typical of a man his age, he carried some weight in his belly. His face was rugged and worn, but his eyes carried the glimmer of a man who was quite happy with what life had shown him—and where it had brought him at this particular moment. He was also the only person I'd seen on the fire line who wasn't wearing sunglasses.

"How we doing today, gentlemen?" he asked.

"I'm good," I said. It was the first time anyone had been friendly to me in days.

"Well, my name is Chuck Fearson, and I am the division superintendent for this section of fire."

I introduced myself, as did Rob.

"I'm here to talk to your boss and let him know I got the help he requested."

"Our sup is serving as lookout—but I couldn't tell you where. The foreman is up in front of the crew, flagging line. He shouldn't be hard to find," Rob said.

"Well, that's who I plan on talking to then," the old man said. "But while I'm here, since I see myself as responsible for everyone's safety on my division, why don't I ask you boys some questions?"

"Okay," I said nervously, sensing a test coming.

"So where is your LCES young man?" he asked me.

"Uhm...." I racked my brain to remember this one-of-a-million government acronym I had already come across in my young life. After three months working for the federal government, I was beginning to suspect the sole purpose of acronyms was to give people in intellectually simple professions the opportunity to sound smart.

"You know, your Lookout, Communication, Escape route and Safety zone!" Chuck said, clearly dismayed that I wasn't even aware of what he meant.

Rob interjected, "Our lookout is Bruce, our superintendent; our communication is channel nine on our team leader's radio; and our—"

"Now hold up there, sir. Let this young man here answer the rest," Chuck said.

"Well, uh...," I had no idea. I now remembered mention of LCES on the line, but I had heard so much incomprehensible jargon over the last forty-eight hours that I just ignored it. Besides, it seemed they wanted me to know nothing and just follow directions, so that was all I had put my mind to—and that was proving tough enough. "I guess down the line to the helispot," I said, finally.

Rob sighed.

"Now I don't like that answer, Jonathan," Chuck said. "That helispot is well over five miles away. That sure would be a long hike if you needed to get out of here quick, now wouldn't it?"

"Okay, I'd run down this hill for a while and set up my shelter on the line," I said, openly winging it.

Rob put his head down. "Sorry, he's not a regular member. He's detailing for an injured guy."

"The fire's not going to treat him any different than a regular member, now is it?" Chuck demanded.

"No," Rob conceded.

"Now, Jonathan," Chuck continued, "you have to make sure you know these things right off the bat—like you know your own name. I am going to expect your partner here to tell you all about LCES right after I leave, and you make sure you understand it perfectly. Even if it takes you the whole shift to do it and you don't get any work done. Got it?"

"Got it," I said, hanging my head.

"And for God's sake, don't ever depend on your fire shelter. It's a last resort at best. Pretend you don't have it."

"Okay," I said.

"You know, back in the late sixties and seventies, when they first introduced those things, a lot of us didn't even want them."

"Why not?"

"Well, for one, damn things weigh a couple of pounds. We'd rather use our strength carrying water or swinging a shovel than on carrying some piece of tinfoil you can't depend on. I guess we just had a sense that we'd been fighting fire pretty well without the damn things, and all's they'd be good for was giving us a false sense of security. They might tempt us to do things we otherwise wouldn't. In some ways we were right, too. You know, a lot of people have gotten in those things and not come out. They're not foolproof I tell you, no sir. A hot fire will burn that piece of tin right up."

"Is that what they are made of?"

"Actually it's a fiberglass cloth laminated to aluminum foil—but see, this is only good for protecting you from radiant heat. Won't help you a bit from the convective heat from the flames themselves. So in order for that shelter to work, you've got to get to a place that's free of ground fuel, where flames won't burn over it."

"But they have saved hundreds of lives," Rob protested.

"That could be true, but then, you never know. Could be that if the people didn't have them, then they wouldn't have gotten themselves in a dangerous predicament in the first place."

"Yeah, maybe," Rob said. "But soon they're gonna give us shelters that can withstand the heat of anything—even a full crown fire. Nobody will get hurt."

The older man shook his head. "That's not going to be an answer, Son. The most dangerous thing you can do is try to take the danger out of firefighting, or try and tell people that we're going to take the danger out. See, you try and take the danger out, and pretty soon people will start taking this out," he said, tapping on his temple. "And they'll start taking this out," he said, patting the left side of his chest. "Be aware of danger, absolutely, mitigate it when possible, sure, but don't think you can eliminate it—and definitely never think that you *have*.

"I've fought fire for over thirty years now," he continued, "and if you listen to only one thing, I say listen to this: Your best shelter is right here," he said, tapping his temple again.

The man in the blue Department of Natural Resources work shirt arrived with the crew of convicts in tow. With his mirrored sunglasses, chiseled face, and holstered gun, he looked like a Chuck Norris knockoff.

"Holding!" he yelled, as he came to a stop.

The order was repeated down the line by a few men but quickly faded away.

The crew boss grew red in the face and yelled, "Bump that goddamn order all the way down!"

The crew complied, some smirking with mild satisfaction that they'd frustrated the authority.

"This here is Tom Hunter, and he is what's called the FCS, or Forest Crew Supervisor, for these inmates."

"Hello," I said.

The man nodded stoically.

"So, um, these inmates that fight fire, I assume they're all low level offenders," I asked diffidently.

"Nope, they've done all sorts of things, some of them. Rape, murder, armed robbery—anything that can get you thrown in the penitentiary."

"And they don't just run off?" I asked.

"No, all these men are in our honor camps, which means they have served the bulk of their hard time

51

and now are in a low level prison—a rehabilitation camp of sorts. They usually only have a couple of years left with us, so they would just rather finish out their term. Beside, you'd be surprised how many of them are scared enough of the woods that they don't want to take off into it on their own."

"So they never escape?" I pried.

Hunter looked annoyed. "I've had two attempts over the last eight years. Caught them both."

"Well, Chuck," Hunter continued, "I am going to go ahead and move my men on up the line. It's best to keep them moving."

Chuck agreed, and the line of convicts began to shuffle past us. They looked ragged and wild, broken and intense—spirited and caged. One or two tried to smile at me; others peered stoically into the distance. One of them looked directly at me—his skin was almost black, so that the red shirt he wore seemed to radiate. His face was worn past fifty, and his guilty hardened yet wizened eyes made me feel as if I was the most pampered man on earth.

"All right," Chuck said to Rob and me. "You all be careful—and learn that LCES! Remember, it might seem like we don't get many big fires up here to a brush fireman, but when we get 'em, we get 'em big! Why back in 1902, we had the Yacolt Burn that killed over forty people—one of the worst fires in US history—and it's all set to happen again."

As Chuck walked away, he noticed Cynthia vigorously cutting line with her Pulaski. He stopped and turned towards me. "Oh, and Jonathan, while you have the chance, make sure to learn from these men and women. They really know how to work!"

I wondered what it was that, in the short period of time we were together, caused him to sense I might need a lesson in that subject, too.

3:29 PM

I looked up the line to see all the sawyers sitting near a large tree stump. Some of the scrapers were there, also, digging through their packs and pulling out food.

Thank the Lord, lunchtime! I thought.

I dropped my shovel and walked towards the resting crewmembers.

"Hold it, Taylor!" Rob said angrily. "Pick up your tool and work your way to the end of the line. This end is just as important as the rest."

I sighed, picked up my tool, and went back to the section of line I had been working on, quietly mocking Rob's words while I dug.

As I got closer, I started to tune in to the conversation the sawyers were having, and I realized it was about me.

"Dude, he didn't know his LCES when the division sup asked him," one sawyer said. There was a ruckus of embarrassed laughter and groans.

"That's great—that's all we need. Everyone's wondering how we're going to do this year 'cause Hank's out, and now it's going to get out that our crewmembers don't even know their LCES."

"Well, I don't think the division sup is going to go around telling people. He seemed pretty old school." In the world of wildland firefighting, the term "old school" signified someone with valuable experience who came from a time that demanded firefighters be more rugged, tough, and when safety was dictated by lucidity and common sense rather than protocol and bureaucracy.

"Maybe he won't say anything, but that still doesn't change the fact that Taylor didn't even know."

"He took a shower last night, too."

"You mean he was walking around base camp in one of our crew t-shirts with a clean face and a wet head?"

"Blasphemy!"

"I tell you, I know Mike hurt his hand, but I say we should have put some gauze on it and got him on the rig. The last thing we need right now is someone that doesn't know what they're doing."

Had circumstances not become so extreme, I may have held a grudge for some time over this insult. But what I failed to really appreciate at the time was that many of these men had worked for years, in the hardest way, to simply get on this famed hotshot crew. Now I was here wearing their crew emblem as a matter of luck, and not taking the position with the pride or seriousness it demanded.

The men continued to talk about past detailers, and this ended up inspiring one man to tell a story.

"I remember the first fire I ever had to take over an engine—a year before I started on this crew. It was the South Dam Fire, and the regular captain had to go take over a division, so he left the engine to me. Anyway, since we were short a person, the park threw on this trail crew guy—Jimmy was his name—to help us out. He was a cool guy, into surfing and snowboarding. Anyway, he was freaking out to be fighting fire. I mean he loved it. Never saw a guy so excited. For the first two days of the fire he would, out of nowhere, raise his fist all excited and yell, 'Yeah I'm fighting fire!'"

The storyteller imitated the gesture.

I rolled my eyes. Over the last two days I had grown sick of hearing fire stories, like so much boasting. To be honest, it created envy in me— perhaps even anger—that such rich tales lived in men so close to my age. However, as time has gone, I've realized that storytelling in firefighting is a tacitly respected art. Far from being an egoistic pursuit of attention, it is instead a means of transmitting essential, possibly even life saving knowledge, from one firefighter to another. It was also the chief method of a vibrant subculture communicating its unifying mores, wisdom, and lore to its newest members.

"Anyway, so it's early morning, and we meet up with the park's Type II hand crew to attack a flank of the fire," the storyteller continued. "The crew boss was this guy named Craig, a real like serious guy, who'd been fighting fire for a long time, and was pretty respected by all of us. So we're going direct with this crew, running hose from the engine up and down this real steep hill. The hand crew was building line, and they anchored it to this twenty-foot cut bank that dropped straight off to the road. Embedded in their trail was a big fucking rock, this big," he said, stretching his arms, "that the hand crew had made part of their line, and that everyone was stepping on as they hiked up and down.

"So I'm walking up and down the line constantly to check on how things are going, and about twenty minutes into it, I step on this big rock and it gives out from under me, and me and the rock both start tumbling down this goddamn hill. Well right in my way is Jimmy, and I end up smashing right into him. So now we're both tumbling down this hill arm in arm towards the cut bank that falls twenty feet to the paved road, and the goddamn boulder is tumbling right behind us, and Jimmy and I are like hugging each other as we tumble down this fucking hill. There's no way we can stop. Everyone's screaming 'rock,' 'cause there's nothing fucking else to do, but it's like way too late to tell *us* that. So right as we get to the cut bank, I grab on to the trunk of this small tree, maybe four-feet high, that is like the last stop before death. The tree bends and we swing out over the cut bank as the rock flies over our heads. Then we get slung back to the lip of the cliff, but not before we see the boulder drop twenty feet and hit the pavement, *wham!*" The storyteller slammed one hand against the other to punctuate the effect.

"So we stand up and everyone's all looking at us real quiet, and Craig says, 'You guys going to calm down now and start fighting fire,' like reprimanding us or something in front of everyone. But Jimmy, he's too full of adrenaline to take shit from anyone, and he yells 'Hey, if you don't start your morning out like that, *then you fucking suck!'* We high-fived and then went and put out the fire."

There was a clamor of chuckles and grunts from the resting men.

I worked my way to the line just as the story was finished.

"Eat a bean, kid, but don't get too comfortable. We'll probably be moving soon," Rob said.

The crewmembers pulled out water, nuts, dried fruit, energy bars, and beef jerky from their packs. The fireline attracts people from various cultural subsets: bikers, rednecks, hippies, REI yuppies, academics, and proud blue-collar types. The Nomex and dirt hide the normal telltale features— but the food they choose to pack is the ultimate giveaway. Hippies—nuts and berries; academics and outdoor yuppies—energy bars; rednecks and blue-collar workers—beef jerky and chew.

I pulled out my last quart of water and drank from it. I licked my lips in between, relishing the salty taste. The warm breeze evaporated the sweat on my face and the air entering my lungs felt almost sweet. Before this moment I never knew how much euphoria could be found in the act of resting.

Within moments my quart canteen was already half empty. Grump had recommended that I pack at least six quarts of water with me onto the line. I saw some of the sawyers pack up to ten, but I wrote this off as a sadistic display of bravado. I simply couldn't imagine needing more than five quarts a day; plus, water was heavy—and I needed to be light. Now the warm, plastic-tinged water tasted like magic, and I fretted over how I could continue without it.

"Okay, listen up!" Grump shouted to everyone at the spot. "This is the deal."

"Skip is flagging the line down the hill right now. We're going to drop off the ridge spine here, and start constructing line downhill towards the creek bed. The con crew is dropping down to the valley as we speak. They're tying their line into the creek bed and working their way up towards us. We've called in for air support to start dropping on the fire. Once it arrives, then we'll start," Grump said. "Everyone copy that?"

Everyone nodded or said yes.

"Now once we start building line, our escape route and safety zone will be back up the line and over the ridgetop to this rockslide that's right behind us," Grump said, pointing to a large rockslide that was adjacent to the ridge spine where we were and dropped off into the northern basin.

Everyone grunted in understanding.

"You got that this time, Taylor?" Grump asked.

"Yeah," I moaned.

"All right, so eat something and rest up. Once we get the word, we'll be going full blast. We work fast and we might just get this thing tied up," Grump said.

Everyone nodded or grunted in agreement and returned to eating.

A few minutes later I turned to Rob. "Why are we waiting for air support? We built line on the ridge without it."

"Fire moves faster uphill. I don't know about you Taylor, but I move slower uphill. So once that thing hits the top of that ridge, it only has to work its way down the hill in front of us, and then we're in a situation where the fire is moving fast and the crew is moving slow. That's not what we want. So we'll wait for the planes—make sure they come. They'll hold the down the flames – give us more time to get the line done before the fire gets under us."

From the bottom of the valley came the sound of saw engines revving up.

"Now that is the con crew!"

"Yep," said Rob.

"Why are they at the bottom of the valley then? I mean, if we are the hotshots and they're the con crew?"

"'Cause we got you, Taylor," Rob said, staring at me stone-faced. Then his look broke into a grin. "Just kidding," he laughed, then continued, "It's their choice, I guess."

"I don't get it."

"Look, kid, being tough is not always being stupid," Rob said, pausing for a moment to collect his thoughts. "Think of it this way: that crew down there has got a ninety-nine percent chance of making it out okay—even with the given fire activity, and all the red flag warnings. Ninety-nine out of a hundred times they'll make it out just fine."

"Okay," I said.

"The problem is, Taylor, that I've fought well over one hundred fires, and I could very well fight one hundred more. Get it? One in a hundred isn't good enough. One in a hundred eventually gets people burned up. It's because of all that experience that we have to watch our asses."

I conceded to the logic and returned to eating a melted snickers bar.

"Damn, all I got to eat in my pack is an MRE," said Phillips, one of the scrapers on the crew.

Phillips's partner, Nelson, replied "Oh, that sucks. Serves you right though, for not being prepared. What flavor is it?"

"Don't know, didn't look when I put it in." Phillips pulled out the sealed brown plastic bag and read the words printed on it. "MRE HAM SLICE. No fucking way! Bullshit! I ain't that hungry."

"Ha. Ham Slice, worst of the worst. Didn't they stop making that back in like the Vietnam War? Serves you right, though. Next time come prepared," Nelson said. "Of course eating that Ham Slice might help make you thick. And you'll need some help if you're ever going to get to that stage of development," Nelson advised with a pseudo-spiritual air.

"Thick! Look who's talking—long time before you get to be thick. Judging by the way you fell back on that last hike on the Olgalby Fire, I don't think anyone will ever deem you that tough."

"Hey, you can't count that, I had a cold. Shit, I had a temperature of over a hundred that day!" Nelson protested.

"Well so did half the crew there, tough nut! Hell, Skip threw up on the side of the trail and still didn't fall back—even when he was doing it! That's thick."

"We all know Skip's thick," Nelson said, waiving off the unfair comparison. "The key to what you said is *almost*. I almost fell back, but didn't."

"Ah, you were starting to gap. I saw the gap between you and Mars. You should be ashamed. You'll never be considered thick this season— maybe never."

"Just eat the damn MRE!" Marcus abruptly demanded.

The two men looked behind them and said nothing. Phillips picked up the brown package, tossed away the main entre of the MRE, and found a package that read "strawberries." He cut open the package to reveal a red square of dehydrated strawberries and quietly ate it.

At six-foot-one and two hundred and twenty pounds, Marcus easily fit the description of "thick."

But it wasn't his size as much has his eight year history with the crew, coupled with his unbreakable tenacity, which had earned him the designation. Throughout his time with the crew, he had never missed a fire, had never fallen back on a hike, and never failed to fell a tree exactly where he wanted it.

As a child, Marcus had suffered from a bad stutter. He overcame it by the age of thirteen, but only after the habit of keeping silent had been ingrained in him. The reluctance to communicate kept him from rising into the ranks of overhead, and at thirty-four he was the oldest and most experienced member to not have supervisory duties.

There was something in the two men's banter that bothered, Marcus. Eight years earlier, when he joined the crew, falling back on a hike would have been so shameful that people wouldn't even speak of it. Now these guys were treating it like a joke. Marcus didn't like the change, not only because it indicated that this new generation of men might be less devoted to their work, but also because it stunk of influence from the "outside world," as he thought of it.

Marcus determined long ago that there were two worlds: the outside world—the world of the urbanite, the office worker, and the bureaucrat; and the fire world—the world of the hotshot, the smokejumper, or any hard working wildland firefighter. One world worshipped comfort and luxury and the other tenacity and austerity. But as of late it seemed that the fire world was under siege from the outside world. Each year more of the modern amenities of the outside world made their way into the fire world. There were almost always showers at base camp now, more comfortable backpacks, televisions in crew rigs, fancier MREs, and on and on. It filled him with a concern that was often difficult to voice, but he knew the outside world would try to destroy the fire world. After all, hotshots labored with their hands, lived with danger and dirt, chewed tobacco, cussed, sweat, suffered, and stunk—all things the outside world viewed with disdain and was intent on eradicating.

3:55 PM

"Whoa! Look at it now! It's going off!" one of the crewmembers yelled out.

From behind the southern ridge, smoke boiled out into a monolithic tower of gray and white pumice that contrasted with the brilliant blue sky. A bass rumble emanated from the direction of the ridge, moving through the air with the depth of a foghorn.

All the firefighters gasped in awe and appreciation. They smiled and joked and became more animated as they watched the force they would soon attempt to halt. Some crewmembers took out cameras from their packs and snapped pictures of each other posing with saw and tools in hand as the plume reigned in the background.

It excited me too, making me almost giddy and a bit spastic. I yearned to be part of the camaraderie and pride shared by the crewmembers, but felt significantly removed from all that. I took out my disposable camera and asked Rob to take my photo. He agreed. It never got developed, but if it had, I assume it would have been a strange image of a person trapped between boyhood and manhood—the lonely awkwardness in my expression perhaps even more striking than the destruction taking place behind me.

A single-engine plane soon started circling the tower of smoke, looking like a mosquito hovering around the shoulder of a giant.

"Lead plane's here! Looks like we'll be getting air support," Rob said.

After the plane circled the fire several times, a much larger four-engine plane came into view and started following it. The small plane swooped down, indicating the path it wanted the larger plane to follow. The large plane followed the path, swung close to the ridgetop, and dropped a load of red slurry from its belly.

"Isn't that red slime bad for the forest?" I asked Rob.

"Who knows? It's suppose to be fertilizer, but whatever they say is good for the forest today, they'll say is bad for it tomorrow."

"Okay! Let's move!" Grump yelled out. "Remember your escape route and safety zone are up the hill and to this rockslide. Let's bang this out, Bison!"

"Pulling rope!" Edgar yelled out, as he yanked on the saw, which sputtered and died.

"Let me show you how it's done there, Rollingson!" shouted Steve Andersen, picking up his own saw and barking, "Coming on!" as he tugged on the starter rope. It didn't start either.

A few sawyers scoffed. Joe Jacobson yelled a warning and tugged on his starting chord. The saw roared as he throttled it aggressively.

Soon the air vibrated from the growls of all four saws, and the men were furiously cutting a twenty-foot swath through the timber. They hooted war cries as they wielded their tools and crashed through the ten-foot tall timber reproduction. After the saws had cut a large enough swath into the vegetation for the scrapes to start working, the squad boss called out, "All right scrapes, let's keep up with them!"

Rob turned to me. "You better be ready to bust some ass now. The crew is pretty pumped."

Vibrant red flames burst from atop the southern ridge. The frenetic bands of fire reached three times higher than the old growth Douglas fir trees they consumed and spewed a boiling river of soot and smoke into the sky, which pooled into a large mushroom head.

"My God," I gaped in awe. Those flames appeared to be over one hundred fifty feet in length, maybe much longer. Seeing these ephemeral giants dance and crash their way on a distant but obvious course for the crew, I was suddenly struck with a new respect for the hotshots. I felt in a position, strangely enough, of honor. It was an honor to be part of the crew. And for the first time, I was ready and eager to go to work.

4:16 PM

Skip looked at his watch. He then opened his small pad of paper and pondered for a moment on the last weather report he had received from the squad boss. The east winds had been replaced by north winds. It didn't make sense. According to the regional weather forecast, a high pressure system was supposed to be creating a light east wind—unless the fire was beginning to make its own weather, creating local winds that were superseding the regional flow.

Skip walked up the hill, following the line he had just flagged through the vegetation. He stopped when he came to a natural opening, which gave him a clear view of the fire, and put a wad of tobacco in his mouth, hoping that the nicotine would end the unease in his gut. He breathed deep, spit, and tried to reason.

The fire was parked on the top of the ridge. The intense updrafts from its own heat were keeping it from moving downhill at a rate faster than a crawl. By the way the plume was growing, though, he could tell that it still had plenty of fuel on the back side of the hill—that's what worried him. If the plume kept getting larger, all that air and matter forced into it could eventually reach a critical mass. Theoretically, the column could collapse under its own weight and send intense down drafts towards the ground, where they would blow the fire in every direction. While exceedingly rare, the phenomenon had occurred in 1990, and the result was the loss of six firefighters on the Dude Fire in Arizona. Thermal drafts around the column did such strange things to local weather that there were reports of rain moments before the blowup and a sudden and unaccounted for drop in temperature.

But collapsing columns are extraordinary events, Skip thought, and he tried to push the paranoid thought out of his head. He was probably just nervous because it was his first time leading a crew during such intense fire activity. Besides, the crew was working hard, and their line would intersect with the convicts' line within the hour. Then they'd start prepping for the burn out.

Skip spit to mark his decision and continued hiking towards the crew. Despite all of his desire for complete determination, he couldn't help but glance over his shoulder to watch for a sign or warning in the ominous mushroom cloud above.

∞

4:22 PM

"Rock!" I heard Rob yell as he dodged the baseball-sized object that sped down the line towards the other crewmembers. Hearing the warning, those nearest to him looked up, echoed the call, and crouched to dodge the stone. Some crewmembers desperately tried to stop the projectile with the blade of their shovels, but the rock bounced too erratically on the uneven terrain. Within seconds it passed all the scrapers—whose silent tools allowed them to hear the warnings—and whizzed down towards the unaware sawyers. No matter how desperately the crewmembers above yelled, the blaring engines kept the sawyers unaware of the danger. Luckily, the rock hit a large boulder and ricocheted off safely into the brush.

"Goddamn it, Taylor!" Rob belted. "That's the third rock you've sent down the hill! Watch where you're digging for fuck's sake!"

"Sorry, I didn't mean to," I said.

"Everyone dislodges one now and then, but you're making it a habit. Pay attention!" Rob said.

"Okay, okay, I got it," I said.

The thrill had faded in the last twenty minutes, and digging was once again just hard labor. Working downhill had proven to be more of a chore than working on the relatively flat ground of the ridge's spine. I had to watch my footing constantly, and the men kept yelling at me about rocks or stepping in the trenches they had built in the line. Eventually the crew assigned me to build the trenches, though what purpose they served, I wasn't sure. In fact, the only thing I knew about the trenches was that every one I made was deemed unsatisfactory.

I hit my shovel on the ground, expressing my frustration to the dirt. Sure enough, another large rock was set free.

"Rock!" I yelled out, as I had been told to do.

Rob tried to block the stone with his foot but was unsuccessful, and the warning echoed down the line as everyone tried to dodge or stop it. This rock did not ricochet to safety after missing all the scrapers but instead bounced high in the air and whistled towards the sawyers, gaining velocity. The sawyers, as before, were deaf and oblivious to the imminent threat. I watched as the fist-sized rock, seeming to move in slow motion, struck a sawyer named Corn directly in the head. He was the same man who had christened my shirt with dirt. His hard hat flew off his head, and he fell to the ground.

In an instant, the sounds of tools clanking, chainsaws buzzing, and shouts of warnings stopped. I froze, wondering what kind of damage my carelessness had caused.

Within the same second, Corn slowly rolled onto his hands, then came to his feet. The atmosphere crackled back to life as crewmembers fired off questions, asking if the struck man was okay. Corn motioned that he was unhurt, picked up his hard hat, and inspected the impact mark the rock had left. His partner came over to him, and the two talked for a moment.

Then Corn's eyes, ablaze with anger, looked squarely at me. My knees buckled. I wanted to vomit. I put my eyes down, my head down, everything down, and focused on building my current trench as if it were my last masterpiece.

Everyone on the crew intimidated me, but none more than the sawyers. They were arrogant and mean-spirited, and they carried the kind of manliness that makes boys fear men, bureaucrats fear criminals, civilians fear soldiers. They were the hotshots of the hotshots. And now one of these bulging-armed brawlers, had turned his intense focus on me.

"You're up shit creek," Rob said.

"I know."

"Too bad you didn't pay attention like I told you," Rob said.

I almost told him to shut up, but instead I kept working on the trench and tried to act innocent.

Maybe if I work hard he'll go away. Maybe he's not coming for me at all. Maybe he's going to take a ...

There was a thwack on my shoulder. I looked up to see Corn. In the same second I was pushed off the line by his powerful shove.

"Come here," he said. "We need to talk."

He grabbed my arm, and I stumbled at the force of the tug. He was my height exactly, and probably the same weight, too—but his was all muscle and grit.

"You know what I got planned when the season is over?" Corn asked, with a sort of feigned informality.

"Um, no, I haven't heard," I said.

"I'm getting married."

"Oh!" I exclaimed. I was trying to sound cheery, but it came out as a screech.

"To my girlfriend of five years. We're going to Hawaii. Got it all planned out—renting this cabin on the beach, just me and her."

"Congratulations. That's great."

"Now don't go congratulating me yet, 'cause it ain't happened yet. And as long as stupid things keep happening it might not ever happen. Get it?" he asked.

"Uh …"

"Now it ain't the fire, it ain't the dead snags, it ain't the burning stump holes, it ain't the snakes, and it ain't the saw that really scare me. What scares the hell out of me is the rocks. I hate 'em! They're just waiting to be set free so they can kill somebody. Now they're bad enough just with gravity helping them out, but when gravity gets put together with stupidity, stupidity like yours, well that *really* scares the shit out of me! Get it, Taylor? Gravity plus stupidity kills people." Corn said, jabbing his finger into my sternum.

"Now we already had two men killed on this fire when it rekindled because of stupidity. I don't want to be the third!" Corn yelled. "The poor bastards really got hit by the stupid bug when they tried to take on a grass fire with just hand tools, in the middle of a hot east wind, after two weeks without rain," Corn continued. "But you can't blame them really.

"See, the way I see it, everyone does something stupid now and then, everyone," Corn insisted. "That's what makes this job so dangerous, the stupidity. There's always the threat of stupidity, no matter who you are! The reason why is this job *makes* people stupid. I mean, when you first pick up a saw, or cut down a tree, or build line downhill, you're nervous. And for good reason! It's fucking dangerous!" He punctuated his point with another sternum jab.

"But after a while of doing it, you don't get nervous—you stop thinking about it being dangerous. See what I mean? You get stupid. Now most of us, as we get older, try to fight off the stupidity with knowledge, but eventually the stupidity comes to you, and if you get bad luck at the same time, well, then you're fucked."

"Okay," I said.

"The problem I see with you, Taylor, is that you haven't been on this line for four days now, and you're already stupid. I mean, me and Mars down there have been doing this job for four years, and we're not even as stupid as you."

"Look, I am really sorry about—" I started to say, but Corn cut me off.

"Now I know you ain't the quickest dog in the race," he said, "but I want to get on that goddamn flight to Hawaii real bad. *Real bad.* So I figure I got to find a way to cure you of your stupidity. So, I'll make you a deal. I'll forget about the fact that if the rock you sent down would have landed two inches lower it would have broken my face, if *you* remember that the next time you send a rock down, and it comes within a thirty-foot perimeter of us sawyers, well ..." Corn produced the rock that nearly killed him. "I am going to slam this rock into your face just as hard as it would have hit me. Got it?" Corn said, sending one last jab into my chest.

I nodded.

"So you got to ask yourself," Corn continued, "am I going to fight fire, or am I going to get smashed in the face?" Corn put the rock in his pocket, spit on my boot, and walked back down the line.

I rubbed the sore spot on my chest and absorbed the ultimatum. Rob eventually signaled me to get back at it. I focused intently on every swing—and for a short while, my fatigue faded from my mind.

4:40 PM

I had to take a shit. Since I had an almost superstitious aversion to using outhouses, or going outside, I had been holding back the need for the last forty-eight hours. Now the demand wouldn't wait.

As far as I could tell, etiquette on the crew regarding the matter was non-existent. As long as it didn't cause a delay, they would urinate or defecate anywhere without inhibition. I also noticed that the desire for privacy was a sign of weakness. In fact, there seemed to be a sense of pride and bravado in being able to piss and shit in front of large groups of people. This attitude was not bound to the males.

I learned this through shock, when, on the first day, I looked up to see Cynthia relieving herself two feet from where we were working. I couldn't help but stare, until ...

"What the fuck are you looking at, Taylor! Haven't you ever seen a chick piss before?" she yelled.

My face flushed red. No, I hadn't.

I decided to follow my suburban inhibitions and walk at least thirty feet away from the others. I slipped away from the line and moved through the reprod until I felt comfortable enough to pull down my pants and pray that I wouldn't need toilet paper.

A raindrop hit my cheek. I looked up at the clear sky, and figured I was loosing my mind as fast as my dignity, but I would learn later that it was no hallucination.

∞

4:42 PM

"A...A-F."

"Yes, Bruce," Skip said into the radio.

"Skip, how's the line coming down there?"

"It's moving along pretty fast. I'd say we'll tie in with the convicts in about a half hour," Skip said.

"Do you think we can continue safely?" Bruce asked.

Skip thought the question was a test—though whether Bruce was testing his ability to keep the men working or his ability to call them off a job that was too dangerous, he wasn't sure.

"Yeah, Bruce, let me get back to you in just a minute," Skip said.

He walked up the line where his men worked, stopping occasionally to look at the fire and its column from different vantage points. He hoped to find an unquestionable sign to tell him the answer, but he saw nothing to sway him.

This would be a great one to hook. If they stopped this flank of the fire, the rest of the fire could be wrapped up in two days. They would go back to base camp with retardant and ash all over them, and word would spread that they had stopped it. If they let it go, then the whole operation would have to take a defensive stance and focus solely on structural protection while the fire ran wild—the domestic firefighters would turn into the heroes of the show, as they saved the houses from the fire the hotshots couldn't stop. People rarely spoke of such things of course; a fire was a team effort between all on the line; but they had a way of being known. It showed in the subtle interactions at basecamp, the grip of others handshakes, the length of time they watched you walk by, the size of the step they took to get out of your way.

The crew had a prized reputation in the fire world—that's why overhead had placed them in this position. But alcoholism had robbed the crew of their highly reputable foreman, and there was doubt whether Skip could fill the critical role. The superintendant job was like head coach, and the foreman, after all, was the quarterback. To turn around now, without an obvious reason and during this critical moment in the fire, would certainly not help his cause.

He was also concerned about crew morale. It would be tough on everyone if they retreated, and crushing if the convicts ended up hooking the line—though he was almost sure the convicts would pull out if the crew did. He knew how it felt to be pounding dirt and sawing brush through years spent climbing the hierarchy of the often-brutal world of fire. He suffered as a crewman sawing in the hundred-degree heat, sleeping on the dirt, eating bad food, thrashing his body, and stuffing the desire for sex and soft company deeper and deeper into his gut. The federal government rewarded his hard work and sacrifice by allowing him to drift as a temporary, seasonal employee paid only ten dollars an hour, without job security, pension or healthcare.

Because of this, he knew there was something else at stake other than reputation and morale. There were those few and far between moments that kept you going as a hotshot—those magical, Zen moments—and he could feel one of those moments coming over the crew now. Work turned to warfare, and purpose and challenge posed themselves on the most basic level of sweat and breath. The crewmen forgot all the meaningless bickering and infighting that invariably develops over months of extreme proximity. Suddenly every firefighter seeks not his own potential, but the full potential of the crew—the whole becomes tenfold the sum of its parts, and the individuals become one unit expressing their will to nature. It was a form of perfection that only came once or twice a season, if it was a good year.

Under the whine of the saws, the clank of the tools and the grunts of the men, he could hear the collective will of the crew:

Don't stop us! This is what we live for! This time when the work is tough but so important, this time when others would cry, quit, and leave. This is when we show our mettle, our value. Maybe we don't exhibit the finest social graces; maybe we hate the doldrums of day-to-day life so much that we cannot win the fruit it offers. But we can work—*hard*. We have the will and vitality that is rarely found in others. Let us use it. Let us release our strength upon the universe. This is our medium in which *to be*. We can risk! We can work! Let us do it! Let us be!

But Skip was no longer a pumped-up sawyer begging for a chance to kill dragons. Now he was the foreman. He had to face the fact that human skin burns at 113 degrees, and fires reach 2000.

He had to acknowledge that even a well-conditioned man can sustain a run of ten miles an hour for only so long, and fire can move four times that fast for an indefinite period. He and the superintendent were ultimately responsible for the lives of the crew, and so he had to deal with these simple but intractable facts. Skip stayed up at night thinking about this new responsibility—these men and women had mothers and fathers. Some even had their own children.

His mind teetered on the decision.

Then he realized the wind had stopped.

A chill went up his spine. The sign had come—but perhaps too late.

"A...A-F."

"Go ahead, Skip."

"We better pull out now."

"I concur, Skip. Good call.

Chapter Three

4:45 PM

"Reverse Tool Order!" The foreman yelled.

"RTO!" The crewmembers loudly bumped the order down the line. Tools immediately stopped clanking, saw engines sputtered out one by one as the men received the order. A collective groan shuddered through the crew as many grunted in contempt of being denied their goal. But within two minutes they were all set to hike up the hill. All except one. Me.

"RTO!? What the hell does that mean?" I wondered as I squatted with my pant waist over my ankles, looking pathetically for something to use as toilet paper. I could tell it seemed important—even demanding. "Jesus, I can't even take a shit outside without being bothered," I complained aloud.

I finished up as quickly as possible, pulled up my pants and went to see what was happening.

The crew had gathered in a tight line above the last trench I had dug, and they were all staring at me. I walked with my head down to avert their glares, and a barrage of angry shouts burst from the crew commanding me to move faster. I looked up and saw the intensity on their faces. They weren't just mad; they were concerned. I scurried toward them and hiked passed the awaiting sawyers to take my place in line with the scrappers. I could feel their eyes blaze with contempt behind their sunglasses.

"We ready?" the foreman asked Rob when I arrived, with the slightest hint of stoic sarcasm.

"Yes," Rob replied. He then turned to me— "Goddamn it, Taylor! How was I supposed to know where you were? What have Grump and I told you a million times in the last two days about buddies!"

"They work together, sleep together, eat together and always know where ..."

"Moving!" the foreman yelled and started to hike up the hill.

"Enough! Just hurry your ass up!" Rob said, giving me a shove so that I complied with the order. We started hiking up the steep grade.

Within seconds I could tell I was in trouble. My dehydrated, out-of- shape body would never keep pace with the crew marching up such a steep slope. I could feel my blood, thick from lack of water, pounding in my head. My heart raced like an overheated piston about to blow, and my legs moved like rusty cylinders seizing in an engine without oil. My breath became erratic and frenzied, drying my throat, so that it felt as if it was swelling. A gap formed between Skip and me.

Rob responded by shoving me again, barking, "Keep up!" And I tried, but it was no use. A sad helplessness started to overcome me, and I felt threatened by tears. Someone behind me shouted, "Move it Taylor. We're getting out of here!"

"Clean that gap!" another yelled. But the gap only grew.

Skip looked behind and saw what was happening. He stopped and let me catch up to him.

"What's going on?" he asked evenly.

"I'm getting dizzy," I pleaded.

Skip looked me in the face. I was beet red.

Cynthia was coming up behind us, and Skip motioned to her to keep moving. She passed us and proceeded up the hill, followed by the rest of the crew.

Skip continued examining me, then said to Rob, "Looks like he's already in heat stress."

"What do you want to do?" Rob asked.

"We can't exactly cart him into shade and let him rest. Have you been drinking water?" Skip asked me.

"I'm out," I said.

He reached into his backpack. "Take this canteen. Drink some." He turned to Rob. "You two grab a quick breath. Catch the end of the train." Then he turned back to me and looked me dead in the eye. "I'm not going to cut this easy, because it can't be. You're going to have to push it. Hard. You got twenty-five minutes of the hardest time in your life right in front of you. Keep up. Make it to the top. You can do it. You must do it."

Skip turned and hiked up the hill, moving past the others to resume his place in the front.

I sipped the water and tried to avoid the stares of the passing hotshots, the men and women whose strength had not failed them. The water was wonderful, but it was akin to suckling mother's milk in front of friends. As I stood there savoring the much-needed hydration, a sudden gust of warm wind splashed my skin, bringing such relief that I enjoyed a momentary euphoria—but its comfort was a ruse.

Thousands of feet above the crew, the balance between thermal updrafts and the weight of the debris and air collecting in the column's head tilted in favor of gravity. The column started to collapse. Air gusted downwards and hit the earth, scattering wind all over the landscape. The wind fanned the fire, which had been moving slowly down the hill on the other side of the valley.

I looked across the valley and noticed the fire's new vigor. Heightened flames still burned mainly in the underbrush, but occasionally they reached into the large conifer branches. A few old-growth trees were overwhelmed in flames, like huge torches. Downed logs wedged between shrubs and tree trunks suddenly rolled free as fire diminished their size and incinerated the trees and bushes holding them in place. They tumbled down the south ridge and soon set a few small spot fires on the bottom of the valley. I remembered Skip's seriousness, and wondered for a moment if humiliation and failure were the least of my worries.

I pushed the unpalatable idea out of my mind. I heard the convicts below us give the command for retreat. Remembering that people were still far behind me helped temper the possibility that my life might actually be on the line.

A few more sips and then the last sawyer passed us.

"All right, Taylor. Let's get it done," Rob said.

I started back at it with Rob behind me. Almost as soon as I made the first step upward, my breathing became labored once again. I struggled to keep my wobbling legs underneath me, fighting through the sting of lactic acid building in my muscles. I maintained for about twenty feet before the space between me and the last sawyer began to grow. Rob kept pushing me, and it helped—but looking up at how far there was to go to the ridge, I knew I would have to stop again soon. Finally I gave up, feeling that if I didn't, I would simply collapse.

"There's no way I can keep this pace," I said through my labored breaths.

"We're in a spot, Taylor. It's okay. Just keep cool. Breathe ten deep breaths. Take a few drinks, and then we'll hit it again." His usual angry tone had been supplanted by something more resolute and cool, but I was too tired to appreciate the difference.

I did as told, and while following directions noticed that the retardant planes were responding to the fire's behavior by swooping in closer to the flames before dropping their red gel. But the wind had become so severe near the main fire's edge that the slurries broke up in ineffectual mist before reaching the ground, and I could tell the pilots were having a difficult time keeping their machines on a steady course in the turbulence. The planes started taking aim ahead of the fire, hoping to coat the area between the flame front and the fleeing crews.

"The planes are trying to buy us time. But we don't have much. We have to hurry. Let's go." Rob said.

"Buy *us* time—there is a whole crew of people behind us" I said.

"Let's go!" Rob insisted.

While singular fatalities are not unusual on the fire line, incidents in which entire crews are lost are exceptionally rare and historical events. In the thousands upon thousands of fires that have been fought in the over one-hundred- year history of Western firefighting, there have only been a handful that have destroyed entire crews. I remembered because the instructors talked about almost every one at fire school, and at that moment I was counting on that statistic to keep me safe. The only way the fire could get to me was if it destroyed the crew below me, and that was too rare an occurrence to really consider.

This must be emotional hyperbole, or practice, or bravado, or an attempt to scare me into going home on my own volition, I thought. Skip and Rob can't actually think this circumstance could get that severe.

I looked up at the ridge I had to climb. It was at least a half-mile, maybe more, but what scared me most was the way the crew made its way up to it. There had been a shift in energy—the group was no longer moving like it was in charge of its own destiny, but as one reacting to a greater force. Small gaps were forming between the individuals, the steps of some were stuttered, and the movement of the entire unit was less rhythmic. I looked behind me and saw spot fires had combined to form a wall of flames burning out of the valley. A bad situation, I knew—but the flames looked far off and spreading slowly.

"Now, Taylor!"

I was shoved forward and so began to walk upward. The consideration that this could become deadly squeezed adrenaline and angst into my blood, and while I pushed it out of my mind as absurd, it did unleash a reserve of energy, and I set my sights on the crew. I didn't want to be left behind. I didn't want to deal with it alone. Rob helped by pushing on my back and prodding me. He pushed heroically, and I noticed that his breath was becoming heavy and difficult, too.

The air began to shake all around us. "Get down!" I heard someone yell. Everyone got on bended knee and placed a hand on their hardhats. Everyone except me.

I was blasted with a smack and blown to the ground. I convulsed, totally confused and thinking, as in the impossible logic of a nightmare, the fire had suddenly reached me.

But I wasn't dead, or burned, or even on fire. I was wet. I looked up and saw a huge tanker zooming over me. I was covered in pink slime. It was fire retardant, and it felt disgusting as it stuck to my skin with the sweat and dirt.

There was no time to complain. Rob dragged me to my feet, and I was about to continue upwards when I realized my hardhat had been knocked off. I looked back to see it tumbling down the hill for what seemed an eternity, finally coming to a stop fifteen feet down the line.

Should I get it? I looked up to see the crew moving ever farther away. Every step down would put me two behind. But if I left it, the cons might pick it up. If they came out of the valley with a hotshot hardhat... I'd learned enough over the last few days about the importance of pride and symbol with these men to know that would be the last disgrace. Just as I was about to bolt down to get it, Rob slapped me in the chest.

"Rest for a second," he said, and set off down the hill at a run and reached my hardhat. As he bent to pick it up, his eyes were focused down the hill, examining the oncoming flames. It was shocking. The wall of fire had become at least twenty feet high and was getting larger by the moment. It had cut its distance from the con crew in half. Rob turned and bolted back up to me, handed me the hardhat and kept moving up the hill. "You're on your own, man. Good luck!"

I was too shocked to protest. "What are you doing?" I finally yelled, but my protest was lost in the wind and roar of the gathering firestorm. It didn't matter anyway, because I knew what he was doing—saving his skin—and after the momentary outburst, I didn't blame him, and I don't to this day. I would call the sensation envy, but that only gives you the proper course—not the proper depth of what I felt as I saw him motor up the hill to catch the crew. I also knew that if it was bad enough to make him leave me behind, it was a situation I shouldn't just run from—I needed to fly.

With trembling hands I put my hardhat on and tried to catch him. Keep him within twenty feet, I said at first. Then the acidic rubber cement filled my legs, making them as useful as wooden pegs. My breath wheezed. My sight grew hazy as I became light headed. Suddenly twenty feet of distance was between us. I bartered with myself, thirty feet, and thirty feet came. Then forty, and forty came, and fifty, and sixty, and soon Rob had caught up to the last sawyer. But even the pack was no safe haven. The crew's typical orderly formation was gone. Gaps formed between individuals. Some people were touching hands to ground as they scrambled to keep up—not to be separated from the herd as the predator approached.

I turned inside myself. I tried to talk myself down, told myself this couldn't be as serious as it looked. I repeated the odds; the odds were on my side— crews never got wiped out. But the more I tried to calm myself, the more I had to deny the unfolding reality. And the more I denied reality, the less I was able to react to it. I became tormented by the dissonance between what I told myself and what my senses told me. I was going mad.

After another twenty steps, the hill had become impossible—like an elevator shaft. The crew had lost all semblance of order. Some passed others; some hiked side by side, as if to pull each other up. Shovels and Pulaskis littered the ground as the scrapers dropped them. Some of the hotshots were even throwing off their packs.

I fell to the ground, scratching at the earth out of panic. The fire's heat began to bear down on my neck. The atmosphere vibrated from its scream, and the air turned red as smoke covered the sun. It was as if some supernatural barrier between the dimensions of heaven, earth, and hell had been breached, and now one was spilling into the other.

I looked behind me to see a wall of flames at least ten times my height lashing up the hill. Large convection currents formed into spinning cyclones of firebrands, ripping small trees from the ground. The silhouette of a convulsing body flashed in the vortex before being thrown back deep into the firestorm. The convict crew had been devoured.

The world became a scrambled puzzle of symbols and horror. I screamed murder and mercy and twitched spastically as the apocalypse came for me next.

Skip called upon all his mental discipline to push what he had just witnessed out of his mind. There was nothing to do for the convict crew that had vanished behind the flame front, or what looked to be their last surviving member who now lay face down on the line fifty or sixty yards below the last member of his crew. He had to concern himself with those whom he was responsible for—he had to stay focused. Find the iron, he thought, find the iron. Think. Think. His crew can make it. *His crew can make it!*

The sawyers were his biggest concern. They had been running the machines for six hours in the heat and now had to carry all thirty pounds of them and the thirty pounds of gear that came with them—the extra saw chains, the saw gas, the oil, the maintenance tools, plus the extra water a sawyer usually needed. Also, they had to shoulder the psychological burden of being in the back of the line—something that has been proven time and time again to slow a man. Skip had never liked the way Reverse Tool Order worked for this reason—but it was the only formation for retreat that anyone had ever used.

Their saws! They're still carrying their saws!

"Drop saws and tools!" he yelled.

Cynthia, who was right behind him, repeated the order, but a fading crewmember gripped with fear did not. Many of the sawyers held fast to their instrument, as their relationship with the machine was akin to the relationship a man has with his dog.

"Bump that goddamn order, Ryan!" Skip yelled at the rookie.   Ryan did, but the order would apparently get lost again as both the fire and desperate breath became too loud to hear anything else.

Skip ran up the hill.   At twenty-seven, athletic, dedicated, and "thick," he could rather easily punch ahead of the average crew speed on a hike. He did that now to get perspective on the crew's position.

He reached the ridge, looked back, and calculated. Cynthia only had thirty feet until she reached the top. There she and all the others could enter the rockslide on the other side of the ridge where they would be safe. He estimated that the crew had spread out two hundred feet. Even the slowest member should be able to cover that distance in two minutes. The fire would be to the top in five minutes—if it didn't double its rate of spread once again.

It'll work out. It'll work out! It'll work out!

Three minutes to get in our safety zone and five minutes for the fire to hit.

It'll work out! It'll work out! It'll work out!

He repeated the equation and its result several times in his head, believing fervently in the idea that thoughts shape reality.

He ran back down the hill to Cynthia to give all the support he might.

He hiked the final few feet in front of her, and as he approached the ridge for the second time, he spotted Bruce walking quickly down the ridge's spine.

Happy to give up Alpha in these dire straits, Skip felt relief as he watched the crew's top leader walk quickly to meet them. But why were Bruce's quick glances away from his path not on the approaching fire but toward the ridge north of them—the safety zone?

He reached the crest of the ridge and understood.

There was fire moving uphill toward the rockslide that was supposed to be their safety zone.

When they had decided to use the large rockslide as a safety zone, they assumed flames would be coming from the south—and therefore would be burning from the top of the hill down. This would keep flame lengths low, and prevent the head of the fire from casting massive amounts of heat into the rockslide. But now with a fire established below, coming toward the top and gathering steam as it did so, the convective heat, the flames, would spill right into it. There was no way the safety zone would suffice for the entire crew.

"We need to shelter up and even then it won't be large enough for everyone," Bruce said immediately once he was within speaking range. "Do you remember another rockslide an eighth of a mile down the spine of the ridge, adjacent to the line we cut earlier?"

Skip could not remember. It seemed that he might have seen one, but over the last eight years he had been on countless hikes on similar ridges. Most of them had rockslides or outcroppings scattered here or there.

"Yes, I think so."

"Okay, I want you to take Marcus, Anderson, Rollingson, and Jacobson and use that rock outcropping. Don't hesitate to shelter up. That's what we're going to be doing here."

There would be shame in using shelters. Hotshots are supposed to know fire so well that they shouldn't ever get caught in such a position. But here they were, and there was only one way now to make sure everyone made it.

"You sure it should be them?" Skip asked. They've been running saw all day."

"They're our fastest guys. They're our toughest guys. They'll make it."

Crewmembers made their way up the hill and gathered around the two men. Their faces were full of sweat, blood, and stress, their eyes unnaturally wide, jaws clenched in deathly determination, or gaping open with breath and fear.

Most realized the issue immediately upon seeing the second fire.

"I need Marcus, Anderson, Jacobson, Rollingson!" Skip barked.

"I'm here," Jacobson said. "And here comes Anderson and Marcus."

"Yeah, we're here," Steve Anderson said. He eyed the fire in the north ridge as he dropped his saw. "What the hell?" he said, looking at the fire like a union worker pissed off at forced overtime.

"I don't know, but there it is," Skip said.

"Rollingson here!" a voice yelled out.

"Just do what it takes! Burn out. Shelter up. Don't hesitate!" Bruce said.

Skip nodded, then called out the names of his makeshift unit. "Marcus, Anderson, Rollingson, Jacobson! Follow me! Let's go!"

The men started to run down the spine of the ridge on the line they had cut earlier in the day.

The men charged down the slight slope of the ridge, the brush alongside the trail limiting their vision. It was as if they were in an alley of green. They would occasionally try to peak over the verdant walls to see how far away the oncoming flames were, but it was futile. They could only guess how long before the flames burst over the ridge and devoured them by the depth of crimson in the air, the heat on their skin, and the din of the storm. Was it minutes away? Seconds?

Skip turned and yelled an order for the men to cover their mouths with their sleeves. He hoped it might give protection to their airway from the superheated gasses that would certainly preclude the oncoming wall of flames. He had heard a thousand times in trainings that the airway must be protected in such an emergency—a person can live with burned skin, but not burned lungs. However, the mechanics of protecting your airway while running from a fire was never really explained—breathing through a shirtsleeve was all he could think of. The men tried to do as told, but at a full sprint, it was nothing but a mimic.

Skip approached a small bend in the line that obstructed his view. Was it memory or hope that made him think the rock outcropping might be behind it? He sped up, desperate to find out. As the bend opened up into a straight view, he saw nothing but more walls of green. He reached a steep down slope that obscured his vision of the bottom of the grade. It might be there, he thought. It wasn't. Soon every slight bend was turned with held breath and gritted teeth, which would be released with whispered cussing. He continually tried to calculate how many seconds they might have: thirty, forty, maybe an entire minute...

He turned his head and yelled toward the men. "Drop your backpacks—keep your shelters!"

The men reached along their waste belts, unclipped the straps of their backpacks and dropped them to the ground. Their web belts, which had one small pouch for a canteen of water and a large pouch for their fire shelter, stayed on their waists.

Edgar Rollingson moved his attention from the bumpy ground he was running on to a stubborn clip, and doing so he tripped and fell to the ground. Joe Jacobson, directly behind Rollingson, hurdled over him gracefully, but Marcus did not see him until too late. He tripped over Rollingson and both men skidded across the ground.

"Goddamn it, Rollingson!" Marcus protested.

"Always a clutz..." Rollingson said as he scrambled to his feet, helping Marcus.

Skip heard the ruckus, turned, and yelled, feverishly incoherent. His eyes beamed with wild anguish. His words were practically rabid in tone. He was completely out of character. The men realized then that he knew of no safety zone. They were on the last seconds of a suicide mission.

The last moments of my life were passing, and my emotions seesawed between sorrow and dread.

One moment it was profound—like a tragic movie or a man's last broken heart, an orgy of self pity, the pain and fear so exquisite as to be almost pleasurable—but as soon as anything like catharsis happened, utter and complete horror once more took its place, the blood curdling fear a searing poker up the ass that demanded one move, or at least squirm feverishly and scream.

I looked up to see the last hotshot reaching the top of the ridge.

They had all made it to the top. The studs had made it. The studs were going to live—to avoid the wall, the rock, the infinite power and awesomeness that was sure to obliterate me in only moments.

The dope was to die. The dope was weak; the dope hadn't pushed himself. I had done nothing, I had been coaxed into doing nothing, I had been hypnotized by an easy life, and now I would be betrayed by it. And that fucking rock jock, that fucker who stole that girl at fire school, that cocky shit head pseudo-hippie asshole, Grump, the boss who had left me to die without so much as a word—he was someone who would make it. In a moment of a million visions, I saw him skiing in the day, I saw him in a bar at night, I saw him telling the story of his hair-breath escape to some hot snow bimbette, I saw her look longing at him, I saw him about to get laid because he had survived some monumental tragedy fire—the fire that *killed me.*

My death would be fodder for a seduction story.

Unless things changed.

My teeth clenched together, and I focused, for the first time ever it seemed, on the problem at hand. A lesson from fire school suddenly blossomed in my mind. In almost all burnovers firefighters made one common mistake. They tried to escape their fate by returning up the same path that had led them to it—the desire to "get back" to where they had come from overwhelmed them—even when it was an impossible endeavor.

Climbing the hill was suicide. I had to think of something else ...

I must use my fire shelter.

I scanned the hill and the timber reproduction covering it. Through the trees, shrubs, and briers, I spotted a rock outcropping below. Twenty feet of Himalayan Blackberries surrounded it, looking impenetrable. There was nothing else—no rock slides, no bare dirt, just a load of densely planted juvenile timber that were so ready to burn they already had a spot fire or two in them.

It hit me like lightning. Yes. *A SPOT FIRE!*

I ran toward a small fire that was burning about thirty yards away, barely able to keep my limbs from shaking into worthlessness.

Left over timber slash from the logging operation covered the replanted clear cut, so that I had to jump from log to log. As I did, branches and sticks caught my shins and groin, tripping me up and causing me to fall in between the logs.

I approached the spot fire, seeing that at the uphill side the flames were at least ten feet high, but on the downhill side, where the fire had presumably started, the flames were gone—only a black scar remained. I hiked toward this entryway and walked into the black area. Inside the small burned space was a small rockslide. I threw my hands out recklessly and dived. I clenched the jagged pieces of hot granite so tightly that the sharp edges cut through my gloves and into my hands as I scrambled onto the clump of rocks and looked for a flat surface where I could deploy my shelter. A flat rock, so rectangular it looked like a table or alter, lay in the center.

My fingers fumbled through the small pouch that housed the tightly packed shelter on the backside of my waist. Finally getting a grip on it, I yanked out the silver brick of folded aluminum. It was covered in clear plastic, with a red tab that seemed to indicate I should pull on it to unwrap. I tried, but the radiant heat had made the plastic so soft and malleable that it would not tear but merely stretch. I started to jump in angst and protest as I dug at it passionately. Finally the covering stretched to its limit and a small mouth opened in the melted plastic. I tore the shelter out, grabbed an end, unfolded it length wise, then whipped it open. The wind caught it instantly and it sprang into the shape of a small pup tent just as it was ripped from my hands and blew toward the uphill side of the spot fire.

Seeing my shining deliverance fly away I pounced at once, landing on the sharp rocks, breaking my ribs, tightening my breath—but I had it in my hands.

Clinging to the shelter, I crawled desperately to the rock slab. I put my hands and feet through the straps at each inside corner, so that the shelter covered my back. Then to my knees, then to my stomach, with my feet to the coming flame front.

What was about to happen to me? Would the shelter be lashed from my hands? Would it delaminate, burning me slowly in ever increasing agony? If I survived, would I forever be a burn victim? Is there a worse fate than slowly being baked alive?

A sudden gush of air shook the tent, spiking the temperature; an acrid smell assaulted my nose.

The wall of the main flame front hit.

The roar was so loud and violent that it crumpled my eardrums—but I dared not cover them. A tidal wave of violent winds heaved and tugged at the shelter so that it took all my strength to keep it on the ground. The heat became excruciating, and sweat from effort and panic poured down my brow, stinging my eyes as I yowled like a beat dog. Tears born of helplessness streaked my face.

∞

As the men galloped in panic, Skip peered ahead, willing the rockslide into existence. He was about to go off the north bank and make a blind run through thick brush as a last-ditch losing effort.

A patch of dead grass along the ridgeline crossed his peripheral vision.

He stopped in his tracks. He had an idea.

The other men nearly tumbled into him as he slowed down to look at it.

"Get your fusees!" Skip ordered.

"They're in our packs! We dropped them!" Edgar said.

"Shit!" Skip said as he fumbled in the pockets of his pants. He found nothing but a can of tobacco. He patted down his shirt, found the small metal box inside, and pulled it out.

"Help me!" he barked. He flipped the Zippo with his finger and shielded it with his free hand. Using his body to push away the bushes that were adjacent to the patch of dead grass, he walked along the perimeter, setting the area on fire.

Realizing what his boss intended, Jacobson picked up a stick, ignited it in the flames his boss had set, and bolted to the other end of the grass patch. He walked toward Skip, mirroring his actions. The men met each other and waited as an ephemeral orange blanket covered the grass.

"Pull out your shelters!" Skip yelled to the men.

In moments the fire and grass disappeared, leaving a smoking black scar. It wasn't a big piece of land, but it was now free of fuel.

Within in twenty-five seconds, the crewmen removed their shelters from their web belts and whipped them open, as they had practiced many times in training. They grabbed one last deep breath of air before lying prone on the still smoking ground and squirmed under the tents as the hot ground scorched their elbows and knees and residual smoke filled the tents

All except Steve Anderson.

Joe Jacobson had just gotten under his tent when he heard Steve yelling, "Dude! Dude! You got to let me in! You got to let me in! My shelter is fucked!"

Joe poked his head out from under his tent to see Steve yelling, face full of panic, arms flailing about him, the shining shelter whipping about in his hand. Unable to understand a word the hysterical man was saying, Jacobson figured the situation when he saw the two foot long rip on the left side of Steve's shelter.

Jacobson calculated the data like a computer:

◊ Chances of survival far from perfect with one person
◊ Worse with two
◊ Breathable air in shelter limited
◊ I = wife and child
◊ Steve = single, erratic
◊ People survived with rips in past

"No! No you can't come in here." Jacobson blurted. "Just ... just get in the shelter and keep the rip under you. I can't let you in!" He disappeared back under his shelter.

Steve screamed for Jacobson to let him in. He reached to tear Jacobson's shelter off the ground.

"Get in your shelter now!" Skip roared as to give a lion pause, as he stuck his head out from under his shelter. Steve froze and looked at Skip. "We've

105

talked about this before. You know what to do. Keep the rip under you. Now!" Skip yelled.

Steve's eyes turned to meet the directly oncoming fire. The monolith of dazzling blood red walls was massive, dreamlike, surreal. He closed his eyes, jumped to the ground and pulled his torn shelter over him.

Within moments, an orange ray of radiation beamed through the shelter, burning a hole through his shirt, and then his skin, seizing him in indescribable pain.

∞

My scream died—but the horror did not. I lay there with my face pressed against the hard rock trying to talk myself out of the claustrophobic panic.

Something positive, I told myself. I must think of something positive.

I remembered sitting on my grandfather's lap when I was four, in the old man's worn out green chair. He would bounce me up and down, tell me stories of his heroics, and sometimes sing me songs.

He told me someday I would have stories, too, someday I would sing songs. I tried to sing the songs I remembered to keep from screaming. The screaming only made it worse.

But just as I began, a searing pain burst so violently into my awareness that the note turned into a shriek. A noxious odor filled the air—the smell of glue and burned meat. It was my calf. The shelter had started to give out and now the hot aluminum was making contact with the skin of my leg, burning it. I was about to throw off the shelter, but tried to sing to stop myself. I sang nothing ... everything ... whatever came to mind, and just as I thought I was getting some control of myself, it got even worse.

The sting of sweat in my eyes ceased. I stopped sweating. *There was no water left in my body. I was being baked alive.*

An insatiable panic rushed through me.

I will run! I will run from all of this! I will run so fast only my feet get burned!

But just as I was about to throw off the shelter and face suicide by taking the blaze on straight, one last sober thought of hope stopped me. The emotional torment and physical stress put a strangle hold on my consciousness, and I slipped into darkness with one last yelp.

Until he saw the rip, it had all been a thrill for Steve. He had been chosen for the most dangerous assignment, a nod to his physical stamina and strength, which clearly stood out even from his formidable crewmates.

It really wasn't surprising. He had always excelled at all adrenaline-inducing behavior. At eighteen he had bypassed college to go conquer complex levels of skiing. In no time he had jumped off every cliff and slid down every thirty-percent slope in the West. Then he snow boarded every acre of backcountry in the Rocky Mountain resort where he lived—and slept with at least half the women there. He moved on to big wave surfing—and by twenty-two he had surfed the biggest breaks in Northern California. The upcoming winter he had plans for Hawaii's North Shore.

He met similar success in the world of fire. After working only one year doing "slug" work on a wildland fire engine, he received a job offer from the esteemed Bison Hotshots because of a recommendation from a well connected boss. His strength and aggressive attitude even earned him the prestigious position of sawyer his first season, a job normally saved for proven veterans. This was his second season, and probably last. He planned to be jumping out of airplanes in wildfire next year, as a smokejumper. All this success in dangerous endeavors gave him an air of invincibility.

But in the shelter a new landscape of the psyche opened up, and it was one of terror. Unlike other dangerous situations he had dealt with, there was no way to swing, hike, paddle, run, or talk his way out. Games requiring nerves and control, such as pool, golf, and bowling, had always caused him contempt—but the practice of such attributes would have helped him during that terrible first taste of his own mortality.

Joe Jacobson watched a bright ember on the tip of his nose slowly cool into ash. It was one of many that had assaulted his face. Despite all his desire to wipe them off, he had to grit his teeth and take the sting. His hands were too busy keeping his shelter from being blown off by the tempest bearing down on him.

He yelled out several times, trying to make contact with the others over the roar—but there was no response. Even in the center, the most protected spot, his lungs burned and gagged on their own mucus, his arms trembled from the strain required to keep the shelter to the ground, and threatened each second to give up the fight. At one moment the wind would be heavy but steady; the next it would scream to split atoms and demand every ounce of strength from his limbs. He couldn't judge from one moment to the next, so he simply pressed to the ground as hard as he could for as long as he could. He yelled out again but heard no one. He fought off the impending sense that he was the sole survivor, alive only because he had greedily taken the center of the burned patch.

He had felt justified in taking the spot because he had the most responsibility. Unlike anyone else on the crew, he had a wife and a child—and if he retraced his steps to the current moment, he would see that his family had both jeopardized him and saved him.

While most crewmembers headed to Mexico or a mountain resort for the off season to ski or surf, drink and cavort, he condemned himself to a purgatory of exercise. Every morning at daybreak, he walked outside his small mountain cabin to put on a sweat-stained, thirty-pound backpack. Then he would hike straight up a two-mile steep grade in the snow. On these cold hikes, Joe whipped himself up the hill like a merciless slave driver. His only way of getting gainful employment was wildland firefighting—it was his only skill—and it was a terrible job for a man with a family. How could he have lacked such foresight? How could he have chosen such a dangerous career that put him so far away from those who needed him?

He met Gina, his wife, for the first time when they were both only four, at Sunday school. She was wearing a green dress made of corduroy. The light from the large windows was shining behind her brunette hair, and he was glad to see her. A few years later, when he was seven, she moved only three houses away. The two became friends, but her family was richer, and she was pretty and soon popular. For most of his secondary education, he yearned for her without hope, like everyone else save the hockey and football players. He was a grease monkey, and he dated girls considered in his league.

When he turned eighteen, his dedication to a high school vocational program in mechanics paid off, and he got a job with the Forest Service through a work-study program. But that was as far as his career as a mechanic would go. Fires broke out that hot summer. The Forest Service sent him to fire school and then he was on a fire, working as a grunt in a makeshift type II crew. Suddenly, he was no longer an apprentice mechanic, or in high school. He was a firefighter—maybe even a hero of sorts—or at least a bonafide man.

When he returned from his first fire, his confidence was at full mast; a kingdom awaited him. He went to his parents' house and saw Gina at the top of the hill; before he could doubt or sweat, he had asked her to a movie. And then they were in love, and then they were pregnant, all within a year. The baby came before they could legally drink alcohol.

There was nothing sophisticated about their bond. They were mammals. And they intended to be nothing other than that. They were warm. They were proud. They were full of lust for each other, full of love for their young, and ferocious when it came to their protection. They made a family. A family that groomed each other, a family that cared for each other, a family that laughed with each other, a family that cried together, and a family

111

that talked to each other, sometimes in words no one else could understand.

But how to support it? He could make more working six months on the 'shot crew than he could in a year working as a mechanic. And the lump-sum of money he would save gave them greater control of their finances. Gina had a small knack for investing and so the money lasted easily throughout the off-season. And since all hotshots were technically laid off over the off-season, he could collect a healthy sum of unemployment. And while he knew in his heart of hearts that he could get a job fixing cars—or maybe really bite the bullet and try to sell them—there was a pride in firefighting, and a freedom, and a bond with his crew that he could find no where else.

And so to justify his decision, he would hike at a brutal pace up the wintery snow-covered slope. His lungs would fill with fluid to protect against the frigid air, and his muscles would whine and twitch with every flex.

After climbing the hill three times, exhausted but purged, he would return to the cabin to shower and light the fire. He would put himself down next to his warm, sleeping wife, and hold her close in the still light of morning. Sometimes they would make love, and sometimes they would talk, and sometimes they would just lie in peace until the child awoke and another lazy, cozy winter day began. Later in the day, when his guilt had collected enough strength again, he would go out into the cold garage to lift weights for an hour.

In a way his self-inflicted penitence had backfired. The stamina he had earned over the winter also earned him a spot on the death run for a nonexistence safety zone.

He cursed himself for not refusing it. But it had all unraveled too fast—and he respected Bruce and Skip too much to refuse their authority at the critical moment. Nevertheless, his commitment to his family had pushed him to take the center spot in the burned out patch of grass, the area most buffered from the flames, the only area that seemed survivable.

He called out one more time to his crewmembers, but heard nothing. He was alone, the only one left. And with his ebbing strength threatening to succumb to the hurricane, fire-filled winds, not sure he would be for long.

Edgar Rollingson moved his weight from one side to another with the nervous grace of an inexperienced trapeze artist as he tried to keep the bottom of his shelter sealed to the ground in the fierce winds. He used his long wiry arms and legs to hold down the tent, and used well practiced techniques to keep his fear in check.

He had spent much of his adolescence scared. At age twelve, his sheltered childhood in northern Oregon came to an abrupt end. His father, a well-off accountant, informed his mother that he was in love with her substantially younger best friend. The two told his mother together in the living room, while he sat anxiously in his room. He remembers the screaming but not the words.

His mother retaliated to the betrayal by making plans to move Edgar and herself, swearing to his father, in front of Edgar, that he would never see his son again. On the way out of town, she explained that she had found a job in Salinas, California, as she wanted to be far away from "the monster." Once in California, however, she did nothing but rigorously attend church, watch TV, and complain with great zeal to her lawyer about his father's "amoralistic" ways. Edgar finally gleaned that no job awaited at all. He later put together that the sole reason she had chosen the area was because of an ex-boyfriend, who turned out to be more than willing to have a relationship with her, as long as it didn't infringe on his marriage. In two months' time Edgar's world had changed from stable to absolutely chaotic. In a new town, with black hair starting to creep from his skin in places where it never had before, he faced the revelation that his father was "amoralistic" and that his mother wavered between fantasy and fanaticism.

A week after arriving in the new state, feeling the ground beneath him was not to be trusted, he went to his first day of junior high. The chaos outdid itself. Kids ran around everywhere in the courtyard, speaking, screaming, and yelling in a language he could not understand. Many of them had tattered clothes and haircuts that would only be worn as a joke in his former school, yet they all walked with a bravado and confidence he'd never seen. His clean and well-kempt Izod shirt, his cropped and dull sandy hair, his blue eyes and pale skin all made him an immediate target. Beads of nervous adolescent sweat seeped from his forehead.

"Look, an exchange student!" a young Hispanic boy yelled.

"Sounds like a spy to me," another said as a group circled and taunted him.

He bolted out of sight, fleeing to the sanctuary of homeroom.

Believing that such circumstances must be temporary, he kept to himself. Most of the kids, whose cultural upbringing made them naturally gregarious, interpreted his introversion, coupled with his new clothes and good grades, as conceit. In a world of alliances, conformity, and bravado, he was alone—unique, tacit, and small.

Within days he found both fists and ridicule aimed at him. The first week he was christened "the

Nazi" by having his head dunked in a flushing toilet.

Bands of boys hunted him constantly when he walked to and from school. Lacking any physical prowess, except for his developing ability to run, Edgar had no way to defend himself. When caught, they would usually just humiliate him by throwing his books, or pulling his shirt over his head, calling him a school boy, a Nazi, a weak white bastard whose mother had moved down to California to get the preferred Mexican dick, and other equally creative taunts. At least once a month they would beat him painfully. The streetwise boys would strike only the body so the beatings wouldn't leave obvious marks. Not trusting the emotional equilibrium of his mother or the care of his teachers, he said nothing.

So he went it alone. At first the fear during fights was too much; it paralyzed him, made his legs like defiant rubber nubs that couldn't possibly move fast enough. But slowly he evolved from a deer in the headlights to a rabbit that could dash for known cover. And as his testosterone levels increased, his anger became available, almost irrepressible, so that he would hiss and strike out like a badger, making room for escape. His intellect grew keen, making him cunning and creative, like a wolf, with not only the ability to run or attack, but also to remain still and poised. And finally, like a human, he learned to adapt to his culture, mimicking those who were strong, so that he would look strong himself.

By his ninth grade year, with many of his tormentors now distracted by the frightening demands of gang life, he had earned enough respect to get what he sought: to be left alone.

But the mark of insecurity and fear followed him to adulthood. The adrenaline sports popular at his college—skiing, rock climbing, surfing—never suited him. He lacked the innate sense of immortality that many other young men had. He did them just the same—it was important to push oneself—but he always did them with a sense of dread, and he never excelled. It was only running, with its singular demand to endure, and fighting fire that he was good at. But unlike all other thrill-seeking behavior, firefighting was different—it was a job, a duty, a mission. Someone had to do it, and this purpose gave him the courage he often lacked in activities done for only thrill or glory.

So now, trapped in his shelter, with temperatures outside well over a thousand degrees, he wrestled with his fear and pain in a well-practiced fashion. He removed himself from his emotions and focused on the task at hand—keeping the shelter on the ground.

∞

Skip's lungs could barely expand enough in the smoke to gather the wind needed to call out to his crewmembers, but he tried and tried, pulling in small puffs of air until he had enough to shout. It only made him dizzy.

By the time the noise began to subside, he found his voice too hoarse and dry to yell at all. But eventually he heard something—was it a yell, a groan?

Gradually the noises started to take form. The lowest voice was Marcus—he was repeating, "Is anyone there?" Then he heard Jacobson, also asking if anyone else was around, then Steve asking the same, or was it Edgar? He couldn't be sure. He waited for the fire to quiet down some more—and allowed his voice to rest—before yelling out.

"Marcus! I am here. Are you all right?" he shouted, turning his head to his right.

"Yeah, yeah I am," Marcus responded, stoically.

"Jacobson, are you all right?" Skip asked.

"Yeah. Think so," Jacobson said.

"Edgar!" Skip yelled.

"Here," Edgar said.

"Steve!" Skip asked.

No response.

"Steve!" Skip demanded again.

Soon the other men started calling for Steve. Skip wished the men would shut up. No one was going to hear anything over their own yells. But he didn't have the vocal strength to shout them down after all the smoke exposure. He stuck his head out of his shelter and a barrage of light and heat struck him.

"Should we get out and look for him?" Jacobson asked.

Skip's face acclimated to the outside—it was tolerable.

"Yeah, I wouldn't mind getting the fuck out of this thing!" Edgar said.

Skip was about to give the go-ahead when he felt a slight visceral tug.

"No...no. Let's wait. Still too hot out," he said.

"Fuck, if you say so," Edgar said.

Skip put his head back under his shelter, and felt a sense of gratitude that his men were still willing to follow him. Even after he had almost raced them to their death, they were still asking for his permission and advice—and through some miracle, he was still able to give it.

In high school he had been a real space case—a gentle soul who wasn't afraid to laugh at himself, and often had reason to do just that. Though was the brunt of jokes, he earned respect and popularity through his humor, keen empathy, and humble character. He enjoyed slow, deep thought processes. He secretly painted in his spare time, and though he received only average grades, by the time he graduated, he had read many complicated works of philosophy and often felt he understood them better than his teachers did. He planned on going to college, picking up an advanced degree, and teaching in some small mountain town where he could ski and rock climb.

That was his plan. Then, in the summer after graduation, he picked up a seasonal job with the Forest Service doing brush disposal. It redefined him. The job involved stacking timber slash from clear-cuts and burning it. But the summer had been unusually dry and hot, and the fire season demanded many hands, so the Forest Service sent the brush disposal crew to help with the suppression effort. Work, fire, and money suddenly filled Skip's life.

It was a thrill. He rode on helicopters, hiked into remote forests, slept under the stars all summer. Base camp was always abuzz with reporters and hundreds if not thousands of people from across the state and the nation, all joined in a common mission. He made close friends; he learned about fire, weather, and geography. He was free from cleaning, laundry, daily grooming, and other mundane chores. On the few days they had off, the crew would go to town with plenty of money, and girls his age smiled brightly when he told them he was a firefighter. The only problem was, he didn't feel like he was fighting fire.

Since the crew was Type II, Incident Command used it almost exclusively for mop-up. Only after the fire had been contained by a firebreak and the flames had subsided would his brush disposal crew be called to put out the remaining hot spots that might throw embers over the containment line. Using hand tools and only limited water, Skip's crew would dig out burning stumps, separate the coals, and spray them with a light mist of water from bladder bags they wore on their backs, called "piss pumps." It was hot and heavy work that was testing, but Skip longed for the excitement of cutting hot line—the work that stopped the fire's spread.

Skip learned that on large fires the crews assigned to go head-to-head with live, active fire were almost exclusively Type I "hotshot" crews. He would watch these crews come in every night to camp and queue up in the dinner line, covered in soot, exhaustion, and pride. They were mature men who enjoyed an easy camaraderie with each other. Though they were all clearly in shape, it was not their muscle but their faces that impressed Skip the most. They were lined with strength, and tempered with hard-earned dignity, almost wisdom. It was a look he had seen before in some of the older rock climbers. He didn't know what gave a man that look, but he sorely wanted whatever knowledge or experience the job gave these men in order to bear such an expression so naturally.

Skip's boss on the brush disposal crew had been a hotshot in Alaska for ten years and had a well-respected name in the fire community. Skip asked him question after question about the experience, and he told Skip tale after tale about life with the 'shot crew, and his travels and adventures during the off-season.

"Jeez, why did you ever quit?" Skip asked once.

"Because it was the job or my wife," his boss said.

"You must really love your wife," Skip said.

His boss recognized Skip's incessant questioning, and the way he sized up the hotshots as they came in to camp. After dinner one night, while Skip watched the Stanislaus Hotshots walk by, the boss came up behind Skip.

"So you want to be a hotshot?" his boss asked.

"Yeah. Yeah, I do," Skip said.

"It's a lot of hard work. Got to be tough. Got to make a lot of sacrifices," his boss said.

"Yeah, well, I think I can do it," Skip said diffidently. He wanted to sound confident and bold, like a hotshot, but he was tripped up because he feared sounding cocky and arrogant. He later learned that a person cannot achieve one without risking the other.

"We'll see how you do the rest of the summer," the boss said and walked away.

The summer passed quickly as Skip's brush disposal crew went from fire to fire, mopping up what the hotshots put out. September came, but the fires still burned, checks still filled his bank account, and he still shared plenty of laughs with his fellow crewmembers.

His boss came up to Skip one evening after a shift and told him that the Forest Service had extended extra emergency funds to keep the crew working another month. He knew Skip planned to start college in a few days, but he would like Skip to see the season out. Of course, the choice was Skip's—he had fulfilled his obligation—but the crew still needed him.

Skip knew what his boss implied: make this sacrifice right now, and I'll give you that recommendation for the hotshots next year.

Skip wavered for a moment as the new offer conflicted with his original plan. But his last year in high school had given him distaste for academic study. His teachers seemed obsessed with mundane names and dates; while he tried to find the edges of the universe, they seemed confined to the lifeless rotating rocks of the solar system. After five seconds of contemplation, with his boss looking directly at him, Skip made a monumental decision. He would stay with the crew.

"Good to hear it," the boss said and walked off.

The next spring, a few days after his nineteenth birthday, Skip found himself the youngest member of a hotshot crew. With his self-image and personality still developing, Skip was immersed in a world that worshiped tenacity, competence, adrenaline and an uncompromising work ethic. The tough and seemingly angry men of the crew called him "Kid," and they tried their best to break him whenever there was a chance.

During one blistering-hot, southern California fire, after cutting line for ten hours, the crew was forced to sit and wait on a burnt, shade less hillside in one hundred degree heat. The sawyers got wind that the Kid wanted to run saw himself some day.

"All right Kid, let's see how long you can saw for," one of the sawyers said as he handed his saw to Skip.

Skip looked around, questioning what to cut, since the line was complete.

"Saw in the black – saw all those damned burned Manzanita bushes," the sawyer said. "I'm sick of looking at them. Besides, the El Cariso 'Shots are down this ridge, and I want them to hear us working while they sit on their asses."

The boy shrugged, pulled the starting chord, revved the engine, and started cutting trees.

"Faster, kid! You got to move faster than that. And swamp that shit yourself," the veteran yelled at him.

Skip, trying to impress the humored crew, moved as fast as he could. Soon his shirt was soaked with sweat.

The men sat and watched the boy struggle at meaningless work. "Keep going, kid! That's it!" a crewmember yelled. "Just go until you pass out. That's your body's safety mechanism. Just go until then and you'll be fine."

Skip's face flushed with blood, and he could feel his body waver with heat stress. But a few of the veterans still pressed him on, so he continued to work, determined to prove to those around him that he had the will and the desire to gain the esteemed position.

The world began to smear in a strange white and purple pattern. He stumbled for a moment, his arms became slack, out of his control, and the saw dropped down, the teeth gouging his chaps as he fell against a tree, trying to brace himself.

"What the hell! What in *the fuck* is going on here?"

Skip faced the angry superintendent who had returned to retrieve his crew. The men all looked down or away, leaving Skip to answer the furious supervisor.

"I just, I just..." Skip stammered.

"You just what? Wanted to waste a saw, some gas, and yourself on some fucking burned brush! Put down that goddamn saw!" yelled the superintendent.

Skip did as he was told, laying the saw in front of the veteran's feet.

"Goddamn it, Rally!" the Superintendent barked at the veteran. "I don't ever want to see this kind of stupid shit again! If that boy goes tits up on the six mile hike out of here, you're the one who's carrying him!"

Skip made it out on his own.

After three years on the crew, the nickname "Kid" slowly lost its stick. It was eventually replaced by a deep respect from all who worked with him. He earned a place as a sawyer, and the transformation from tender high school kid to hotshot was complete. He developed excellent self-discipline in order to keep his mind on task and focused, instead of allowing himself to drift into the dreamy outer reaches. Keen awareness of his outside environment now replaced his former spacey introspection and intuition. He came to disfavor those who were unaware of hazards, forgetful with their tools, or prone to complaining. His life became one thing: the job.

During his fifth year, he was shown a picture of a fire the crew had been on. In the background, a man with a solid, callused, and tough expression on his face caught his attention. It struck him to realize it was his image that bore such hardness and depth. A momentary pride filled him, but dissipated just as quickly. After all the work and sacrifice, it was simply an even trade.

Now he laughed rarely—usually only in unguarded moments after beer and tequila. During such times his face would light up, almost like a clown, his limbs would become loose and gangly, and a smile would radiate from his face with such warmth and joy that crewmembers would almost be confused as to who they were with.

Other vestiges of his former self remained, also. Sometimes when all logic pointed to a certain course of action, his intuition would rise up inside him and turn his stomach into a knot. When he heard no response from Steve, and the fire appeared to have passed, it seemed sensible to throw off his shelter, tough out the heat, and find his missing man. But his gut wouldn't let him do it. As the winds returned to violently shaking his shelter, and the temperature once again spiked to lethal levels, Skip felt thankful to an old forgotten self.

Chapter Four

I came to in a void without form. Not quite black, but rather streaks and smears of formless, imaginary color, in which hue and brightness were one and the same—like ghosts of bodies that never were. And then there was a throb—almost peaceful at first, until it turned to a thud, more painful with each repetition.

Then a streak of light—a ribbon of it ran around me. A sensation of open nerves being scraped.

I was aware of my eyes first. My eyelids scratched them like sandpaper. The throbbing became painful and intense. Then there was a tingle all over that soon turned into a terrible ubiquitous itch, and then I felt the hot burn on my calf.

Was I dead? In a hospital? In a car wreck? Was I coming out of a coma?

The day's events suddenly unfolded in front of me in a frightening epiphany. I spasmed in latent horror and threw off the shelter, immediately assaulted by the brightest light in my life.

I squinted, coughed, gagged and waved my arms around, as if trying to fight off the entire place and time. Eventually I regained some composure and slowly stood up. I wasn't dead, but hell surrounded me.

The juvenile trees and timber slash were gone, replaced by a cover of black and gray soot. The only trace of what had been was the occasional blackened stump, which cracked with flames and puffed smoke. They popped and crackled as a slight breeze rustled—but otherwise it was quiet, almost peaceful compared to only an hour before. I could not believe that only earlier that day this place had been full of life and activity; such ugliness had to have always been.

The fire shelter rustled at my feet. Its silver sheen was gone, covered with brown and black corrosion, and it looked like it would turn to dust with a touch. I felt a moment of uncomfortable wonder at how such an insubstantial item allowed me to survive such destruction, before turning my attention back to my surroundings.

The large stands of timber still stood on the opposite ridge of the valley, keeping it predominately green. But through the limbs I could see that the ground was covered with black ash. Columns of smoke rose through the branches.

The only place that did not look affected by fire was a thin strip of vegetation running down the valley center. I wondered why it would remain so untouched.

My knees buckled at the conclusion. The image of water, streams, lakes, waterfalls, clear, pure, unadulterated liquid, seized my mind. Water was suddenly the answer to everything. Water was sex, money, fame, fast cars, beautiful women; water was healing, redemption, love, enlightenment. And it was likely water that kept the valley floor safe.

I had to get to it.

Though my intellect reasoned that any water in the valley was most likely subterranean this time of year, my instincts compelled me toward it. I wanted to sprint, but it took all of my animal will to slowly put one foot in front of the other. My legs were unwieldy, and I stumbled and fell often into the loose, powdery soil. Soon soot covered my face; grit got in my nose and already parched mouth. My skin itched terribly, and my tongue felt as if it had swollen to the size of balloon. But the desire for water kept me in motion.

Finally I reached the first brush of the riparian zone. I pushed through the shrubs back first, and while doing so, noticed something dark, like a shadow moving down the hill. I tried to get a good look, but saw nothing specific. I turned and went on, unable to spend time or energy on phantasms created by my thirst.

Under the limbs of a few deciduous trees, I saw the first ridges of a cut bank. I began to tremble. Below the bank that indicated normal winter levels was the streambed with nothing but a trickle running over it. However, there were various small pools of stagnant water covered with decaying leaves and brown with algae. A small cry burst from my lips. I found new strength and ran over to the nearest one, stuck my hands in it and lapped it up, giving no care to the mosquito larvae spinning in the murky pool.

The water moved through me instantaneously. First it brought a cool sensual joy to my center, which transformed into a warmth so strong it seemed as if my stomach might glow. It pushed through my center to my eyes, lubricating them to the point of tears. Then it streamed through my arms and legs, giving them strength, then to my toes and fingers so that I regained my balance and felt the air anew.

Greedily wanting more, I looked around, stood up, and ran down the stream looking for deeper pools. I found one that was larger and clearer than the others. I wanted to rip off all my clothes and jump in so that I could feel the luxurious substance over all my skin, but the pool was barely big enough for my head, so I stuck it in as deep as I could and felt the liquid inundate my scalp. The water that had rooted in my center drenched my mind, causing an experience of rapture that surely even those possessed by heroin or love could not know.

Finally I pulled my head out to catch my breath from the ecstasy that overwhelmed me. I sat with eyes closed, focusing on the water sweetly dripping from my hair and caressing my face as it rolled back towards the earth. I savored the breath filling my lungs.

At the sound of rustling branches, I opened my eyes. In front of me was a silhouette of a muscular, shirtless bald man coming towards the riverbank. The dark figure leaped into the air, his arms spanned out like a crow and then he slid gracefully down next to the pool, where he began to drink and laugh spastically. It was the criminal I had seen earlier in the day.

Skip threw off his shelter and was met with the smell of burnt aluminum and smoke. He stood up. The smoke was so thick he could barely make out the two fire shelters on either side of him. The heat from the remaining fire was still rather intense, but he ordered the men out of their shelters anyway. Jacobson and Edgar both emerged from under their shelters, and somewhere out of sight he heard the rustling of another tent.

"Call out!" The foreman demanded, as he peered through the clogged air.

The two men in his view called out, as did Marcus, and Skip found his outline in the thick air.

"Where's Steve?" Skip asked. "Is Steve with you, Marcus?"

"I don't see him," Marcus said, as the men began to roam aimlessly through the smoke, looking helplessly as they called Steve's name.

A draft of wind blew along the ridge, giving the men better visibility and fresher air to breathe.

But Edgar's breath stopped cold.

"Oh, shit," he said.

"What? What is it! Do you see him? What did you find?" Skip asked almost angrily.

"You guys better come over here ..." Edgar said.

Skip and the others walked over to Edgar and saw in front of him a spent fire shelter with a distinct rip in its shriveled remains dancing mournfully in the breeze. Skip paused for a second, then charged toward the brittle shelter and grabbed it like a foe so that it crumpled and tore. He threw it back on the ground in disgust.

"Goddamn thing," he whispered. "Anderson! Anderson! Steve!" he yelled.

The men continued roaming aimlessly about.

"Skip! Guys! I see something!" Jacobson said. The men came immediately up to him. "He's over there," Jacobson said evenly in his shock, as he pointed down the hill.

The men followed the direction he indicated. But after a few minutes of walking down slope, they saw nothing. The smoke gathered around them again, and soon they lost confidence in their direction.

"I saw ... I saw something," Jacobson said.

"Was it ... was he standing?" Skip asked.

"I don't know, I don't want to ..."

"*Hey, boys*," said a raspy, almost inaudible voice.

The men swung around towards the voice, and saw a human figure sitting on a rock.

"Steve!" Marcus yelled, and the men ran towards him.

Their momentary excitement turned to horror as Steve came into view.

He was unrecognizable. His face was covered with black patches, he had no hair, and the tip of his nose was missing. His jaw hung open from strips of wrinkled skin. A milky ooze ran over his shriveled lower lip and mixed with the blood dripping from his facial wounds. His eyes were open but almost lifeless as they fixed on oblivion.

His body fared no better. The vestiges of his Nomex pants covered only his front thighs, waist and hips. The rest had been burned off. His shirt was a tangled mess that exposed huge gaping burns all over his torso. The fat cells under the skin were exposed in some places where the skin had been completely destroyed. The only sign of life was a terrible gurgling that came from his chest every few seconds.

But it was the smell that was most unshakable—a waft of sulfur, singed meat, and a metallic, almost copper like odor hung over him assaulting the already rattled men .

"Oh my god, man!" Edgar said as he got close.

"Steve...Steve. Can you hear me?" asked Skip.

"Steve, talk to me," Marcus said, and waited for a response. None came.

"Come on Steve, we know you can do it. It's Marcus, your saw partner. Your buddy. Talk to me," Marcus pleaded. But there was no response.

Marcus leaned back and examined the man from a distance.

"Look, just hang in there, buddy. We'll get you out of here!" Marcus said.

Skip grabbed Marcus and motioned to the other men to follow him. He walked about fifteen feet from the burned man, where they gathered around him.

"We got to get him out of here! Now!" Marcus said.

"Jesus," Jacobson said, trying to catch his breath and control his emotions. "He's at least eighty percent burned. How are we going to move him? He's really badly burned," Jacobson said. "We're going to have to carry him at least two miles to the next L.Z.," he said, referring to the landing zone for a helicopter. "I mean, he's really burned bad, really bad," he repeated, shaking his head in shock.

"We have to move him. We have to get him some help. I mean, there's just no other choice. We have to move him," Edgar said.

"Look, I know," Jacobson said. "I'm just saying. God, I'm just saying he's really badly burned, like eighty percent—third degree."

"Yeah, well maybe if you would have let him in your shelter he wouldn't be that bad!" Marcus bellowed against Jacobson's judgment—eighty percent—third degree meant almost certain death.

Jacobson looked as if he had just been punched. "Oh, come on. I got a family!"

"Well then you can just get away with whatever, 'cause you got a goddamn family! What the fuck are you a hotshot for then if you got a fucking family! And what the fuck *are we—strangers*?"

Marcus yelled in a voice clinched by threatening tears.

"For all we know he panicked and threw his shelter off!" Jacobson said. "How do you know he wouldn't have done that with my shelter? I mean, you heard him trying to get in my shelter, and I didn't see you inviting him into yours, and you're his goddamn buddy!"

Marcus stepped back for a moment as the words hit him, then sprang forward with his arms outstretched towards Jacobson's neck.

Skip leapt in between the two men before they made contact.

"Take it easy, goddamn it!" Skip said.

Marcus backed off, his eyes and face gorged with blood.

"Keep it together for fuck's sake," Skip said as he walked back to the burned man. The others slowly followed.

"Steve, we're going to get you out of here," Skip said.

Steve didn't respond.

"Can you hear me? Talk to me. I know you can," Skip continued. He waited for a few moments, then turned away and hoped for some inspiration as to what to do. Jacobson was right about one thing, the landing zone for a helicopter was at least two miles away, and carrying the burned crewmember with the delicacy required without equipment would be almost impossible. He looked at his men, who now gathered around them. Their hung heads and dumbfounded looks offered no answer.

"*No, I ain't burned*," Steve's raspy voice said softly.

∞

The convict and I remained kneeling over the pool of water in silent worship. Finally I could drink no more, and I leaned against a rock, my stomach sloshing with water. I studied the man in front of me, who was making slight sounds of contentment as he drank.

The man's black skin rippled from the large muscles of his arms and shoulders. Burn scars left from an old injury ran down his pronounced lateral muscles. All over his naked torso ran fresh scratches, some of which bled. Pieces of his red shirt hung off his waist, and his pants were torn in many places. He was bald, and he carried some extra weight in his mid-section, but despite the signs of middle age, he beamed with a wild vitality.

But beyond his scarred, strong, and aged body, I wondered what history was inside him—what put him in the penitentiary? I remembered all of the possible crimes that convicts on the fire crew might have committed, and I assumed his was not white collar. Maybe he was a bank robber, a car thief, or perhaps even an aged drug king-pin, who commanded minions through charisma and intimidation. Or was he a serial killer—a mindless shark who followed no cognition, only violent impulse?

"Hoaah!" the man suddenly yelled as he threw his head up from the water. "Goddamn that was hot! Wasn't it? Damn hot as it can get, I tell you. Wasn't it?"

"Huh?"

"Wasn't it hot! Boy, didn't you hear me?"

"Oh yeah. Glad it's over," I said. I puffed out my chest. Knowing I was likely talking with a violent criminal, and a long ways away from any help, I wanted to sound tough. I wanted him to think I was a real hotshot, and a strong one at that. "Shit yeah," I amended.

"Damn this water is good," the convict said. "Bet those poor mofos I was fighting fire with would like some of this right now."

"What happened to them? Did they ..." I started to ask.

"Oh yeah. They's all dead. No one left but me," the convict said. He looked out into the air for a moment, contemplating, then turned his attention back to me. "What happened to your crew? You all had a big lead on us getting to the top. They make it?"

"No. Well, I don't know. I guess everyone made it. Yeah, I'm sure of it, actually," I said. I wanted to sound together, but could tell I was doing a poor job of it.

"Well, which one is it?"

"They made it," I said. "I think."

"Then where in the hell are they now?" the convict asked, stretching out his arms around.

"Up on top of the ridge I guess, or on some rock outcropping on the other side."

"Left your ass behind."

"Well, kind of ..." I've never been good at lying.

"Couldn't you keep up with your own damn crew?" the convict said, and laughed.

"Uh, I was taking weather when they RTO'd out."

"Well if you was taking weather, where is your radio? Don't you need a radio if you going to tell your crew what the weather is?"

"Yeah, I dropped it. It got burned up. I can't find it."

"Uh-huh," the convict said, narrowing his eyes a bit. Then he let the inquiry go, opening his arms

141

and face. "Well, at least you still got one!" he said with a laugh.

"Still got what?"

"A crew! You still got a crew!" the convict said, shaking his head and laughing. "So they going to come and get you?"

"I guess," I replied, trying to think quickly. "Yes. For sure. Soon."

"They're probably already back at camp, eating steak and potatoes and just starting to realize they're a man short!" he said with another laugh. Everything seemed to be a joke to him.

But I winced at the thought, believing it all too possible.

"How did you ... make it?" I asked.

The man shook his head. "I saw all those fuckers running up that hill, and I said to myself, 'Gregory, that's got to be at least a half mile up that hilltop. Ain't no way any of us is going to make it— especially your old ass.'

"But the foreman had his mind set. He kept hollering and yelling at us to keep moving." He shook his head some more, then looked straight at me, as if telling a secret. "See, that foreman, he didn't want to face up to his situation. He didn't want to take the shame and pain and fear of having been caught somewhere he shouldn't have been in the first place. He denied it. He could've told us to shelter up; then at least we'd have a chance. But uh-uh. He kept denying the truth. See, that's the difference between one that makes it through and one that don't—the one that makes it through don't try and reject what's really going on."

He relaxed against the rock and looked at the sky.

"Can't blame the others so much," he said. "After a man has been told everyday when he can shit, sleep, eat, and piss, it's hard to use your own mind. Even when it's your life. Hell, part of me just wanted to do as I was told and drive up that mountain, too.

"Coming up," he continued, "just as I started to really feel the heat coming up from behind, I saw a rockslide to my left. It was surrounded by briars, but I took off running towards it anyway. I knew it was my only chance. The foreman started hollering at me. May have even pulled out his gun, but he was the last of my worries. I just thought, 'come and get me.' He was too busy about to get his ass burned off to do anything to me.

"I saw that rock slide! The blackberries were thirty feet thick and ten feet high!" I said.

"Hey, didn't tickle there, boy. But you'd be amazed at the shit you can pull when you're about to be burned up. Tore my shirt to shreds, my skin too," he said, looking down at the deep cuts over his chest and arms. "God has put some work on me!"

"So then I pulled out that damn shelter," he continued, "and I remember thinking, 'after all this, I'm going out like broiled chicken!' Served me right, I figured. But I made it. Somehow I made it—just held on tight and made it through."

The words took me back to my last moments of consciousness in the shelter—and suddenly I felt like I was going to throw up. I remembered the searing pain in my calf. Then I looked down at it, and what I saw didn't look human.

It looked like a piece of costumed zombie skin. A black burned swath ran from my upper calf down to my boot. Blood and a milky colored substance dripped from it and oozed down over the leather. Yellow pockets—probably subcutaneous fat—and angry red skin with pustules surrounded the scorched area.

"Damn! That's a nasty looking mark you got on your calf there, boy!"

"The shelter started to give out on me. The hot tin, or aluminum, or whatever they make those things out of, was touching my skin." I almost started to cry while speaking but became too light headed. My calf throbbed and burned, and in a moment all the euphoria I had felt from the water was gone. The world started to spin and the only thing certain was how suddenly excruciating the burn was.

"I know, I know, believe me, I know. Those burns don't feel good at all. Going to need some medical attention on that," the convict said.

I knew he was right. I needed attention, and fast. The pain was too much to take. My breathing became thin and labored, my peripheral vision constricted, and I felt as if I was going to pass out. In less than five seconds I had gone from satisfied to mortified. I was slowly slipping into shock. I looked around, but there were no planes, no crew, no helicopters, no rescue—just the woods and a man who could not be more different than me, and who was most likely extremely dangerous.

"*I ain't burned*," Steve said again. His damaged mouth produced garbled words that the men could barely understand. "I thought I was getting burned ... hurt real bad ... shelter got blown off ... hurt real bad ... but then the pain stopped ... everything was all right ... I could just walk right through the fire. Now .. .just thirsty ... just a little thirsty."

He began to drift back into a catatonic state, but was shaken out of it by a thought.

"*... got any ... water?*" he asked.

The men had thrown their reserve water away with their packs, and the water on their web belts had been used earlier in the day during the intense downhill line construction—before the blowup.

Except Edgar. He knew there was a quarter of a liter on his web belt. And he had been saving it— looking for a chance when the others weren't looking to greedily gulp it down. He had imagined drinking it hundreds of times in the shelter, and used the vision to give him something to fight for.

He pulled it from his belt and held it to the sun, where it illuminated like a promise. His mouth and eyes started to itch, and he shuddered with desire. He unscrewed the cap and handed it to Steve.

Steve attempted to reach out for it, but his hands were useless. The tips of his fingers were missing. Edgar drew his extended arm in half way and paused until Marcus grabbed it from him and sat down next to Steve on the rock.

While the two men were buddies, Marcus rarely said anything complimentary about his saw partner. Even though they were considered the fastest saw team on the crew, they would often be seen bickering at each other about who had put the saw chain on too tight, who had dulled its teeth through careless use, or who had misjudged the bind while cutting timber.

Marcus was much older and more reserved than his partner, and he was easily annoyed by Steve's swagger. But whether personalities click or not is unimportant; men that hike, run, hunger, thirst, sweat, and fear together form an unconscious bond that is often only felt in times when there is distance or danger—like an appendage only noticed when it is in pain.

Marcus's hands trembled and his eyes welled as he put one arm around his partner's once sturdy body. He brought the water bottle to the man's singed lips and tipped it up with his free hand. Steve swallowed as the water flowed into his mouth, but the muscles would not contract properly, and the water ran all over his front. Short spasms ran through the burned man's body.

"*Didn't quite make it,*" Steve said.

"No, no it didn't. But we'll give it another shot," Marcus said as he tipped the last sip of water to his partner.

The convict propped me up on the cut bank of the stream.

"Boy, you never look at a wound until there is something you can do about it. Now just calm down. It'll be okay."

I looked up at the trees and tried to force my breathing back to normal. Eventually the panic subsided—not because of some great mental discipline on my part, but simply because there was nothing else to do but calm down.

"You feeling better?" the convict asked.

"Yeah, I feel a bit better."

"Gregory," he said.

"Jonathan," I said.

We shook hands.

I looked up at the sun and figured it to be around six in the evening. That left two or three hours to find a search and rescue team and get flown out. I knew the helicopters never flew at night, no matter what the circumstances. So I committed myself to doing whatever was necessary to get out of the woods by sundown.

Chapter Five

I lobbed stones into the pool and waited, assuming that any moment I would hear a helicopter or see the hotshots or other signs of search and rescue. But after twenty minutes the air was as silent as an empty church. Occasionally I looked at my new companion, hoping he might say something meaningful, but he just sat quietly, clearly in no hurry to have the moment pass.

I shifted and fussed over the pain. My hunger grew more demanding, too, and within every joint I felt an eerie creak—as if a fever was starting to brew within the space between my bones. I forced myself not to look at my calf again, but I couldn't erase the picture of it from my mind.

As time continued to pass, I started to envision bacteria entering the wound—millions of them invading my blood. My white corpuscles, desperate to save my body, were going valiantly into battle against the massive security breach—only to be overwhelmed by the nefarious germs.

The disgusting intruders were eating my heroic corpuscles, polluting my blood stream with their death and sickness. I could almost hear my immune system scream for help.

The Infecticons laughed at my body's vain attempts to protect itself as they began to ravage the cell membrane, crushing the cytoplasm, chewing the mitochondria, and finally to the nucleus where they would insert their...

"That's it!" I said, chucking the last stone. I stood up. "I don't know where in the fuck any of those guys are, but I can't wait around here any longer. Time is just passing by!"

"As it always is there boy," Gregory said, like this was some higher wisdom. "You best just sit down and relax. Ain't much else to do right now."

"There's a huge rock outcropping on top of this hill here. I remember seeing it," I said, motioning to the hill behind me. "I bet they could land a helicopter on it and get us out of here. It's a hike, but at least it's under the trees, in the shade. Better than hiking up the hill we just came down, where there's not one wick of it."

"But ain't that the side your crew is on?" Gregory asked.

"Screw them. They must've hiked out or something. Besides, the helispot we came in on was miles from where we started work. I'm not hiking that far. No way."

"Well, your idea of hiking to some nameless rock in hopes of catching a helicopter out of here doesn't sound too air tight, either. But hey, do what you want. Right now, we's free. I'm going to sit here and enjoy my solitude. My life's been lacking it."

"Okay, well, good luck. I'm not sitting here any longer. That's for sure," I said.

"You sure you want to do that?" Gregory asked.

"Yeah."

"Well...best to you."

"Thanks," I said, and headed off into the woods by myself.

∞

"I can't get hold of Bruce," Skip said, clipping his radio back on his belt. "I'm going up the ridge to see if I can get some better reception. Edgar, why don't you come along?"

Edgar nodded, thankful for the chance to take action.

"Take care of him the best you can," he said to Marcus and Jacobson. "We'll be right back."

The two hiked swiftly up the hill. To ease the pain of anyone in such a condition would be worthy of tough work, but for a crewmember who had realized a fireman's most apparent fear, it was sacrosanct.

Once on top of the ridge, Skip pulled out his radio and called for his supervisor. He tried several times and finally got a response.

"This is A," Bruce said. "Who am I speaking with?"

Skip felt a moment of release, relieved to be turning over the decision making. "A this is A-F. We have been burned over. BREAK."

"...We have one in critical condition. We'll need a medevac. BREAK."

"This is Bison A. Who is calling?" Bruce said.

"Fuck!" Skip said aloud. "My batteries are too low. I can only receive, not transmit."

"Shit," Edgar said.

The two stood in helpless silence, thinking.

"If this is Skip please key your radio twice," Bruce said.

Skip pushed down twice on the soft button.

"All right, Skip. We'll keep with this code: key your radio once for no, and twice for yes. Do you understand?"

Skip punched the button twice with his thumb.

"Have you been burned over?" Bruce asked.

"No, we flew over the fucking mountain!" Edgar said.

"SHHH!" Skip said. The foreman indicated the positive to his supervisor.

"Did you survive the burn over without injury?" Bruce asked.

Again Skip gave the affirmative signal.

"That is good news, Skip, BREAK."

"...Unfortunately, we have had problems. Cynthia and Nelson both have severe burns on their legs and arms. BREAK."

"...They will need to be medevaced as soon as possible. BREAK."

Skip uttered a word of frustration as he saw the situation getting more complex. In hopes of getting Bruce to understand that he hadn't made the correct assumption about the state of his men, the foreman started to push the transmitter in quick succession. After five seconds of this he stopped, hoping Bruce had gotten the point. There was a long silence.

"A...A-F," Bruce finally announced.

Skip keyed his radio twice.

"Skip, is something wrong?"

The foreman signaled yes.

"Are you—or your men—injured?"

Skip signaled the affirmative.

"Skip, I want you to key the radio once for each man that is injured," Bruce said.

Skip gave one long press, trying to send the urgency he felt through the radio waves.

"Is it critical?" Bruce asked.

Skip gave two presses.

"Skip please confirm that you have one man, and only one man, in critical condition.

Skip signaled affirmative.

"All right Skip, I'm going to give you some information, and you're going to have to make a choice. BREAK."

"...We have two badly burned people that need immediate medical attention. BREAK."

"...They can make it. But they are in the red. BREAK"

"...The fire has blown up, and has trapped a small community. All air resources are being diverted to buy time for an evacuation. BREAK."

"...Other crews have also been burned over, and are requesting medevacs. BREAK."

"...I have been able to secure one helicopter trip for the whole day. I can get that ride immediately or I can wait until after seven o'clock. BREAK."

Skip listened and tried to deduce what was happening. Incident Command probably assumed that by seven o'clock the battle to save the town would be over. Fire activity would probably die down as the evening cool-off came, making bucket and retardant drops less crucial. They were hoping to get the crews out between seven and dark—they wouldn't fly at night. He didn't know what time it was but figured it close to six.

"Skip, this is where we have a problem. BREAK."

"If I take Cynthia and Nelson on the next possible helicopter, their chances of survival are high, and it will limit their suffering. BREAK."

"...But if I do this, we will be moved to the bottom of the list. We won't get another helicopter until late, or even tomorrow morning. BREAK."

"...There are a lot of people suffering right now, Skip. Our crew isn't the only one, and resources are scarce. They'll use them to save civilians first. After all, they didn't sign up for this. We did. BREAK."

"Now if you think your injured man needs to be on that bird with us enough to prolong the suffering of others and lower their chances of survival, then I'll tell the Air Operations to come later. We're all in this together. BREAK."

"...But if he's outside the red ... then we need to make the tough decision. BREAK."

"...This is a matter of triage, Skip. It's your call. BREAK."

"...If you want us to wait until seven, key your radio twice. BREAK."

"...If we should go now, key your radio once. I'll give you a few moments."

Both men sat in silence for a moment, until Edgar exploded.

"Fucking foresters!" He blurted. "This is all politics. Firemen die, and it's tragic with a touch of heroism. But you have civilian casualties, and it's bad press and lawsuits. People will find out that this happened because of poor forest management and fuel loads. And then they'll sue—the same people that would have raised hell if anyone came even close to suggesting putting down a prescribed fire last year!"

Skip did not have the luxury of complaining, so he turned away from Edgar as his thoughts contracted painfully on themselves. A brutal but obvious decision awaited him. The odds of Steve surviving were next to none, even in a hospital, let alone after being carried over miles of rough terrain in the hands of men so exhausted they could spare no effort to proper care. Then again, Steve had willingly taken the more dangerous route so other crewmembers could be safe. He had followed his orders and gotten under his own shelter. Wasn't that worth something?

Before the weight of the decision could play on his mind anymore, he quickly pressed the transmitter button, once. The motion slowed. The feel of the soft rubber falling under the pressure of his fingers seemed to go on forever. When it finally hit its contact, it sent a painful vibration back to his brain.

Skip looked at Edgar, hoping to see some confirmation, but there was only confusion.

"What are you doing?" Edgar asked. "Push it again! We can't leave him here!

"God damn it Edgar! It's simple triage," Skip flared back in his own defense.

"Fuck triage!" Edgar said. "How can you do this? Steve's one of the best guys we got. He works hard as hell. He wouldn't have been sent with us if he wasn't one of the best. Is this how we repay him? Is this how the crew's going to repay him? He risked his life for them! Why can't they risk their lives for him?"

"Calm down and use your head, damn it! You saw him! He's not eighty percent! He's ninety-five percent! He's dead already!" he said, choking on the last words.

They stood looking at each other until the radio crackled back to life.

"I copy, Skip. BREAK." Bruce said.

"We'll get Cynthia and Nelson out of here soon. A out," his voice cracking in the last phase.

"He is now," Edgar said, turning his back to his foreman. He walked a few steps up the ridge to distance himself from Skip, but was suddenly confronted by a large burnt tree. What remained of the limb structure indicated the tree had been an oak—a species out of place for the elevation. The still thick trunk, though encased in black soot, proudly supported its few remaining branches. With every leaf gone, and pockets of fire still slowly eating at it, the tree had no chance of survival.

Skip came up behind Edgar and examined the tree, perplexed at how stubbornly it reached out from the ground where everything else—shrubs, weeds and conifers—had all succumbed completely to combustion.

"It must have been two thousand degrees on this ridge," Skip said.

"Yeah, it's amazing that it didn't burn up completely. Won't be standing much longer, though."

Edgar looked around his immediate landscape. The ground was uniformly covered with black ash. Small fires lashed out from the remains of fallen timber. Smoke billowed from stumps. It looked like a medieval hell. He'd been surrounded by such environments many times, but never had they made him so anxious, so nervous. It dawned on him—he was scared. With a twinge of shame, he realized he wanted Steve on that helicopter so he could fly from this place with him.

"Let's go," Skip said.

The two gathered their strength with a sigh, knowing they would soon witness something like the oak but a million fold more grisly.

For the first few moments hiking up the hill, I was almost elated. It felt good to move. It felt good to be alive—I was safe from the fire that threatened me, free from the crew that demeaned me, cured of the thirst that had tortured me, and away from the convict who had troubled me. I was taking command of my own destiny, and I was sure I could whip the grade, no problem. I'd climb it, flag down a helicopter, and be back in California in no time, with one hell of a story.

I had failed as a hotshot, true—but I had survived one wicked experience, and with a few small omissions, and a revision or two, the story would earn me respect. I'd survived a life threatening experience. I suppose we all want to consider ourselves survivors, but up until then I had avoided self-evaluation on the topic. I'd been coddled by my mother as a child, and I knew it—my dad made sure of that by bitching about it, and his whining was no model of masculine perseverance either.

After a few minutes of hiking, however, movement lost its novelty. I grew tired, and started to curse the hill. It was steep, and the thick gray ash made walking difficult. My burn started to throb, and I looked at it again. The black patch of excoriated skin wept opaque and bloody slime even more than before. It made me sick and panicky. My breathing became irregular and thin. A great fatigue overcame me in a wave, and with it I dreamed of sinking into the earth, to sleep forever.

I knew walking on my wounded leg would do more damage. I could sit down and prop it up, but if I did that, it would certainly mean staying out over night—and now I was in a place that would be even harder to find than the creek bed. I peered through the trees hoping to see some sign of the hill's end, but there were only groves of conifers in front of me. I sat down to think.

The hike could be futile—I hadn't seen a helicopter all day, and perhaps, like the convict said, it was just some nameless rock. My legs were so tired that I might not make it until nightfall anyway.

But I wouldn't be found here, which left me only one other real option: to go back to the creek where the criminal was. He was the last sort of person I wanted to spend the night with in some burned up forest. Besides, I could hear him laugh and say, "I knew you'd be back, 'cause there was no way you's going to climb that hill!"

No! I resolved to climb the hill no matter how tough it was! I'd do it! I'd get there before dark!

Having given myself this internal pep talk, I stood and started limping up the mountain with as much charge as I could muster.

But it wasn't long before the pain in my calf and my exhaustion started to convince me it was all for naught. My pace slowed to a dying trudge, and soon I fell to the ground. I leaned up against an old growth tree—jumped as my butt found a hot spot—then flailed and probed until I found cooler ground, leaned back against the trunk, and let my tired mind rest. Maybe they would find me ...

Skip knew his conviction must be complete. He would present his decision to the men as fact. He would offer them no hope of saving Steve—he wouldn't even hint that it might have been an option. It would be the situation's certainty that would allow them to let their friend go and not look back. With even a glimmer of hope, the men would try to fight on. He just hoped that Steve was not lucid enough to ask about his own situation.

After a few minutes, the three awaiting crewmen came into view. Steve was lying on his back while Marcus leaned over his torso and pumped his fists into Steve's chest. Jacobson knelt over Steve's head, intermittently leaning down to the fallen man's mouth to deliver breath to it. CPR. Skip and Edgar ran towards them.

"What happened?" Skip asked Jacobson.

"About two minutes ago he went into convulsions. Then stopped breathing. He's lost his heartbeat, too," Jacobson said, between giving rescue breaths to the burnt man.

Skip squeezed between the two men giving CPR, grabbed Steve's wrist and searched for a pulse. Nothing. He scanned the body—the brown and black skin covered with pools of red and yellow fluid created a disgusting collage—death had to be imminent.

But Marcus kept counting out compressions, calling out each number with such passion and battle that Skip couldn't tell everyone to stop. The question Skip had wanted to answer before it was asked had already been posed in his absence— there was no choice but to continue the fight.

"Still no pulse," Skip said, taking his hand off of Steve's wrist. "Okay, let Edgar and me take over for a while."

Though his face was flushed with exhaustion, Marcus pulled off with noticeable reluctance. Skip hunched over Steve's chest and Edgar kneeled next to his head, taking a look at Steve's mouth. The sight of the shriveled lips lined with burns and pus created a reaction so strong in Edgar, it overwhelmed him—he had dealt with fear many times, but not such intense disgust. The feeling seemed to jump in and out of him, pounding on his heart, twisting his stomach, confusing his thoughts. It was a personal demon, an internal gremlin, and it was wrestling for control. It laughed at his noble desire to perform the repugnant task. "Remember all the women ol' 'Stud' here has been with. He bragged about always riding bareback. If you even touch him you'll become like him!"

Edgar looked away from the mouth, hoping to cut his newfound alter ego off its source of strength. He tried to focus on Skip, who was counting aloud each time he pushed on Steve's chest. But the image of the orifice had burned on his mind's eye. He pleaded for his mind to silence—for the ability to do what lay in front of him.

"SEVEN!" Skip yelled.

The voice of authority cut through Edgar's scrambled thoughts. He regained himself, took a breath, closed his eyes and put his mouth to

Steve's, exhaling forcefully. The air filled Steve's lung's and before Edgar could sit up to breathe again, he tasted its return—its dead, singed, salty taste—like burned asphalt.

He breathed again, put lips to mouth, and in doing so got a mouthful of pus. The gremlin rematerialized from each cell in his body, clenched Edgar's stomach, and spun his world. With all his will he exhaled, then turned away from the orifice and spit out a glob of salty discharge.

"Go," he said to Skip. He turned his back to the scene and tried not to vomit. But the muscles of his viscera contracted anyway, painfully up his chest and throat. The dry heave left an acidic taste in his mouth.

"1...2..." Skip yelled out, returning to deliver the chest compressions. In seven seconds Edgar would have to do it all again.

"3...4..." Edgar turned to watch Skip, and seeing Skip's hands push so deeply and unnaturally into the chest—with seemingly no regard for the bones or the internal organs—only intensified his nausea.

"5...6..."

As the time grew closer he felt the demon squeeze his neck; he felt as if we was about to faint.

"7!" Skip yelled again.

Steve's body lurched, as if responding to the command. A gush of liquid came from his mouth. The burnt man suddenly sat up, eyes wide open, then fell back to the ground and became lifeless except for a gurgling sound from his chest. He was breathing again.

The men stepped back from the body, dumbfounded.

"He's living!" Marcus suddenly burst out. "He's living! My buddy's living! Skip, we got to get him out of here! He wants to live, don't you see! We got to get him out of here!"

Skip kneeled next to Steve. "Anderson! Anderson! Steve," Skip said, as he placed two fingers on Steve's neck, and searched for a heartbeat.

"He's got a pulse," Skip finally said.

"Yeah, he's breathing ... so he must," Jacobson said out loud, trying to remember his CPR facts through a fog of stress. Like most wildland fireman, he was not as practiced in medical emergencies as his structural fire fighter counterparts.

"You never know," Jacobson continued. "He's got a shot. Old Stud's got a shot!"

"You bet he does!" Marcus said. "Goddamn, he's tough as they come, I tell you!"

Skip nodded in recognition, trying to hide his confusion. He had let the men continue CPR because he felt they needed a chance to fight for their crewmember, but he didn't think they'd actually get him back. Now Skip doubted the judgment he had made on the ridge—maybe Steve had a chance, and he had taken it away.

He looked at Edgar, expecting to see indignation, even hostility—he even feared Edgar might blurt out the decision made earlier. Instead he saw Edgar staring at Steve in blank dismay.

"Look, I talked to Bruce," Skip said, avoiding Marcus's eyes. "We can't get a medevac, not until well after seven. Probably even longer."

"Why the fuck not?" Marcus demanded.

"The fire's gone to shit, Marcus. Not just on us, everywhere. All air support is busy with urban interface, and—"

"Skip, it doesn't matter," Marcus said, shaking his head impatiently. "My buddy wants to make it out. Don't you see? He'll do it, if we help. Now let's just get him to a landing zone, and you can tell me the situation when we get there."

"It seems like he's fighting for it, Skip," Jacobson said.

"So let's not waste any time," Marcus replied. "Come on! Help me lift him."

Skip felt his resolve fade. "Okay. We'll give it a shot," he said. "You guys take the top. Edgar, help me with the legs."

The flaccid body was hard to manage. As they climbed up the steep, ash-covered hill, the men carrying the shoulders could not coordinate their movements with the men carrying the legs. The body would slacken and sag towards the ground one moment, only to become taut the next, as the men tripped and stumbled over their load. Unable to support all the joints of the human body, appendages would sling from the men's grasp, and bend towards the earth. The neck was especially difficult to control, and the head often dropped to the ground. The skinless face quickly became covered in soot and ash.

Within moments it became clear that they wouldn't make it to the ridge top without taking a break. Labored breaths and muscles whining with lactic acid eroded the men's zeal. Instead, they found motivation to continue in a proud, unspoken principle: no one wanted to be the first to quit. Soon each man was getting through every step, each breath, each second, only by hoping that another would capitulate in the next. But the surrender didn't come, and another painful moment would slide by, endured only by the anesthesia of quiet hope.

Finally the body stopped moving. No one conceded. The body that had been carried with such jolting disharmony simply came to rest on the ground in perfect unison, as if a tacit agreement had been made between the men's unconscious minds. And no one objected. They sat down and tried to catch their rapid, shallow breath.

"Jesus Christ, I am spent," said Jacobson.

Chapter Six

"Looks like the timber on the south side is about to slick off in a reburn," Edgar said watching the large timber that had survived the initial conflagration slowly become overwhelmed in flames. It was a menacing site, but at least it turned his attention away from the terrible sound of Steve's labored breathing.

"We should start moving again," Marcus said.

Jacobson clenched his fist in dread. His face prickled from heat. His breath was shallow. He knew carrying Steve under the sun even a hundred more yards would mean sweating out the last salty reserves of water he had—and this would mean heat exhaustion, or worse.

He had been through it before. In the summer of '96 the crew had been assigned to cut line directly next to flames in a large manzanita field. The ambient temperature in the southern California fire was over one hundred degrees, and the fire would torch through the manzanita brush, sending shards of additional heat on the men working next to it. A few hours into the shift, his sight began to fade into a milky haze. His thoughts became irrational—he confused the direction the line was being built in, thought for a minute his partner was joshing him when he redirected him twice in a row, and soon started to suspect that the whole crew was in on the joke. Confusion threatened horror when the whistle that often sounds from burning manzanita morphed into a scream. Their twisted red branches seemed to want to hold him prisoner, as if to force their agonizing fate onto him.

Just as nausea, thirst, and confusion were coming to an apex, the crew finished the line and were told to hold. Jacobson hobbled to an isolated spot, unbuttoned his shirt and pulled down his pants and underwear to help his body cool. Feeling humiliated and exposed with his testicles in the wind, he wanted to swear he'd never succumb to the condition again, but from his training he knew that after having it once, he'd actually be more prone to it.

Now he faced having to carry a dying man for miles with no water, no shade, and the same haze threatening to strangle out his sight. But he could not request clemency.

While hotshots espouse the policy of "safety first" like a mantra, they also earn and maintain respect by being able to perform outside normal limits, especially in regard to arduous labor in hot conditions. Therefore, almost all crewmembers at some point must ignore the first signs of heat exhaustion to get their job done and avoid the shame of being outworked. So now, in a time of crisis—one that Jacobson felt at least partially responsible for—he ignored his body's warnings. He would not rest while the others struggled on.

He stood up first, and he stood quickly, deciding it best to attack the problem.

"All right, let's do it," he said, shifting his feet as he stood.

The other men followed suit, squinting their eyes and also swaying as they stood. Grunting and heaving, the men overcame the lying body's inertia, and for the slightest instant it felt light.

Jacobson's strength lasted only seconds. His pulse slammed through his ears and eyes, bringing an intolerable headache and then dizziness. He breathed faster, more desperately. His straining arms slowly gave way to gravity.

After five more steps he felt an eerie visceral tear. There was no specific physical organ or structure related with the sensation, but instead it seemed to come from the ethereal life force in his belly. From the rip leaked a gelatinous substance, which spread to his diaphragm and lungs, robbing him of some essential tension he had not known existed. The substance spread to his arms, and they became hopeless and limp, so that he dropped the body. The ooze reached his legs and head, so that his knees buckled and his world spun into a smear. In the next instance it reached his eyes, and as they closed the ground leapt up to smash him.

∞

I sat stiff, a statue made of black ashen wood. I tried to get up, but the material my body was made of would not bend. The most I could do was send desperate vibrations of my will through it so that I shuddered. I was in agony. My calf burned with a circle of red-hot ashes growing slowly. As the ring of scorching cinder continued to grow, it left white, spent ashes in its center. Then out of the growing circle rose a bird, black as a shadow. It began to flap its wings as if to fly and in doing so sent streaks of pain up and down my leg and spine. But it could not rise into the air; it was only able to lift one skinny leg at a time. It began to peck at me, move its wings in frenzy, and scratch with its talons. It began to walk along my leg up to my stomach, sending searing pain with every step.

The orange ring shone with greater intensity and began to burn along my leg faster and faster. The air around started to shudder with a dull roar. The bird flapped more desperately. It twisted it talons in my stomach, causing my gut to clench in agony.

I awoke, startled. A deep black face stared at mine. It was the convict.

172

"Get up, motherfucker! Get up!"

I came to, blinking my eyes.

"What is it? What do you want?" I asked.

"We best get out of here right now," he said.

"Why! What are you doing?"

"The fire, the fire is coming up the trees. Hear it?" Gregory said, his breath heavy from climbing the hill in a rush.

He reached down, grabbed me by the collar, and effortlessly brought me to my feet before I could protest. I squinted my dry eyes and looked around. There was an orange-tinted light filtering into the forest, indicating that the sun was lower. Looking down the hill and through the trees, I saw a large amount of smoke rising up from below. A low rumble moved through the air.

"It's not moving fast, but it's moving—and right at us," the convict said. "I was hanging near the stream when the wind started to pick up again. The little fires near the creek started grabbing onto the bushes. Pretty soon it got into the branches of the big trees. I figured your tired ass would be sleeping on this hill somewhere, so before the mess got too big, I came looking for you," he said.

"It's cooking now, though. Ain't no way we can go back down without risking walking straight into it. The only way is up. We got to make it to the rock."

"You mean we can't go back to the stream? Damn, I'm thirsty again," I complained.

"You best forget about water and worry about getting your ass up the hill!"

But I didn't want to forget about water, and I sure didn't want to run from fire again. The thirst I felt continued to get worse, like a great, demanding emptiness.

"Did you bring any water?"

"Water! Now how in the hell am I going to carry any water? Come on, boy. Let's get going!" He turned towards the hill and started hiking up it. I reluctantly followed.

The convict moved fluidly up the slope, showing athletic prowess and good conditioning. I could barely keep up. My legs moved as if made of wet cement, and it wasn't long until he gained a substantial distance on me and my passionless plodding.

I was being left behind again.

∞

The men, heavily engaged in their own internal struggles, took a moment to recognize why there was suddenly extra weight. They looked up to see Jacobson's face flushed and contorted. He tottered away as if struck—a sudden flash of stunned surprise upon his face—and then he crashed to the ground face first, kicking up a cloud of ashen soil.

They placed Steve on the ground and ran to Jacobson, cursing. Skip kneeled by the man's head and motioned for the others to help him turn Jacobson over onto his back.

"Jacobson, you okay?" Skip asked, placing his hand on the man's neck to find a pulse while searching to see if he was breathing. He had both signs of life.

Jacobson's eyes opened halfway and replied, "Never better."

"Track my finger," Skip said as he moved his hand across the man's field of vision.

"It's the heat. I got to get in the shade and rest. I don't think I'll be able to help you guys," Jacobson grunted.

"I think you're right," Edgar said, feeling an inexplicable need to laugh beginning to boil out from under the taxed layers of control.

"Could you help me get to some shade?" Jacobson asked.

Edgar's urge to laugh suddenly changed to a threat of tears. The corners of his mouth started to turn down, and he forced his lips tightly together in an expression that was the last balancing point before sobs—a method of concealing emotions he hadn't used in years.

"We'll get you to some shade, Joe. Don't worry," Skip said.

Skip turned to Edgar and Marcus. "Let's take him over to that rock. Should be enough shade over there," Skip said, pointing to a boulder about one hundred feet away. "Marcus, grab the feet. Edgar and I will take—"

"No, no. I can walk there," Jacobson said. "Just help me to my feet."

The men made haste to get him in the little shade the rock provided.

"How you doing now?" Skip asked after they propped Jacobson on a rock.

"I'm just so goddamn dizzy. I won't be able to help you with Steve," Jacobson said.

Skip told him to hang on and went with the two other men to bring Steve to the shade.

As they put Steve next to Jacobson, Skip's sunglasses fell off, and he caught an unfiltered look at Edgar. His dry, red face and purple lips looked almost as distressed as Jacobson's. He turned and studied Marcus, who also had the same telltale signs of heat stress. An obvious but ignored fact struck Skip like a slap: all his men desperately needed water. For heat did not actually cause the condition, but thirst. The human body can withstand the heights of almost any ambient temperature Earth's atmosphere can throw at it—if it is hydrated. The problem is that to keep cool, it can sweat up to one gallon in an hour but only absorb about a liter of water in the same amount of time. They had spent every drop surviving in their shelters, and now they were all deep in heat exhaustion and fast on their way to heat stroke.

"How you two doing?" Skip asked.

"I've been better, I guess, but I'm holding out," Edgar said.

Marcus nodded and said he was okay.

"That old division superintendent told me there's a creek at the bottom of the basin we were working in. It'd be a ways—maybe a mile—but it's downhill," Skip said.

"Until the way back," Edgar said.

Skip nodded. "I want you guys to go and fill up the four water bottles we have. Can you make it?"

"How are we going to get Steve to the—"

"Marcus—I don't know. We need water. All of us. We won't make it without it."

Marcus didn't like it, but the limitation was obvious.

177

"Can do. We'll be quick," Marcus said.

"No—don't rush. You guys will stay at the creek bed and drink slowly. Let your body absorb it. Drink till you piss. Because you won't get any of the water you bring back. That'll go to Jacobson."

"And Steve," Marcus insisted.

"Yeah," Skip said.

The two men patted their pockets to confirm they had canteens, then started to head out.

"Drink some for me," Skip yelled in a raspy voice, realizing the intensity of his own thirst, and that he too teetered on the brink.

Small embers from the fire below began to float gently through the air around me, falling gingerly, like burning snow. They landed softly, quietly, burning bright orange for a second once on the earth before quickly fading into the gray, ashen ground to be forever indistinguishable from it. It was mesmerizing; I allowed it to hypnotize me, and eventually gave up on the march.

"What are you lagging behind for, *hotshot*!" the man above me demanded. "Can't let some old con out-hike you!"

His powerful voice startled me out of the trance. "I'll be there in a minute! Just keep going," I yelled back.

"You better hurry up. That thing is like a slow train—might take a while, but you sure as hell don't want to be in its way when it gets here," he hollered.

"Yeah, yeah," I said, staring once again at the field of falling embers.

He shook his head in contempt and continued to hike.

I turned my attention back to the convict. He was now thirty feet away, moving in and out of sight as he weaved between the tree trunks.

Deciding to ignore this, I turned the other direction, but the column of smoke behind the tree limbs and the orange glow emanating from below was no more comforting. I cursed the signs of fire and grew angry at its coercion. A defiant strategy came to me: I would deny the fire. It would control me no longer. I had already proved myself in this circumstance. I had suffered, I had sacrificed, I had tried, and I had survived. By anyone's just measure, I deserved a break. I determined that justice would rule over nature. If I wanted to walk, I would walk—and if I wanted to rest, I would rest. Whatever threats the fire used to inspire fear and movement, I would disregard.

I sat down and watched the falling debris. The pieces burned brilliantly, only to fall into total obscurity. They did not fuss or scream or run: they simply accepted the trajectory gravity and combustion gave them. I would seek a similar acceptance, a similar peace. I closed my eyes and tried to relax.

But relaxing was not so easy, either. The fire's constant rumble continued to call my instincts into action. I fought the urge to fight, but this of course was fighting. A series of irresolvable twists, bends, and shifts of logic nettled my mind. Finally, in the anguish of it all, I stood and started walking again.

But I was still uninspired. The ashen, spongy ground, the steep hill, and the trees that obligated me to swerve my path all seemed to indicate I should just have remained seated. I paused every ten feet, tempted to stop in one last defiant gesture against fire. At the same time I was hopelessly pushed to comply with the instinctual impulse to go on. No matter what I did—struggle awaited.

"Boy, we had better hurry up," the convict said, surprising me with his sudden proximity, as he leaned against a nearby tree.

"Look, man, I just..."

"You just got to hike up this damn hill!"

"I can't go on any longer. It hurts too much," I said.

"What do you mean 'it hurts too much?' You got no choice!

"Look," he continued, "we can't have much farther to go. That fire's moving about four miles an hour. You're moving about two. Now we've got enough space between us to make it, but you've got to start fighting a bit."

"Fight, fight, fight! I've been doing it all day! Look at my leg, man! You see how burned it is? I'm going to have a huge scar! For the rest of my life! Shit, if I don't get it treated *I am going to lose my leg*!" And for the first time I realized this was a very real possibility.

"They'll cut it off! *They will cut it off!* I'd rather burn up than have that," I spit.

Something in the convict's face gave a subtle sign of agreement—but he didn't let it win the moment.

"You going to give up that easy?" he chided. "You so weak that you're just going to give up 'cause it hurts, 'cause you're going to have a scar? Look at these scars! You think it tickled me when I got 'em? I got prison waiting for me! You got picnics, wine, and cheese and crackers waiting! You got your whole damn life, and you whine and piss at me 'cause you might lose something. Men lose shit all the time. They lose their money, they lose their house, they lose their jobs, they lose their families! All sorts of bad shit. And they go on! Life makes 'em go, see, just like it's making you go. 'Cause life is never done chewing you up. It likes you good and soft before it swallows. Ha!

"Now you stop this horseshit, accept that there ain't no accepting—there ain't no quitting—life won't let you. So move with it and get up the goddamn mountain!" With this, he grabbed me by the collar and dragged me up.

"Okay, okay! Jeez! Just let me go. I can do it myself," I said, trying to wrestle his hand from my shirt.

"That's the spirit! You just quit your bitching and keep up, and I'll leave you be."

We hiked together for a moment in uneasy silence.

"Thing is with you," Gregory said, "you're afraid of a scar. Hell, a scar is something to be proud of. Means you been fighting, suffering, living! It's a tattoo from God himself! Everyone your age goes around getting this pierced and that tattooed— don't mean shit. You going to go to heaven and God's going to say, 'What the hell you been doing down there? I don't see no scars!' You'll show him your tattoos and he'll just laugh and say, 'Get your ass back down there! You ain't been living for shit!'"

"Yeah, well," I said, bitterly, "I don't have any tattoos."

"Ah, well now that's good! May be some hope for you after all. No tattoos and one hell of a scar."

182

A fleeting moment of joy passed through me. I liked having this man's approval.

But soon thereafter I was hit by a wave of nausea that nearly brought me to my knees.

"You okay, boy?" He asked.

"Yes, yes, let me rest."

"Don't' give up now. We can make this. We're not that far."

"I know, so just let me rest. Go on. I'll be up in a minute." I suddenly wanted to be rid of him. I wanted to suffer in solitude.

"I'm not going to carry you. You got to make it out on your own," Gregory said.

"I don't want you to carry me! I want you to leave me alone!" I shouted.

Gregory looked momentarily hurt—then relented. "Suit yourself, I suppose."

He slipped ahead, quickly fading out of sight behind the trees and the smoke.

I indulged in a moment of surrender. I gave no resistance to anything—not even gravity. I fell, landed on my hands and knees, and began to weep. As my self-pity came to its highest crescendo, I replayed all the past defeats my short life had dealt me. I had been poor at sports, with humiliation being evermore present than victory. I was mediocre in school, finding myself too distracted to do well. I was even mediocre at video games, with all the hours wasted for a product that by its very nature became outdated within a year. And girls, the ultimate sorry story, with one unrequited love after another.

That was it. It was over. No more trying, and no more failing. The defeat would be complete within an hour—and it was to be my last. The world wouldn't have Jonathan Samuels to kick around anymore. I licked my tears as they rolled down my face, savoring the mild saline. And there I stayed crying for at least ten minutes, until I could no longer hear my sobs because of the increasing roar of the fire. As the roar became louder than my cries, that instinct—that fear—grabbed hold of me again, demanding that I move. And so I did, lamely crawling on hands and knees.

The warm ash covered my tear-stained face and coated my tongue. Occasionally a knee or hand would land in a pocket of intense heat, scalding it, and making me curse the God who I begged for mercy.

The ambient temperature began to increase—and while it was not terribly hot, it was an aggressive, radiant heat that beamed into my skin. The atmosphere trembled from the thunder of the approaching fire, and the brilliant orange and yellow hue that started to bounce off of every object could not be ignored. I cast a glance down the hill.

It was the most massive thing I've ever seen. The flames, though still a quarter of a mile away, towered well over my head, spastic and dazzling in an almost supernatural way. From them came a column of smoke, rushing out like a tumultuous river, pooling into a large head thousands of feet above. The magnitude of the crown fire burning through the old growth was four times greater than the earlier fire. The forerunning flame wall did not move with the demonic speed of the earlier fire, but it was gaining momentum, just as Gregory had said.

The immensity overwhelmed my mind's ability to comprehend, and all self-pity was displaced by awe. When the awe ebbed, I was left with one desire, which seemed to scream from every molecule that made me: live.

Marcus and Edgar moved down the ridge in an exhausted catch-and-fall movement, which spared their muscles at the expense of their joints and jarred them from feet to skull. While it took concentration to keep their feet planted firmly, they could not help but notice at times the huge, rumbling reburn running through the canopy on the opposite side of the valley. After winding their way around smoking stumps, still a-crackle with fire, they reached the valley floor and entered the small, half-burnt riparian zone of the stream.

They looked down at the stagnant pools, momentarily contemplating the murky water, filled with decaying plant matter.

"Well, I guess a little beaver fever never hurt anyone," Marcus said. He kneeled down next to the water, took his hardhat off, dipped his clasped hands, and began to drink.

"We'll win every fart contest for a week," Edgar said as he also kneeled down to drink.

The water quickened the men almost immediately.

Edgar felt the sweet slosh in his belly and leaned back against the nearest rock—and for a moment he felt free of the entire event. However, pieces of burning debris rolled down from the fire on the north bank, and served as a constant reminder of where he was.

"Damn it," he whispered aloud after dodging a small, burning piece of wood that had rolled into the stream bank. "Can't this fucking thing leave me alone for a minute?"

"We can't wait around long here anyway. We have to get back," Marcus said.

"It's best if we're strong," Edgar said.

Marcus filled his hard hat with water, then threw it out on the ground and refilled it once more, then shimmied to a nearby stone and sipped from the improvised canteen.

"I should have put him in my tent. I should have done it. I heard him. I heard it. I pretended not to. I pretended I was too much in my own world, and maybe I was, but I heard it. I know. I know."

"We can't worry about that now," Edgar said.

"Well what are we suppose to worry about!" Marcus demanded. "We can't just sit here."

Skip watched the two men trod down the hill, wondering if at any moment one would fall, tumble down, and succumb to the thirst. But they didn't, and eventually they disappeared out of sight. He had fallen into an 'event cascade,' when an emergency causes a person to focus on only one problem, and in turn, lose site of the bigger picture. A fireman runs to get a hose, while thinking only about the burgeoning fire, and gets hits by a car. A ski patrolman attempting to help an injured skier, ends up in an avalanche zone. Skip had let his concern for Steve cloud his concern for the other men, and now everyone under his care was about to succumb to heat stroke.

He turned towards Jacobson—who was babbling incoherently—and unbuttoned the man's pants.

"Don't take this personally," he said, as he unzipped them, and pulled them down to the supine man's knees, exposing the waist, thighs, and genitals. Skip then took off his Nomex shirt and began fanning it over the crewman. It was the fastest way to cool a body without water.

Soon he became tired and, worried about his own state, rested to save his strength. He leaned against the rock and realized that the gurgling from Steve's chest had stopped. Steve wasn't breathing. He placed his hand on Steve's neck, so that two fingers overlapped the jugular vein. A light but persistent pulse thumped through it. Skip put his face up to the mouth to attempt rescue breathing, but then gave pause. He placed two fingers back on the neck.

The beat was still strong, still resolute, still demanding. But Skip knew he could only give witness to the struggle, not aid. A tragic intimacy formed between Skip and the heart as it continued to pound, a last rage against its dying. And Skip, drawing on some personal depth or inborn wisdom, decided that he should give it what perhaps strength and beauty ultimately wish for: a medium of expression. The final moment was coming. The pulse grew strong for two beats, and following the third, a monumental contraction. In that moment Skip had a vision of Steve, standing in victory, his saw thrown over his shoulder, his handsome face beaming with sweat and a smile of pride after he had just dropped his first C class tree with near perfection.

Then the pulse was gone.

The wind ceased, as did Jacobson's banter. For a moment, complete stillness dominated the world as a perfect neutrality enveloped everything.

Skip finally exhaled, and the world was sent back into motion. He released his hand from the dead man, slumped against the rock, bit his fist, and cried.

Chapter Seven

Fire simplifies matter into its constituent parts, and the mere vision of it did the same to me. No dream, no hope, no idea, no thought existed. Even pain made no sense. The languor and helplessness that had become an almost inextricable part of my person from years of over-institutionalized socialization, electronic entertainment, cable television, and parents more concerned with the price of their living room coffee table than the development of their son's vigor and fortitude— cracked, split, and tore away. All that seemed left was blood, salt, and a thump in my chest.

I came to my feet and began putting one shaking leg in front of the other with the same pure will that drives sperm to egg. I conserved no energy. I did not plot a course to the rock; I paid no attention to the path of least resistance. Instead my boots tromped through trees and burning stumps, stumbled into deep holes, and tripped on remaining roots. When I fell, I scratched at the powdery ash while returning to my feet, as if trying to move farther up the mountain with the aid of my fingers.

But even sperm tire, and soon the refuge of thoughtless panic gave way to fatigue. My lungs could not expand wide enough, and my legs trembled in such a chaotic frenzy that forward movement became impossible. Angry at my weakness, I yelled out at my limbs, demanding they flex and push me away from the fire.

But the fire continued to gain on me. Swirling slowly, like a massive inverted vortex, it forced all matter to instantly recognize its potential as energy and sent it into the ethereal plane with a merciless roar. Within minutes it would do the same to me.

I would soon pass out. The sensation rushed over me like so much dark water until it seemed I was to float off into the ease of painless drowning. All I had to do was let go.

"Hurry it up, boy!" a voice called out, garbled by the roar of the fire.

I looked up to see the convict hanging on the edge of a large wall of stone about twenty feet in front of me. It was the base of the rock butte.

For a flash I was torn—I was about to escape the easy way, and suddenly a real chance at survival presented itself.

"Hurry it up boy, goddamn it! Don't give up now!" Gregory yelled. He had one hand and leg on the rock while the others hung free so that he could look at me.

His words tilted my decision towards hope, and suddenly I was desperate for it, scrambling towards the rock with both hands and feet, fearing that any moment hope would be crushed again.

I reached the rock, wild and mad, and clung to it like a lover.

"Good job, boy. You're half way there."

I looked up to see the butte was at least six times my height. Hope was crushed again, and I fell to the ground.

"No, goddamn it! Don't give up now!" Gregory growled as he came down off the rock to pick me up. He shoved me back on it.

"Come on! Move!"

But I was frozen—I could barely cling on to the rock with my trembling hands

He jumped back up on the rock face so that he was even with me.

"Look, you in pain! You're fearful. Achilles himself would feel the same damn way! But you suppose to feel that way! Accept it. Don't resist it. Don't call on nobody to save you from it. It's here to save you! Let it save you! Let it move you! Climb the fucking rock!"

At least that's what I think he said. The words were practically unintelligible, but their passionate expression, perhaps their truth, perhaps that some random stranger from a completely different background simply chose to care, emboldened me to at least try. I tentatively loosened my grip with my right hand, and with a trembling caress searched for a hold higher above. I found a hold, clenched it with all my strength, and wondered what to do next. I was stretched like rubber, and there was nowhere else to go. I raised my foot to find a higher hold for it, but the clunky work boots were rejected at every shuffle—there was no crack or divot that would accept them. I bent my knee toward my chest, as high as I could get, and eventually found a nub that the toe of my boot could barely get on. But it was the best I could find. The calf of my other foot began to shake violently, and knowing it would give in at any moment if I didn't redistribute my weight, I trusted the nub and pushed on it, feeling as if I'd fall to my doom through the entire motion.

"That's it! Accept what you *must* do!" Gregory yelled.

I heard that phrase clearly. I moved my hips closer towards the rock wall for better leverage and began to slowly move up it as I pushed further—a unicycle on top of a rickety ladder, seemingly against the laws of balance. The move was a success.

"Can't just stay there, boy. You got to move!" Gregory yelled.

I found the hero inside. I freed my left hand, let it creep slowly up the rock. The ledge was there, and I took it.

"Good! Keep moving!" yelled Gregory, who was off to the right and above me, climbing the rock like an experienced old pro.

The rock unchangeable, absolute, supreme. Harder than the law, it cut into my flesh as my hands continued to use it. The consummate hardness of the rock struck me in the heart, with its perfect apathy. And I resisted it, pushing against it like one does the punch of a bullet, and for the briefest moment, when a move was executed, it congratulated me.

"Come on, boy! You're almost there!" Gregory yelled, as he reached the top.

The fire behind me began to scream into my eardrums. It would slam against the rock face and my body in moments.

I reached my hand over the top of the ledge, patted it on the flat surface. Gregory grabbed my wrist, and with a sudden pull, I was on top. I had made it.

"We got no time! Get to the center!" Gregory bellowed. He thrust me forward, toward the center of the rock. We quickly covered the hundred feet of distance or so, running and stumbling.

He pushed me to the ground. "Get down! Low to the ground is the best chance we got!"

I followed his directions, and as I did, the head of the fire hit the edge of the rock slab, burning the trees that towered around it. The roar vibrated through my body like the laughter of Zeus, an unceasing shockwave that threatened my sanity. Trees simultaneously exploded from the heat, causing a violent blast to sound out over the already impossible ruckus. Hot air rushed towards the sky, forming a vacuum that tugged on our clothes and threatened to suck us up into the sky on fire. I clenched the ground with my remaining might so that it would not be so.

While I lay on the rock, the fire still did its bidding on my back, piercing through the Nomex with intense razors of heat. What Gregory's bare skin went through, I can only imagine.

∞

By the time Edgar and Marcus reached the ridge top they had already sweated most of what they had consumed climbing the hill, and their thirst returned with vengeance. The water bottles sloshing on their sides heightened their anguish, but they saved each drop stoically for their crewmembers.

They walked towards the rock where they had planted Steve and Jacobson, and they saw Skip in his crew t-shirt. He was using his yellow Nomex shirt to fan off Jacobson, whose eyes were half closed as the blood gathering in his face was swelling them shut.

"Hey!" Marcus yelled out to Skip, who was too involved creating breeze to notice their arrival. "What are you doing?"

"Cooling him off!" Skip said in between heavy breaths.

"How's Steve?" Marcus asked.

Skip stopped fanning his shirt and turned towards the men. "Steve's gone," he said.

"What!" Marcus yelped with the shriek of a dog slapped by its master. He rushed behind Skip to find the body.

"He died ... he passed a few ... he passed 20 minutes ago."

"Did you try CPR? Did you try to revive him? We did it once before. We can do it again!" Without waiting for an answer, Marcus knelt over the body as if about to start resuscitation. "Come on Edgar, you do the breath while I do the compressions," he demanded anxiously.

But Edgar stayed still.

"Come on! What are you waiting for?" Marcus yelled at Edgar, who slowly turned towards Skip.

Skip slowly shook his head at Marcus. "It's over."

Marcus's eyes opened wide with bewilderment. He shot up and charged Skip in confrontation.

"What do you mean? What do you mean!" he demanded.

Skip stood stoic. Marcus eventually looked away from him and cast another glance at his fallen buddy. Flies and bees hovered over the corpse and landed in the cold pools of fluid that seeped from the many cracks, openings, and skinless patches on the destroyed body.

He turned away and hung his head.

"Fuck," he muttered.

He raised his head up high and yelled the same word. He looked back at the body that had once been his saw partner—once so full of strength, courage, and youthful beauty, now lifeless and covered with insects. He cursed out once more to the air and kicked the corpse. It moved lifelessly, already getting stiff with death. He kicked it again, harder.

"Marcus!" Skip said, reaching for him. "Come on, take it easy."

Marcus pushed his foreman away and kicked at the dirt, spraying the dead man's face. Then he walked away.

∞

Eventually the sound subsided and the upward suction of air ceased. Small embers started to land on my hands, on my neck, and on my back. The roar dimmed into a growl, and the heat waned. We stood up and looked at each other in disbelief.

All around us were burned trees, pockets of fire still eating at their remains. I pictured how the fire must have looked from a bird's-eye view. Certainly no one would imagine that life of any sort could survive in the center of such destruction. But we had—we had been in the middle of a bomb, and I still breathed with no more injury than my earlier wound and some small red spots on my wrists and neck.

"Holy shit!" Gregory blurted. "Twice in one day!"

I sat for a moment, solemn, looking at the utter destruction, the volcanic sterilization of all life. "Yeah, twice in one day ...," I said.

"If I was you, you know what's the first thing I would do when I get back to base camp?" Gregory said.

"What?"

"Ask for a fucking raise!" he bellowed.

I mustered a small laugh and continued looking at the scene around me.

As far as I could see to the north, a desiccated crust of black ash blanketed the Earth. Remains of trees, knocked down and stacked on each other like toothpicks, covered the hill, while crackling pockets of fire devoured their remains. Farther away, a tremendous plume rose from the earth. It was the northern edge of the fire that had passed over me hours ago. Its faraway rumble was now only a background noise.

"I hope they hurry," I said.

"Hope who hurries?"

"The rescuers, or whoever is going to get me the fuck out of here."

Gregory scoffed. "Look around, man! You think they're going to look for survivors in this? Better to look for a whale in the desert."

"They've got to find me!" I protested. "Look at my leg! Look at me! There's *got* to be a rescue mission going on!" I wanted to throw myself down on the rock to beat it, like a child having a tantrum.

"Okay, okay there, boy. Don't get yourself all excited. Save your energy. You going to need it."

"I don't have any energy. Look at what we've gone through. Someone should look for us. Someone should save us!"

"Yeah, well 'should' ain't much of anything out here. It's a mirage. Look at that fire—look at that town way off there. They're going to save them folks, not you. Not when everyone thinks you're dead already, and probably even if they didn't …"

"Don't say that," I said.

"You're not making it out tonight, man—we're not going anywhere but here."

"Look at my leg!"

"Yeah, looks like shit. You best stop thinking about it, and think about how things are, not how they 'should' be. How you going to deal with this."

I almost spit profanity in his direction. But then I remembered, I owed him my life.

"Look, I owe you a big thank you. So thanks, thanks a lot."

"Ah, no big thing. Now, let's make ourselves comfortable—seems like there's nowhere to go, and a show to watch," Gregory said, gesturing toward the fire plume far away.

"Why was this in your pocket, Marcus?" Skip asked as he looked at the radio battery, and picked a piece of chewed gum off of it.

"Good luck, I guess," Marcus said.

"You got any food in there, too?" Jacobson asked.

"You're not ready for food yet," Edgar said.

"Hey, I'm standing, aren't I?" Jacobson said. The water and the evening cool off had revived him, but he was still very shaky, and felt as if he might tumble if he didn't keep sipping on the plastic canteen.

"We'll try it," Skip said, as he tried to hail his superintendent over the radio.

"Good luck. That Big Red that was stuck to it, looked like it was chewed sometime ago," Edgar said.

"Shshshsh!" Skip said, as a voice came through, garbled in static.

"If this is Skip, key your radio twice," Bruce said through the speaker.

Skip did so.

"How many are in your party, Skip?"

Skip keyed his radio four times.

"So you are without one?" Bruce asked.

Skip keyed the radio twice to indicate the affirmative.

There was a brief pause.

"I am sorry to hear that, BREAK" Bruce said in a voice sodden with disappointment. His voice then abruptly changed to cold and businesslike.

"Rob reports that the detailer was left behind. Is that correct?"

The detailer! Skip hadn't had time to consider the outcome of that earlier problem—the person he hoped would rise to the occasion, when the situation was concerning but not yet dire. He remembered the mental picture he had taken of the man shaking on his knees as the fire was seconds from overwhelming him, the man that up to that point he had assumed was a convict. It was a haunted and heartbreaking image, and now one filled with guilt, as he realized it was one under his supervision.

Skip responded in the affirmative.

"So we must presume the worst?" Bruce asked, his voice drenched in disdain.

Skip wanted to explain: he had had a crew to lead in the midst of a rapidly deteriorating situation; the best option was to trust Rob and hope for the best; but he could make no excuses, only push the button to indicate the affirmative.

And he did so.

"I see. Skip, all helicopters will be busy doing medevacs for civilians and firefighters until dark ... BREAK ..."

"I have one helicopter scheduled to pick us up in fifteen minutes. It will fly two flights for us. BREAK."

"That is just enough to take everyone here back to camp. BREAK."

"You and your men will have to stay out for the night. Do you copy?"

Skip had to muster his strength in order to push the button twice. The sudden sterile and cold tone of his superintendant rang with contempt. Was Bruce going to blame Skip? Would Skip be found guilty of the mistake that had led them all here? Would Bruce try to make it look like he had failed his duties and put the crew in the position they were now in? Would he blame Skip for not calculating that there was a weak link in the chain? His breathing became shallow and clenched. But he mustered the will to confirm the transmission.

"Skip, I am looking at my map. There is a cabin about three miles east—in the middle of the burn ... I spotted it in the flight over. BREAK."

"They sent a crew out this morning for structural protection. They may have been successful. It's two basins over, to the south. BREAK."

"You should be able to see it from the ridge south of you to confirm that. BREAK."

"There are likely to be some provisions in it. Do you copy?"

Skip pushed his radio twice.

"Tomorrow—at sometime—they should be able to get you out. But it will likely be a while. Do you copy?"

Skip again keyed the affirmative.

"I recommend you hike to it in the morning, get your men fed and safe. BREAK."

Skip again keyed the affirmative.

"A—Out," Bruce signaled, and was gone.

Skip was to blame. He heard it in Bruce's voice. And suddenly he could almost read the report that would be done, the investigation. They would have to blame someone—they always did. Skip felt belted, then crushed. He replayed the discussion he had with me, the weak detailer, the command he had given Steve, "Get in your shelter!" And then he thought about the weather report he had been given, his time standing on the stump long before the fire blew up, the hike in, all things leading up to this, and he became his own prosecuting attorney, seeing how people would say he had ignored all what could appear, in hindsight, to be obvious signs of a coming firestorm.

"Skip?" Edgar said, watching his leaders eyes turn blank and almost lifeless.

Skip turned towards the men and was about to tell them what to do, but he tripped on his tongue.

Words wouldn't come. In fact the plans, ideas, thoughts, and concerns would not even form— they were discarded before they could even manifest.

"Skip?" Edgar asked again. "What should we do?"

But only scattered, fearful wisps, incapable of causing action, filled Skip's mind. The only force strong enough to turn into drive was the want of water, and so he simply started walking down to the creek. Edgar and Jacobson shrugged their shoulders and followed.

"Wait!" Marcus demanded. He walked a few feet to Steve's body. "This is the last time we'll see him."

Marcus kneeled down over his fallen partner and shooed the flies away. He took off his yellow Nomex shirt so that he was wearing only his crew t-shirt underneath. He wrapped the Nomex shirt around his friend's face.

"It could get cold out. We don't know how long we're going to be out here," Edgar said.

"I don't want the bugs getting on him, not on his face at least," Marcus said.

He finished covering the face and head. The men bowed their heads in silence for a few painful moments. Then they slowly turned away and left.

∞

"It's Gregory, right?" I asked, wanting to make sure.

"Still is and always will be," he said.

"And I am Jonathan," I said.

"Still is and always will be," he said again.

"Ha. Yeah."

We sat in silence for a few minutes, watching the billowing column of smoke that was now so far away.

"It's kind of our fault," I said, looking at the massive plume.

"I didn't do shit!" Gregory protested.

"I mean man did it. These fires are happening because of man, not nature."

"You mean because man's been putting 'em out for so long?"

"Yeah, I mean, fire is actually good for the forest. It cleans up a lot of the diseases and insects. In fact, it's evolved from fire. Even before the Native Americans came to North America, lightning strikes would happen and start a blaze. So trees developed thicker bark to protect themselves. Heck even some seeds, like pine, will only sprout after they've been exposed to fire—they need it. It also clears out the underbrush and allows for new growth. Funny, up until today it was just some shit I memorized for class."

"But man saw the fire," Gregory said, "and decided it was dangerous. It was burning up the trees that he wanted to cut down. Decided it had to be stopped. He was going to save the forest, and so he started putting the fires out."

"Yep, now the whole thing is out of whack."

"Reminds me of this story I read about porcupines in the Southwest," Gregory continued.

"Porcupines—what, they were killed by fire?"

"No. They're killed by wolves and coyotes. But see wolves and coyotes also eat cattle and sheep. So the farmers all decided they'd get rid of the wolves and coyotes. They killed 'em all. Shot 'em dead. Till there were none left."

"Okay," I said.

"Well, the porcupines had a hay day. They ate and screwed and everything must have been good for them 'cause there were no more mean old dogs trying to eat them up. The population exploded."

"Uh ... good for the porcupines," I said.

"Not so much, because then they started eatin' all the saplings and little trees. All of them. Pretty soon all their food was gone. Then they all starved. Them porcupines all died. Extinct."

"Oh ... bummer ...."

"As goes the predator so goes the prey."

"Okay ..."

"Just like this here forest," Gregory said.

"So you're saying porcupines are like ... fire?"

"No, I am saying wolves and coyotes are like fire," Gregory said.

"Okay, then," I said.

Gregory turned and looked at me as if I wasn't taking him seriously, and I wasn't.

"After all you been through today you still don't get it, do you?" he said.

"I get that man made a mistake in engaging in fire suppression. I get that very well, after today. Heck, I get that *I made a mistake* in engaging in fire suppression! Look at my leg!"

"But what I'm telling you about the porcupines; it's clearly something you need to know. You need to know it right here," he said, tapping his chest.

"Uh, I don't ... own any porcupines."

Gregory looked perplexed; then he laughed. "No shit! Me neither!"

"Well we got that in common," I said.

"Sucks don't it?"

"The worst!"

The plume in the background suddenly illuminated, its pumice-like texture momentarily vivid in the light of the dimming rays of sunset. A lightning bolt shot out of the column and hit a tree just outside the fire's perimeter, causing a smaller fire that was immediately assimilated into the larger one.

"Whoa! That thing must be huge!" I said.

"That's man saving the forest," Gregory said.

Saving. It reminded me that there was something else I wanted to save—my leg. I put my right hand on the base of my neck and noticed the glands there were swollen. A feverish chill shook me. I lay down, looked up at the sky, and hoped for a miracle in the final moments of light. I prayed that a helicopter, an angel might come if I just kept hoping and staring, begging and praying. But sleep came sooner than providence.

Skip saw the creek, walked up to it and threw down his hard hat. With the care of a dead man, he threw his head into the first big pool he could find. The water flooded his mouth, his viscera. His brain sizzled with momentary euphoria. For a passing moment, there was no fire, no crew, no blame— just ecstasy.

The three men looked awkwardly at him , slightly perplexed by the foreman's breach in crew procedure—normal protocol was for the crewmembers to be nourished before overhead. But they were too thirsty themselves to give the behavior much thought. They found smaller pools nearby and drank silently as daylight slipped away.

"Looks like it's time for me to get a new line of work," Jacobson said.

"Yeah, what are you going to do? Get a job in a bank?" Marcus asked.

"Right, let me figure out how to balance my checking account first," Jacobson said.

"People still do that?" Edgar asked.

"Only since I got a kid," Jacobson said. "Fuck, I'm putting them through a lot right now... ."

"Well dude, you're kind of going through a lot yourself right now," Edgar said.

"They probably think I'm dead."

"Well, think how good the survivor sex will be," Edgar said.

"Just hope Sancho doesn't try to get to her first," Jacobson said.

"Fucking Sancho—we should start a vigilante group of hotshots that goes after each and every one."

"Would we get hazard pay?" Jacobson asked.

"Fuck that! We do it for free," Edgar said.

"I just need to stick around home more. It's clearly getting to be time for a change," Jacobson said.

"What would you do?" Marcus asked.

"You could log. You're good with a saw," Edgar said.

"No way. Too dangerous," Jacobson said.

"And fighting fire isn't?" Edgar asked.

"My dad died logging," Jacobson said.

"Oh—I'd never heard for sure."

"Yeah, well, that's what it was. I don't remember much—a hospital, my mom crying a lot. I was only seven.

"I didn't believe it—I never got it until I was like 12," he continued. "I just kept figuring he would come back someday. I'd seen the way that guy could work, figured nothing could kill him. We had this patch of forested land, and my dad wanted to clear it so my mom could have a garden. I remember him hauling these huge rounds of timber with his bare hands and chucking them like sticks. He taught me how to work. Man, he pushed me. Taught me how to use a saw when I was six—bought me a little miniature one."

"Well, no wonder you're so good," Marcus said.

Jacobson's carriage lifted. It was rare to get a compliment from anyone regarding ability, and unheard of from Marcus.

"He made sure I earned it. Stern as hell. But at the end of the day, he'd grab me by the shoulder, and say, 'good work – now let's see what your mom's got cooking. You deserve it," Jacobson said, choking on deserve.

The men stood in silence as a light breeze moved through the air, allowing Jacobson to collect himself.

"There are few things more wonderful than to be loved by the strong," Marcus said, breaking the silence.

Edgar turned his attention towards the large man. "Now where in the fuck, did *you* come up with *that*?"

"I think I read it somewhere," Marcus said.

"I didn't think you knew how."

"Fuck you, Edgar," Marcus said.

"That's why I like this job so much, I think," Jacobson said. "Sometimes when I am busting my ass, when it's hot, and I'm pushing it with all I got, I can feel him ... close to me."

"That's cool, man," Marcus said.

"Yeah, well I don't want my kid to just feel I'm close—I want him to know I am," Jacobson said.

"You could always try to get on as a structure fire fighter somewhere. Slick yourself up—wear a uniform—shave everyday," Edgar said.

"Fuck that shit," Marcus said.

"It's getting dark, Skip—should we hit it or just stay here for the night?" Edgar asked.

Skip blinked at the request, stunned to be asked for direction. "Yeah, let's do that," Skip said.

"Do what? Stay here? Go?" Jacobson asked. "We won't make the cabin before it gets dark—no way."

"Yeah, but we can cut some of the distance. We don't want to spend too much time traveling in the heat tomorrow," Marcus said, casting a glance at Jacobson. "We climb the hill now, in the cool air—then tomorrow we can get to the cabin before the heat of the day," he continued.

"Yeah, you're right," Skip replied. "Let's try to get to the top while we still have some light."

The men lined up behind their foreman and followed him as he marched along the creek, then turned directly up the hill. No longer bogged down by dehydration, they moved swiftly. The sound of a burned tree falling to the ground would occasionally rake the air like thunder, reminding them to stay alert for such hazards.

They reached the top of the ridge in the waning twilight. Their surroundings were lost in the darkness, and so was the view of the opposite end of the rock.

But they could see the tremendous column of fire to out north.

"Jesus! It's nine o'clock and that thing is still going off," Edgar said. "This is going to be worse than Yellowstone."

"Might not even get a ride out of here tomorrow," Jacobson said.

"Fuck it. We'll walk out of here if we have to," Marcus said.

The men then lay unceremoniously on the ground, keeping their hard hats on, and looked up at the stars. They had done it hundreds of times—but normally they at least had the modest comfort of a space blanket. In normal conditions they would welcome the opportunity to show they could function fine without. On this night, though, the small symbol of security was missed, and they stared nervously at the sky.

"I don't like the idea of him out there, with nothing," Marcus said.

"We did what we could...I keep telling myself, anyway," Edgar said.

"Steve's so damn tough, even dead the coyotes won't mess with him," Jacobson said.

"That's why he always pissed me off. On PT runs, I'd have to bust my ass all off season, drink plenty of water the night before, get plenty of rest, eat right—optimize as much as possible—and then I'd barely do it. When I finally got to the stage where I'd pass him, he'd reek of booze and cigarettes from the night before," Edgar commented.

"And have a dip in," Jacobson said.

"Well, he was young," Marcus said, his voice cracking.

"Yeah, give him a few years and he'd been married with kids, himself," Jacobson said. "Nobody would want to live that way at thirty-five." He paused for an awkward moment. "Except you Marcus—'cause you're so damn tough yourself."

"Eh, don't worry about it," Marcus said. "We all do our own thing."

Lately Marcus's age seemed to haunt him more and more. He couldn't run as fast as he used to. His number of pull-ups, while respectable, was no longer on the top of the crew roster. He couldn't help but notice the lines that broke the once smooth skin of his face.

But for certain, on any hike, at anytime, no one could outdo him. And that's what hotshots did. They worked and they hiked—and while PT tests were always a way to earn a badge of respect, at the end of the day, it was your ability to hike and to work that mattered. His respect had been redoubled a few weeks earlier when the flu ravaged half the crew with fever, and a bad patch of San Bernardino poison oak had given everyone the rash. His temperature was well over one-hundred, and inflamed skin covered his entire torso and neck. The incline was fifteen percent, and it was a six-mile hike through dirt, in ninety-five degree heat. Even Steve, suffering the same affliction, had almost faltered and had to hand the saw to Marcus in order to avoid forming a gap between himself and the member in front of him. Marcus pushed on his back with one hand while holding the saw in the other. Other crewmembers with lighter loads and younger bodies had fallen back, but he and Steve kept up with Skip, who had set the crew on too fast a pace. Gaps formed all over the line—the only time in crew history. But Marcus kept up.

One rookie on the crew, after seeing the event unfold, looked wonder-eyed at Marcus and asked in awe, "How did you do it?"

"One foot at a time," is all Marcus said.

There was more to it, though, that the young rookie wouldn't understand. Marcus knew himself well. He wasn't quick, he wasn't educated, he wasn't funny, and he wasn't particularly sociable. He was tough, and that attribute alone formed his identity and self worth. Therefore, it wasn't just momentary embarrassment that was threatened by falling back on that hike; his whole self image had been at stake. He couldn't afford to compromise the one thing that made him valuable to himself and others. Every step, every flex, and every breath became a war for that value. That's why he made it. There was no choice.

But he still could not completely explain why he never claimed the responsibilities and comforts of domestic adulthood.

The outright answer was obvious: he didn't want to. The idea of middle class domestic rigor—the car payments and house payments, the cleaning of dishes and floors, taking out garbage, and taking care of the needs of a wife, the slow and steady pace of safe responsibility—gave him a headache, and he knew he'd be bad at it. He was geared like a dinosaur, and in his mind, despite efforts to see its reason, modern life seemed artificial and hectic. It was plagued with an underlying sense of impending doom—people acted with fear when there was no reason to fear. Society told you that you had to mount up and fight, not because of life and limb, not because the fire threatened you, not because your survival and your honor were at stake against deadly circumstances, but because an electric company needed you to make a payment.

Then there were babies. What a horrid scene. Not that the creatures themselves were so bad, but the silly bright colored toys that parents inundated them with and the strange scent of helpless purity that permeated their environment. It was repulsive. In Marcus's world, tough was the gold standard, and babies were not tough.

But as he looked into the night sky with the image of his dying friend seared on his mind's eye, he recalled the horrifying panic in the tent and understood for a passing moment the desire for help—arms to hold, blankets to cover, milk from mother. In the tent he too shook like a baby shakes, and though the men could not hear him over the fire, he too yelled—screamed, cried—like a baby. It was like being in a new world, like a newborn. He resolved next time he saw a baby, he would be nice to it, and give it the feeling of safety it deserved for entering such a chaotic world.

"Jacobson, shaving every day might not be so bad," Marcus said, but no one heard him. The men had all drifted into sleep.

Chapter Eight

On any wildfire, sleep is not slumber. Dreams are fitful and uneasy—perhaps not nightmares, but hardly places of peace. The mind busies itself preparing for the next day: the countless hours of hot labor, the possible dangers from flame or rock, the bickering and social threats from constant contact and competition with fellow crewmen, and the lessons of the day before from which one might glean some insight on the day to come. It is not rest but rehearsal—the sharpening of fortitude and focus, a desperate search for common themes in a constantly changing and chaotic environment.

And this night, on a breezy ridge, would give the men even less respite than usual. Their dreams were terrors charged only with processing the agony that had passed them and the ordeal to come. The intensity of these mental aftershocks awoke them often from the thin layer of unconsciousness with their eyes dry and itchy, pangs of hunger in their stomachs, the calls of distress bursting from their lips and ringing in their ears like an echo from the trauma before. They would awaken, push away the headaches and the need in their guts, try to calm their panic, and conjure up apathy towards the situation. But sleep would return, and the symbols of pain and need would surface in the mind's eye, becoming visual forms in dream time, where the hard won filters of self were worthless.

The shimmers of daylight finally came. Edgar watched the stars fade away, and for a moment found solace in the interlude between night and day. The images were gone; the demands had not yet arrived. But the stillness did not last long. Streaks of mauve and orange soon shot through the sky. Skip stirred, and Edgar knew within moments his foreman would rise and tell them to get to it.

But by the time the orange light of morning flooded the sky another concern arose. Skip was still lying in the dirt, and so was everyone else. It was light enough to move, and they needed to do so while it was relatively cool. He could tell his foreman was awake by his rustling, but he was not getting up. The other men were awake too, they stirred, but it was the foreman's job to get up first, and no one wanted to break hierarchy.

Finally Marcus came to his feet and dusted himself off, grumbling. All the men rose. Without a word Skip got up, dusted himself, and instead of issuing any kind of command, simply started to walk in the direction that he believed would lead to the cabin. The men followed out of habit.

They came to the southern ledge of the butte, which gave them a vista to the landscape, and they peered out hoping to find the house. A layer of smoke, influenced by a small inversion of air, hovered a few feet over the ground and covered the land below them. From this blanket, dead trees glistened with black ash, like the hands of burned witches, reaching out to touch the radically auburn and maroon horizon that dominated the awakening sky.

They quickly spotted the cabin below. It was nestled in a shallow valley one ridgeline away, in a small, unburned pocket of the forest. It was not very big, but because of a roof that gleamed as if it were metallic it was easy to see.

"Does it have an aluminum roof?" Marcus asked.

"Maybe, that might explain why it survived," Skip said.

"No cedar shakes to grab the fire," Jacobson said.

"Might as well get to it," Marcus said.

"Yeah, I smell food," Jacobson said.

"That's a ways. We could head back to our original LZ, stop and drink some water at the stream. At least we know there's water there," Edgar said.

Skip looked towards the basin they had been in the day before. Edgar's idea wasn't crazy. The LZ was a long ways away, farther than the cabin, but a more predictable place to get help. The cabin was closer, but the roof, if it was aluminum, might indicate a barn, not a house. The Forest Service was notorious for putting ten thousand dollars worth of effort to save a thousand-dollar structure that often turned out to only house mice and bats. He scanned the roof, but it didn't look like tin—it just shone too brightly. Anything that bright had to be maintained.

"There could be a phone there," Jacobson said. "We could call in help."

Skip pursed his lips. He realized the men were waiting for him to make a decision, and he resented them for it. He didn't want to make another decision in his life. His judgment couldn't be trusted, and he could no longer weigh pros and cons and come to a conclusion. He had let early morning slip away because he had lain there wondering whether the men would benefit more from the cool of morning or an extra hour of sleep. A mind undulates between the logic of any possible action and seizes on a particular peak that is dictated ultimately by intuition—but he could seize nothing. Instead of thoughts consisting of clear reason and keen instinct, Skip's mind went in dizzying circles of ceaseless worry offering no resolution. Somewhere he knew the men were being driven by primal needs, not foresight. They wanted food, a domicile, connection with civilization, and he had no conviction to resist their desires.

He finally gave a small nod, and the men all waited for him to set a course. Finally Marcus turned awkwardly towards the hill facing the cabin and started walking down it. The men followed, not in the normal tight line, but in a disorganized group.

The sun rose into full light. Their water was quickly gone, and the desire for it grew strong— even their surroundings agreed. Burned and desiccated trees reached toward the sky, frozen in the moment of agony's peak, screaming to heaven for the rain that could have saved them.

The ground was a desert. Deep gray powder kicked up high as the men walked down the hill, getting up inside their pant legs, embedding itself in the Nomex fabric, so that the chalky substance scraped against their thighs with every step. The morning air was cool, but the sunlight was already starting to beat down, causing the first droplets of sweat to bloom on their foreheads. They would all be facing severe dehydration again soon.

They reached the valley, and as they did, they lost their view of where they were going. Soon progress was harder to notice, and their direction lost some of its conviction.

"Goddamn!" Edgar said. "Feels like we're in a void."

"To get some place we don't even know exists," Skip said. "This cabin could be nothing more than a barn."

The men shot a look of resentment at their foreman. Skip avoided their expressions, and a wave of wordless self-deprecation crossed his mind—why had he not had the gumption to voice this concern earlier. But they just kept walking, their minds too numb to consider another course.

"Talked to my wife, before we went out yesterday," Jacobson said, his voice raspy. "My kid, he's starting to try to stand up; he's trying to walk. He's going to take his first steps any day now—and I'll miss it."

∞

A crow's persistent squawk woke me up. My sleep was so shallow that I felt practically no disorientation, but I immediately started assessing my health as I sat up.

My limbs felt heavy and cumbersome; my head ached enough to inspire the image of a spike running straight through it. And I was so thirsty—beyond reason it seemed. All night I had dreamt of drinking water without one wick of relief. Looking down at my leg, the reason was clear. My right calf oozed so much pus that it had formed a large puddle on the ground beneath me. I was leaking.

"Boy, that looks nasty," Gregory said.

I groaned and lay back down.

"Boy, I told you not to look at a wound when there's nothing you can do about it," Gregory said.

"Well, it's kind of hard not to look at it when you're talking about it," I complained.

"Ah, calm down, I just saw something that might make you feel better."

"A helicopter?" I asked.

"No, not a damn helicopter. But it's something," Gregory said as he helped me to my feet.

He led me to the southern side of the ridge, and there we found a vista. I saw the landscape unfold in the morning light, an endless skeleton cemetery for trees, like a cursed land from some mythical time.

"Jesus, feels like we're on the moon or something," I said.

"Yeah, but the moon doesn't have one of them," Gregory said as he pointed. Looking in that direction, I saw a glint of sun reflecting off the metal roof of what looked to be a cabin.

"Think there's anybody in it?" I asked.

"I doubt it. I'd a gotten the hell out of here yesterday if I could of. Can't see anyone doing any different," Gregory said.

"Well how far do you think it is?" I asked.

"Hour or two walk I suppose. Maybe longer," Gregory said.

"I can't walk that much," I said.

"Well, what else do you suppose we do? Sit in the hot sun all day waiting for some helicopter? I sure as hell ain't going to carry your ass there."

I pictured myself lying on the sun-beaten ridge with no water and no shade, listening to Gregory talk about some homespun philosophy explained in rodent metaphors.

"Well, guess we better head there now, while it's cool," I said. "Besides, no fire's going to get us in there—nothing left to burn."

Gregory's face beamed with approval.

"Good choice, boy. Glad to hear you don't want to just sit and wait for someone to save you. Now let's find ourselves something to eat!"

And with that we started down the hill.

Jacobson could deny it no longer; the pale shimmering blotches, the blank patches in his field of sight were returning—a sure sign that his body was again under heat stress. The ground began to sway. His pulse was thin but hyper.

But they had to be close. There was only one more slight incline to cover, and then it would be downhill into the small basin where the house was located. Arguing with himself about whether he should stop the men for a rest, or simply slow down—the conclusion suddenly hit him: he was about to pass out. He sat without a word, then lay down in the ash and gazed upwards as the burned trees overhead swirled together. The painful nausea reached a crescendo as he slipped into unconsciousness.

It took a full minute for Edgar to look back and notice Jacobson was down. "Holy shit!" he yelled, and ran back to where Jacobson had fallen.

He reached his crewmate and knew the problem immediately. Skip and Marcus followed behind him, and he looked at Skip hoping for a statement of action, but could see the foreman seemed lost in thought, a vacuous glaze still over his eyes. Then Edgar turned to Marcus, but while he respected the older man's tenacity and work ethic, he did not so much trust his judgment. So Edgar came up with a plan of his own.

"He needs water. One of us needs to get it—from the cabin, hopefully. They can also call in help. Maybe we can get a medevac."

"I'll go get water," Skip said.

But as Skip started walking in the direction of the cabin, Marcus threw down his hat.

"No way! We can't just sit here and wait! We got to move him to the cabin!" He demanded.

"What?!" Edgar exploded "What are you talking about, Marcus! If we do that, then we'll all be sick. Dude, we can't go on any longer. Think about it logically. We should just stay in one place and wait. You know, like when you're a kid and get lost."

Marcus almost succumbed to the logic, but an anger bordering on rage boiled over him and spit from his tongue.

"Bullshit! We're hotshots! We don't need to sit around waiting for somebody to save us while our man goes into heatstroke! We're hotshots! We're hotshots!" Marcus repeated the statement over and over again. There were thousands of thoughts moving through his head that he could not articulate, so he just repeated the phrase, because to him that phrase said it completely.

And Skip understood. Yes, logic—logic of the outside world at least—would dictate that they do the smart thing and wait for help, but the reasoning of a hotshot's mind did not account for outside help. Hotshots didn't get help; they earned their inches. They had to get their man out on their own. Besides, somewhere in his stunned and reeling mind, he knew the odds of either strategy working were even.

Skip walked back over to Jacobson, lifted the sick man up, and put one arm around his shoulder while Marcus did the same with the other arm.

Edgar sighed in resignation and went along with the effort.

I sat down, leaned against a burnt tree trunk, and spat out the realization like so much bitter fruit.

"You've gotten us lost!"

"I got us lost? You the big hotshot woodsman—I didn't hear you say nothing about the way we was going!"

I was getting use to the repeated disappointment—it was just one more Herculean effort that would go unrewarded by God and Universe. I had mustered what little reserves I had to make it down the first valley and over the next ridge in the cool morning air. When we had reached the next ridge top, the cabin appeared close enough to touch—its shining roof seemed like a beacon of hope that could not be lost, and so I didn't worry much about keeping my bearings. But after walking for twice the time I assumed it would take to get to it, I realized that I was no longer sure of where the cabin was.

We walked through the burned moonscape, our feet crunching on the gray ash, weaving around the black, desiccated trees with the timid steps of men who know, no matter what direction they take, it will likely be the wrong one.

Occasionally a far off tree would succumb to gravity and fall with a crash that sounded like a canon as it echoed through the charred forest, making us jumpy and nervous, until fatigue dulled our concern once more. Finally, I decided just to sit. The sun beat down with greater intensity, and I wiggled to make the most of the strip of shade provided by the tree trunk.

"You're the woods master here. Bet you've been on tons of these fires," I said.

"You're a hotshot!" Gregory protested.

"No, I'm not. I'm a scab. Nothing more. So cut me some slack."

"A scab?"

So I told Gregory everything. Even how I fell down in front of the rig with underwear hanging out of my zipper. I'd practically forgotten about it, as it seemed like a lifetime ago—but he had a real good laugh, and eventually I did too.

"I knew there had to be something strange going on. You didn't seem like no hotshot," Gregory said.

"And after seeing these guys, that's fine with me! I mean, they're nuts. You know half the members on the crew had poison oak from head to toe on this fire, and they just went about it, like nothing. They just laughed about how having it on their cock made it bigger. They're missing a few marbles, I swear."

"Maybe they ain't missing nothing. Maybe they just know something – something you don't, something you deny and avoid."

"What's that, bacteria?"

"They know life ain't about being some angel sleeping in a clean white bed. It ain't about peace. Death is about peace. Life is about struggle, conflict, suffering. Life is dirty, life is gritty. They know this, and that makes them strong—makes them able to handle things you can't, even enjoy things you detest."

"Well I agree, for them life is dirty—it tends to be that way when you don't shower for three weeks!"

"Yesterday, when we was talking about the forest and fire, you didn't even mention the most important thing about it, the thing that proves what I am saying!" Gregory said.

"Are you talking about the porcupines again?"

"Fuck the porcupines! I'm talking about fire. Fire, whether good or bad, is always going to be there. As long as there is carbon and oxygen and any spark, be it by lightning or Man, there is going to be fire. And when there ain't fire, then all that wood and brush just grows right up, until there is a fire, and then it burns like all holy hell.

"So see the fire's most important function is not to kill bugs, or even germinating seeds, its most important job is keeping itself in check. Fire must happen now, or they'll just happen worse later! Cause that is the nature of carbon and oxygen. That is the nature of the forest.

"And just like fire there's always going to be suffering and conflict. When you suppress it, it just builds up. It's going to come back at you even harder."

"Didn't know you were a scientist."

"I read *National Geographic.*"

"So, what you're saying is, if it wasn't for fire we wouldn't need fire. Kind of like lawyers..."

"Kind of like food, too, if you think about it. If there wasn't any food, we wouldn't need it for long, would we? Or anything else, I suppose."

"So this is why they don't shower?"

"All yesterday, and even right now you been trying to deny something. Something they get."

"Get what?"

"Bad things are always going to happen, and by always trying to stop the bad, you just load the system with more of it. The hotshots know bad shit happens; they don't run from it in their lives. They take it. Makes them strong. You on the other hand don't accept it. All day yesterday and even right now, you feel like what is happening to you is wrong, unjust, and you keep thinking something should come and save you from it, as if you're owed that much."

I hung my head. Here I was in the exact position I was trying to avoid. "Fine, let's get going," I said. "The house has got to be around here somewhere..."

As I stood up, I leveraged my back to the tree, which gave out with a sudden groan. All support slipped away and I fell. The tree's groan rose to a screech until it crashed to the ground just a foot away from me, forcefully spraying ash and dust in my face and down my shirt as the thunderous blast shook my core.

Gregory jumped into the dust cloud asking if I was all right.

I was far from it, but I wasn't hurt any further, if that's what he meant. My stunned, ash-covered face contorted by shock made him laugh.

"See, boy! No damn peace in this place!" Gregory said, laughing.

Edgar had taken Skip's place propping up Jacobson, and so he and Marcus lumbered up the incline towards the break in the trees, which indicated where the house was.

Upon seeing the house, Skip observed that the most striking feature was the roof, which was not aluminum but rather covered in solar panels. There was a field surrounding it, perhaps an acre. Remnant fibers of burned grass coiled in a flat, charred weave that covered the ground. This paper-thin sheet crunched under the men's feet before being blown away in the light breeze, leaving tracks of earth-brown footprints. The house was at the far end of the field and was surrounded by a thirty- or forty-yard perimeter of golden grass. Both the house and the grass survived because a bulldozer had upturned a wide ring of soil around them. A large, red portable tank at the edge of the grass had hoses running out to inoperative sprinklers.

It looked promising. The house had the firm look of a maintained home. There were even a few ornamental flowers outside, and two days earlier the brown house would have fit well into the green forest surrounding it.

"This is weird," Edgar said. "A well maintained home, and not one road to it, just out here in the middle of nowhere.

"A hunting cabin for a family to hike in to?" Marcus proposed. "It's clearly off the grid."

236

"Who puts solar panels on a hunting cabin?" Edgar asked.

They came up to the red water tank. It was empty. But then they spotted a large hose leading to a stone well house. They angled towards it. They sat Jacobson, now half conscious, against the well house and started cranking up a bucket of water.

Skip walked away from the men as if to investigate the house—but once around the corner and out of sight, he sat down on a small step in front of the front door, relieved to find a moment of solitude.

The swarm of unformed thoughts buzzing through his mind had only gotten worse. No plans, analysis, or even excuses of what did happen or what should happen could form. The only thing he was sure of was how uncomfortable he was being in his skin. His arms dangled about as if he did not know how to swing them, his carriage seemed either too high, or too low. At times he felt as if he had forgotten how to walk altogether. He hoped getting away from the men might relieve some of this unease.

But it did not. It made it worse. He shuffled his feet over the ground; he could not decide where to focus his eyes. Finally he felt as if he might cry or shake, yell, even convulse. A phrase finally formed in his head, and he could not shake it. Soon it was on his lips.

"They died on my watch. *They died on my watch. They died on my watch*," Skip repeated like an evil mantra. It was about to drive him into madness when Edgar came suddenly around the corner.

Skip stood up with a quick jerk, acted as if he were trying the door.

"Is it locked?" Edgar asked.

"Yeah," Skip said, twisting the knob in a perfunctory motion, which opened the door. He closed it, turned away and walked around to another side of the house without as much as a glance, let alone an explanation for Edgar.

Turning the next corner, he saw a cache of tools scattered in the grass. As they moved closer, the familiar objects became clear: there were several Pulaskis, a shovel, a McLeod, two saws, and two drip torches, which are steel canisters with steel tubes and wicks, for placing burning fuel on grass and shrubs.

"Who saved the house, and why did they leave their tools behind?" Edgar asked.

"They must have been in a hurry—probably figured their line didn't stand a chance," Skip said. He bent down and examined the saw. It was clearly a shot crew, because engraved on the saw was a title.

"Papa Chub," he said, reading the name of the saw out loud.

"Nice name for a saw," Edgar said with laugh.

"It's Tulume Lake Hotshots, I'm sure," Skip said. "They saved the house."

He gripped the steel bar handle-grip tightly and wielded the tool as if he were about to use it. A shiver of power ran through him, like a master violinist about to run bow over strings. His relationship with the tool was equally as meaningful, and earning it just as daunting. He yelled, "Pulling rope!" and fired the machine up.

When Skip first earned the position of sawyer, he was an enthusiastic twenty year old whose face still bubbled with acne. He wanted nothing more than to be respected, and he was determined to use his all to make it so. He assumed being a good cutter was a matter of simple strength and determination. But his efforts quickly became frustrated.

No matter how hard he worked, or how fast he tried to move, he was the slowest sawyer on the line. His sawing became a source of ridicule, not respect. The sawyers yelled at him for his wild, chaotic style that often sent branches and vines whipping through the air. He would leave the fire line with welts on his face from all the slashes. And it exhausted him, making him even more erratic and dangerous. Each shift tested his mettle to the last fiber, so that he shivered from fatigue.

Assuming he wasn't strong enough, or tough enough, he lifted weights and ran during the next off season, often twice a day, and built his forearms with ropes and handgrips.

When the next season started he focused on enduring the pain and fatigue caused by the saw's vibration and limbs whipping in his face. He accustomed himself to the acidic burn in his throat and lungs from the saw's purple and black exhaust. This strategy relieved him from being the slowest, but it did not make him respected. And one day this singular, overpowering approach failed him completely when he cut into a nest of meat bees. They burrowed into his face and beard as he ran spastically down the fire line, giving each crewmember a story to tell for years to come.

But later that day, while still in minor shock from the stings so that he was no longer able to overpower everything, he almost unconsciously disposed of a large tangled brush in three quick strokes, perfectly aimed. It dawned on him that sawing was not about brute force, but about understanding the relationship between the vegetation that was being cut. He began to study the interlinking chain of fibers that surrounded him, and he realized that each vine and limb, brush and tree was under the influence of either tension or compression as it twisted and turned around its counterparts. The limbs formed a weave of sorts, a natural artistic architecture, which if discovered could be unlocked with relative ease and speed.

The emphasis on study soon made him the slowest sawyer again. But he studied with diligence and learned how each cut was directly related to the one before and after it. Cutting was like language. There were words—simple cuts bare of meaning without context. There were phrases—groups of briars and bushes bound and twisted together in a simple statement. There were forests—themes to the way vegetation would grow in a certain acre, or even region. And like learning a language, he began to dream about how different binds could be cut depending on how they bent, connected, and pressed against one another. By the end of that summer he was the second fastest sawyer on the crew.

The third year he discovered rhythm. Vegetation did not grow based simply on geometry but also according to a hidden beat. Each forest, each grove, each patch had a secret time signature. The saw had a rhythm, too—a pace at which it wound and unwound with each rev of the throttle. He became the conductor who aligned the two, the beat of the forest and the pace of the saw. This rhythm was never fully understood, only pursued, and the process of this pursuit became meditation. Sawing was no longer just an act, but a realization of the present. His ability became legend not just on the crew, but to anyone who happened to catch him gracefully doing the work of three men. He cared little about the admiration, however. The function had become the reward.

Over the last months, he had been so focused on mastering the position of foreman that he had almost forgotten this part of himself. But with the saw in his hand, revving it up and down, loudly, a feeling of potency returned to him. He may not have been the kind of leader he had hoped, but he was still a damn good sawyer.

He killed the engine and gently placed the saw back down on the ground.

"There water in that well?" he asked Edgar.

"Yep," Edgar said.

"Well, I had better get some," Skip said.

At the well Marcus was dumping a bucket of water on Jacobson's head. Skip bent down and looked at Jacobson. His eyes were open and showing signs of lucidity.

"How's it going?" Skip asked.

"Just the usual drama," Jacobson said.

"You're getting good at it," Skip said.

"Thanks. It takes practice."

Marcus pulled up a new bucket and handed it to Jacobson. "Kind of full, give me a minute." Jacobson said, waving it off. Marcus handed the bucket over to Skip, who drank from it eagerly.

"How about we see if there's any food in that cabin?" Marcus suggested.

The house was simple and clean, with wood floors and nice wood cabinetry. There were no decorations, just some spare furniture and a small bookshelf filled with literature. In the family room was a TV.

The men rummaged the kitchen and refrigerator, finding canned soup, candy bars, and a running tap, all of which they indulged in.

After Skip had a can of beef stew and candy bar in his hand, he went into the family room, turned on the TV, and flipped through the four analog stations—an old episode of "*Star Trek*," an aerobics show, a black and white movie, and golf. He turned back to the aerobics show and watched the sweating, clean people wearing gratuitous smiles and loud spandex outfits.

"Wanting to get in shape?" Marcus asked, coming into the room.

"I want to find some news," Skip replied.

"How about "*Star Trek*"?" Jacobson asked.

"Seen it—it's the one with the flowers and the spores that turn everyone into a sap, even Spock," Edgar said.

"Something about this house doesn't make sense," Jacobson said, looking around.

243

"Like it's in the middle of nowhere with no road," Edgar quipped.

"Yeah, but more than that. It's loaded with solar panels, but there are only three lights, one outlet for the TV. But the solar unit has enough batteries to power three times that," Jacobson said.

"Maybe there's a secret hot tub," Edgar said.

The aerobics show faded to commercials—and a blurb for the local news appeared. "Today, Anna Benett will be reporting more details on the tragic wildfire near Yacolt that has disrupted so many lives, next ..."

"Sweet—a break," Edgar said. "Hopefully they'll say something worthwhile."

The aerobics show resumed.

"I'm going to keep looking around. I can't watch this shit," Marcus said.

"Not so bad, I haven't seen a woman in makeup in almost two weeks," Edgar said.

Five minutes later Marcus marched back into the room. "Found the secret," he announced. "You guys gotta see this," he insisted.

"I'll stay here and tell you when the news starts," Jacobson said as the others followed Marcus.

Marcus led them into the kitchen, where in the corner was a trap door, which he pulled up to reveal a set of stairs. The men walked down into a dim room, lit by light that seeped out of the small crack between two canvas curtains. They could hear the sound of fans in the background. The air smelled like pungent dirt. Marcus opened up the curtains, flooding the compartment with the light.

Their eyes adjusted, and the men walked through the curtains into the larger section of the basement. A series of shelves housed large green plants, their roots submerged in tanks.

"Cannabis," Skip said.

"It's a grow op," Edgar said.

"And an expensive one at that," Skip said, examining the healthy green leaves and the crinkled buds.

"Smells like college," Edgar said. "Been a long time."

"Probably not the time to start," Skip said.

"Those damn Park Service drug tests," Edgar said.

"All this good kush, and no one to smoke it," Marcus said, looking at Skip. The Park Service had a no-tolerance policy towards drug use, and tested employees at random. Moreover, Bruce was completely intolerant of any drug use other than alcohol, and placed marijuana on the same shelf as heroin. So the crew's culture was against it. But Skip, Edgar, and Marcus both spent the off season in the ski resorts and beach towns of California, socialized with rock climbers and other outdoorsmen, and as such, smoked on occasion.

"You think the crews here earlier saw this?" Edgar asked.

"Doubt it. How often do you go into house for structural protection—especially if no one is home," Skip said.

Then Jacobson yelled that the news was on, and the men went back upstairs.

They gathered around the TV as the broadcast began.

"Rick, today the mood at base camp is somber and shocked as firefighters try to piece together the shreds left after yesterday's events," stated the twenty-something brunette reporter, who was dressed in a yellow Nomex shirt that clearly just came out of the package. Behind her were large tents, firefighters, and Forest Service Officials that indicated she was at base camp.

"As most of you at home know, the fire, located twenty miles northeast of Portland, Oregon, caught firefighters and surrounding communities completely off guard. The 'Black Canyon Fire' as it is called turned into one of the worst tragedy fires in modern wild land firefighting history yesterday, when it surged from five thousand acres to over eighty thousand in a matter of hours."

Pictures of fire trucks, ambulances, burned down homes, and displaced people filled the screen, and then a map of the fire, with an animation showing its recent growth.

Skip grabbed a napkin and a pen he had found in the kitchen and started scribbling.

The reporter continued: "The fire started out on Washington State Department of Natural Resources land, but has since grown into the Gifford Pinchot National Forest. In doing so, the fire struck the community of Yacolt, causing panic and demanding a diversion of all efforts for its evacuation. Even so, three civilian lives were lost, many more injured, and over fifty homes burned to the ground, leaving hundreds displaced and countless in shock."

The story cut to a rotund woman in her late fifties with tangled hair and crooked yellow teeth. Behind her was a burned-out trailer. She spoke into a microphone shoved next to her mouth in a shaken, high pitched voice.

"We've lost everything. Everything. Even our little dog, Sadie. All's I got left of her now is this picture of her," she said, producing a wallet size picture of a small white pit bull type dog. "And now I hear there are dead firefighters, too … just terrible. How could this happen?"

"Jesus Christ!" Edgar protested aloud before Skip could shush him.

The shot cut back to the reporter who continued, "And indeed a lot of people are going to be asking that, particularly in light of what the woman mentioned. Early reports are that there might be as many as ten fatalities, though that number has not been officially confirmed, and sadly is likely to rise as more information comes in."

The clip cut to a Forest Service official. "We can't say at this time how many firefighter fatalities we have, and certainly we can't say why or how they happened. These men and women are well trained, and we are all saddened by the reports we are getting. Unfortunately we have not been able to gather information through formal channels, as all of our efforts have been focused on civilian evacuation. There will be a full investigation, but for now we have to focus on getting the firefighters who are still in there, out."

The news anchor was back on talking to the reporter. "So there is no indication of why the fire got so suddenly large and how the firefighters were trapped?"

"Well, as the information officer indicated, the Incident Command unit has been focused on evacuating civilians, so no formal information is available at this time. However we have heard reports that an ill-planned backburn may have cut off some of the firefighters' escape routes.

"*So that was it!*" Edgar spewed. "Someone fucked up! That Division Sup!"

Skip shushed Edgar.

"So what's the plan for today?" Rick, the anchor, asked.

"Well luckily, Rick, the Forest Service and the National Weather Service are not expecting anything like yesterday, though they do expect to see some fire growth. The forecast is calling for winds to be light and out of the northeast. It should be a bit cooler with higher humidity, which should dampen fire activity. Drought conditions still do exist, though, and the potential for spread is there, making communities around the fire very nervous. As a precaution, officials are asking for the voluntary evacuation of anyone who lives within ten miles of the fire's perimeter."

The map of the fire terrain reappeared.

"And what about the firefighters still in the fire? How are they going to get them out?"

"More helicopters are expected today, and at least some of those will be dedicated to finding those who are still unaccounted for."

The anchor reappeared on screen. "Let's hope they do their best, Anna. Thanks for the report. Up next, a local man in Kelso was caught stealing from a PayLess."

Skip turned off the TV.

"Someone set a backburn behind us!" Edgar said.

"That's on the Division Sup. He shouldn't have let that fucking happen," Marcus said.

"I think it was from the division next to us. Contract crews, mainly."

"You know what that means," Edgar said.

"Division Sup was probably a Forester who had been pushed up the chain without any Type One experience."

"I'd like to get my hands on whoever did it," Marcus growled.

"Doesn't matter. We were still going downhill. We still lost someone. They'll say we were somewhere we shouldn't have been," Skip said. "Their investigation will place at least some blame on us, maybe all of it."

"That's bullshit. They do that every tragedy fire. Armchair quarterback the hell out of it with all their hindsight. Supposedly so it doesn't happen again, but we know what's written in between the lines—it was some firefighter's fault."

"We were building line downhill. We violated a Watch Out," Skip said.

"Everyone builds line downhill. Half the time it's the only way to get anything done," Edgar said. "They might as well say wearing Nomex is a Watch Out situation."

"Humidity, I bet it was at eight when that blow up happened, and we had a detailer we knew nothing about," Skip said.

"Yeah, but what was it at when we decided to go downhill, like thirty-eight I bet. We had air support. And we didn't give that detailer his red card, the Park Service did."

"They'll say we broke Fire Orders. We broke Fire Orders. They'll pin it on us."

"Fire Orders! Those are as vague as good and evil. Look at number three: 'Base all actions on current and expected fire behavior.' Duh. The only reason people get caught is because the fire does something *unexpected*."

"It's our job to know. It's my job to know," Skip said.

"Look man, it's fire, it's a weather-based phenomenon. It's chaotic by its very nature. Think about it. Think of hurricanes. The oil companies spend millions of dollars trying to predict hurricanes that might hit their ocean rigs. They hire mathematicians, meteorologists, and super computers to try to figure out what's going to happen, and they still get it wrong now and then. So how are we, a bunch of laborers, armed only with wet thermometers and a local weather report suppose to do any better?"

"Because it's our job."

"Ah. See. That's the worst. It's like the bureaucrats come up with their ways of blaming us, and that sucks, but when the guys on the ground do it—when the guys on the ground blame other guys on the ground for tragedies, that's what really breaks my heart. You saw it in Storm King Mountain, man—and it made me sick. They insinuate by repeating catch phrases, like 'there were mistakes made' or shrugging shoulders and repeating some isolated fact: 'downhill with 14 percent humidity...' I always let them get away with it, but in my gut I want to say, well, dip shit; it probably wasn't 14 percent humidity when they started. Such arrogance! But my favorite, the one that really gets me—'there was a loss of 'situational awareness.' Yeah, no shit. That is true with every tragedy from the kid who got hit by a car to Pearl Harbor. That's not analysis, it's restating the obvious."

"The art of politics" Edgar continued, "is positioning yourself so the blame of life's inherent pains fall on someone else. And these bureaucrats are good at it—I tell you."

"Can we talk about what we are going to do now?" Marcus interjected.

"Yeah, we can," Skip said. He produced the napkin, and on it was a sketch of the map the news report had shown.

"The reporter said that winds will be coming out of the Northeast. That means Incident Command is going to be worried about the southern edge of the fire. Light winds and higher humidity will mean the fire will be somewhat active, but not too active."

"Active enough to be threatening, but not too much that they can't take it out," Marcus said.

"Right. The towns to the south are nervous, and they'll want make sure that edge gets secured."

He pointed to the southern edge of the fire on the map.

"See this long green finger that juts into the black on the southern edge."

"Yeah," Jacobson said.

"There is a large conical hill right here, probably right at the edge of the perimeter, if the map they showed is accurate—it has an old clear cut on the top of it—I noticed it on the flight in because the hill was so symmetrical."

"Okay," Edgar said.

"It would be a perfect place for a helispot. It's likely, if they want to hold that line, they'll be sending crews in all day—and use that as a place to land them."

"A ride out," Jacobson said.

"Yep."

"I see what you're saying, but it's outside the fire perimeter. What if it's active, how will we cross over it? And if we do cross and the fire livens up, we're stuck on a hill. Pretty shitty place to be," Edgar said.

"It shouldn't be much of a problem to cross over. And you're right, it might not be the best if things got weird—but it's a downhill run away from the fire. There is plenty of space behind that hill. We could find somewhere to burn out a safety zone if it came down to it," Skip said.

"Leaving the black, sounds risky," Jacobson said.

"It is," Skip said. "But the way I see it, we have three options. One, we stay here and wait a few days hoping someone finds us. Two, we hike through the black to where we came from and hit up our old LZ—that'll take at least a day, through heat, maybe longer. Or three, this option, and get out to base camp ASAP."

"Base camp does sound nice," Jacobson said.

"We can get Steve out soon that way, too," Marcus said.

"Two hours of hiking does sound better than two days," Edgar said.

"Then let's get some food and get a move on.

Each man took a can of soup and a candy bar, and each filled his one canteen with water. They also

254

grabbed some of the tools left behind by the previous crew. They grabbed a saw, a Pulaski, two drip torches, and as many fuzzies as they could stuff in their web belts.

As they were outfitting themselves, Marcus grabbed Skip and pulled him aside. "That Op inside," he said.

"Yeah?" Skip asked.

"Well, if they got an indoor op this far out, don't you think they also got an outdoor op?" Marcus asked.

"Maybe, yeah," Skip said.

"If they have an outdoor op around, they probably also have—"

"Booby traps," Skip answered. It was not an unknown threat to crews that spent time in Northern California.

"Yeah."

"We'll keep an eye out," Skip said.

The men, now loaded with food, water, and gear, lined up behind Skip. He started the saw one more time and revved it loudly as if roaring to assert his own confidence. Then he shut it off, threw it over his shoulder and yelled, "Moving!" The men followed him out of the valley and towards the fire line.

Chapter Nine

"There it is!" I said, excitedly, hearing the far off growl of a small engine.

We had heard the chainsaw earlier and wandered towards the noise, but soon became unsure of its exact direction or whether it came from the cabin at all. But this time the pop and chug of the engine was clear and close as it revved for a few short seconds before cutting out. It would be easy to track.

I peered through the forest hoping I might even see the sound's source. But it was for naught. The same gray ash covered the ground; the same countless barren trees hindered my sight—their bark transformed into black metallic scales with a reptilian symmetry that shimmered in the sunlight like so much polished coal.

But the sound was enough. I limped spiritedly through the forest, my morale awakened by the hint of people and by a sense that a solid and real path out of this lunarscape was about to take form.

Within a few minutes I found the clearing that surrounded the house, and soon spotted the house thereafter. I began to jog towards it. "Hello! Hello!" I shouted with as much force as my chafed throat could muster. But no one was in sight. I reached the house, looked around all four corners, found the front door, and pounded on it demandingly—but still no one. Gregory soon reached the house and the outside well. When I finally gave up on the door and rounded the corner, I found him reeling up a bucket of water

"Might as well drink up, Kid. Looks like we missed 'em."

He handed me the water, and I drank it like an alcoholic to wine—using it for just as much solace. Here we were again, aimless, blind and alone.

Then we entered the house and rummaged through the cabinets, grabbing cans of food.

"Jackpot!" Gregory barked. He produced three cans of beer from one of the shelves.

"I'd puke after a sip," I said.

"That's right, that's right, you probably would. Best save it for me," Gregory said with a laugh.

We found a can opener, ripped off the lids, and received the nourishment of beans, corn, and chili.

I searched for a phone while slurping at the contents.

"I can't believe this Grizzly Adams bullshit. No phone!" I protested to Gregory a few minutes later, when I walked into the living room where he was sitting in a recliner.

"Hey, Grizzly Adams might know exactly what he's doing," Gregory said, taking a swig of beer.

I sat down on the couch, flustered.

"Well, what do we do now?" I asked.

"Relax, Kid," he said. "This is an oasis and there ain't many."

"Oasis my ass," I protested.

"Look, Kid, we don't get beer in prison. Let me enjoy the moment," he said.

I sat back—conceding to the point. But the silence started to bother me, and there was a question nagging me.

"So, can I ask..."

"Ask what?" Gregory said.

"What happened? To you, I mean..."

"Why I went to prison?"

"Yeah..."

"Aggravated manslaughter," he said.

"Ten years? For that?"

"Twenty."

"Oh."

We stewed in the awkward silence.

"Dreams die hard, Kid," he finally said.

"Dreams? What kind of dreams?"

"Dreams of bliss," he responded.

"Bliss? What, were you on drugs?" I asked.

"Ha! No. Not exactly. But I guess all dreams of bliss are like drugs, in their power to deceive."

I grabbed one of the beers on the table and cracked it open. As a sign of solidarity I even tried to take a sip, but my tongue recognized the bitter taste as a poison it would not tolerate, and I gagged.

"Domestic bliss—that was my drug, you could say, that was my high..." Gregory finally said.

"I'm not following you."

"My dreams of domestic bliss led to disaster," Gregory said slowly. "I wanted a life I had not earned."

"You mind starting from the beginning on this one, 'cause I'm not following."

Gregory took a long pause and sighed, as if to collect himself.

"I never graduated from high school. Quit when I was sixteen. Worked at a gas station—then as a janitor. By the time I was twenty one, I had a job at a university, cleaning the place—night shift mostly. Cleaned the library building. And when I was done with the toilets, I was done for the night. Just me and a bunch of books. For six years all's I did was give myself an education. Read the smart ones and the dumb ones, the science and the philosophy, the literature and the psychology. Even some history. Took notes. Figured if I couldn't get a degree, I could at least be smart.

"Then they moved me to swing, when I was twenty-six. Still only had to clean up the toilets, still had plenty of time to sit in the library and read, but got to watch a lot more of the pretty girls walk by.

"Of course, they didn't want much to do with me. The older janitor guy. But one day in Spring, I was sitting there reading a book—Herman Hesse as it turned out—and one girl did want something to do with me. This little twenty year old sister, pretty as could be. She asked me about what I was reading—turned out she was going into some lit class, and she was suppose to have read that same book, but she hadn't. Wanted me to tell her about it. So I put on my best game and sounded real smart. She listened real well and spoke up in seminar and sounded real smart, too.

"On her way back from after class, she told me what a help I was. I was plumb proud. I asked her what book she was reading for next week, and she let me know. I told her to stop on by, and I'd give her a rundown if she needed it. She blushed and said she'd probably take me up on it. And she did, and so it started. Me reading her books and given her the run down.

"Eventually I asked her out. And she said yes. Hell, I was a janitor, but I was handsome in my day!" he said, patting imaginary hair on his bald head. "And I could sound intelligent as anyone, I guess, if I put my mind to it.

"So we fell in love, or something close to it, and to make a long story short, I asked her to marry me. Said I'd pay for everything, her education—the house, all that stuff. Suppose the offer was too good to refuse, as they say. So we did get married, and for a year, maybe two, we were happy."

"Sounds fun," I said.

"Yes, well, I was no longer sore alone, like before," Gregory said. "But she graduated and decided to make a go in real estate. I told her to go do something she needed a degree for, but she knew where the money was, so she would have none of it," Gregory said.

"She got on with a firm, worked real hard, stopped coming home at the same time, and starting making big money—bigger than a janitor at least. Much bigger.

"I guess you could say I was becoming dead weight, and dead weight fast. I could hear it in everything she done. Or didn't do.

"So I noticed she talked a lot about Mike, her boss—like a lot. In fact her eyes would only light up when talking about making a sale or talking about Mike. Then she just stopped talking about him—but she'd sure dress up for work. So one day I went home, when I usually don't. Figured I'd settle this raw, nagging feeling in my gut. And well, let's say I didn't settle it, instead I...I..."

"No way..."

"Yeah, caught her and Mike in the act," Gregory said. "Still tough to put in words, even after all this time."

"Fuck, Man, that's tough."

"No. The tough part is still on its way. See, I didn't take it too well. I didn't take it at all. I just decided that the lie should burn—that the whole thing we created, I created, should go away. I was not going to confront them. I was just going to end them and everything. I went to the garage. Grabbed a can of gas. Poured it all through the house—even got some on myself," he said, motioning to his burns.

"Lit the match, and boom. The whole sin, the whole evil was on fire. To be gone. Or so I thought, or so I felt, rather."

"So you...killed them? They burned up?"

"No.... They didn't burn up. They got out. They got burned, and they got scars—but they made it out. They made it out...."

"So, man slaughter? That means someone died?"

"Someone did die. The man, Mike, he'd brought his little boy over—a little four year old boy. He was playing in the room next door."

"No way! Who brings their kid to something like that?"

"That all came out in the trial. Mike got up there, with his burned legs—all that shit. Said he was stopping by to talk. Said they both knew it was wrong and they were just going to put 'closure' on it—you know work it out. Well, course they worked it out, in more than one way. Yeah, that's what they did..." he said, his eyes suddenly turning as dark as a moonless midnight.

He broke from his trance.

"She said the same thing. Then the mother of the boy got up. Held it together at first—said both Mike and me, and my "tramp wife," had ruined the only thing in her life, said how her little boy was special, smart, the only thing that gave her a reason to open her eyes, the only reason to eat, or to breathe, to do the laundry, clean the toilet. She mentioned every bit of shit a day demands. Then she was talking nonsense, and started answering questions the lawyer wasn't asking, and then she wasn't talking to the lawyer at all. Started talking backwards, talking to demons. Finally she started singing, right there on the stand—"This Land is Our Land," or some shit like that. She was gone. They hauled her off. And there wasn't going to be any light sentencing."

I sat there, blinking at him for a moment. I didn't feel contempt or sorrow or disgust or any empathy or condemnation—I can only describe it as *latency*—the condition a computer suffers when too many commands are stacked at once. I sat there hour glassed for at least a few seconds.

"There's got to be a phone around here," I said finally, standing up to leave the room.

Gregory glanced at me in a half beat. "Order in a pizza—will you?" he said.

The four hotshots reached the crest of the ridge and started to enter into the valley below. As they dropped below the crest of the ridge Jacobson suddenly stopped.

"You guys hear that?"

"Hear what?"

"I don't know, like a baby crying, someone trying to get our attention."

Everyone tried to listen, but all they heard was the whisper of the wind grazing the blackened trees and the lifting of ash.

"You guys don't hear that?" Jacobson asked. "It almost sounds like someone asking for help."

"Maybe it's time we sit down, take some shade," Skip said—looking suspiciously at Jacobson.

Edgar and Marcus agreed, and found a tree to lean against. Jacobson followed them, but only in protest.

"I'm not crazy. I heard something, someone calling for our attention."

"You feeling hot?" Marcus asked.

"No! It's not heat stroke. I drank water. I ate a whole can of white beans—plenty of potassium."

"So you're telling us that can of beans saved you from death's door?" Edgar asked cynically. "And that there is a baby in these here woods?"

"Fuck you," Jacobson responded. "I just thought I heard someone yelling for our attention. Maybe it was the wind."

"Skip, I say we don't take five here, I say we take ten, and we take ten every half mile, for that matter," Edgar said.

"I concur with that," Skip said, looking at Jacobson..

Jacobson shook his head. This is why admitting or showing any weakness was a mistake. Now he was being watched as if he was an invalid, a sick and crazy old man.

∞

After a few minutes of fruitless searching, I walked back into living room.

"You get pepperoni?" Gregory asked.

"Sorry, we're just out of their delivery range."

I sat down, and the awkward silence returned.

"So what are you going to do with yourself once you finally get out of here?" Gregory asked.

"I don't know, but that pizza idea has really got me thinking."

"I mean in general, whatcha going to do?"

"Go back to my normal job, I guess."

"Your normal job?"

"Yeah, I'm a botanist for the Park Service."

"Aha. A botanist. So is that what you're going to do for your career?"

"I don't know. I majored in it at college. There was a job in it, and I took it. But is that what I want to do? I don't know."

"Well what did you major in it for?"

"I don't know. It was easy for me. And there was a girl I liked who was studying it—I guess that made it more alluring."

"A girl?"

"Yeah, a girl. Stupid I guess. And they're plants—I mean, it's cool and all, but I don't know if it's really what I'm into. To tell you the truth, I don't think I give a shit about plants. I mean the taxonomy is kind of interesting, but—I guess I just couldn't find anything better."

"Never had any dreams?" Gregory asked.

"Nothing realistic," I said.

"Nothing at all?"

"Well, I wanted to be a gigolo, but I couldn't meet the prerequisites."

Gregory laughed. "A noble goal at least!"

"Yeah, well, dreaming was considered just that in my house, I guess. And I guess that is a pretty natural one."

"Sounds like you're sounding sorry for yourself."

"You should be used to that by now."

"It never *gets* old—it just *comes out* that way."

"Fine. There was one thing. .."

"Yeah, what? Out with it!"

"I...I wanted to make roller coasters. Design 'em."

"Like Disneyland shit?"

"Yeah, like Disneyland shit."

"My parents would never take me to them," I continued. "But one summer we visited my mom's cousin in California, and Six Flags was nearby. My cousin said we should go—but my dad would have none of it. He hated lines. Finally my mom's cousin's husband decided to take me. We went to this place, so colorful and fun, and I went on this roller coaster, and it blew my mind. Like, I was free for the first time or something. I got off that ride, man, and I knew what life was for, just for a minute. I looked around me, saw the people working, the carnies, the vendors, all the costumes, and I thought for sure this would be the greatest place in the world to be forever.

"I kept talking about it on the ride home—how I wanted to work there and be one of the people that ran the rides. My mom's cousin's husband was a judge, and thought he should steer me away from the carnie lifestyle, so he told me 'You know Jonathan; you could be a designer of those rides.' I couldn't believe something like that existed, but clearly it did—I started to dream about it—I even drew out different ideas I had, what would make them scary, fun. I couldn't stop thinking about it."

"So what happened?" Gregory asked.

"Nothing—just a stupid dream. They pass, right?"

"Did you even try?"

"I actually took an early engineering course in junior high. Got a C. My dad pointed out that a C didn't prove much talent. That made sense."

"So you gave it up?"

"It just kind of—dissipated. Besides, I'd have to learn a bunch of math, and who knows if I really had any talent. It was just a childhood dream— like quarterback of a pro football team."

"So now you're going to get a comfortable job? Going to be a botanist for the Forest Service."

"Park Service, but yeah, maybe. I don't know— working for the federal government—you always end up being a bureaucrat in one way or the other. Office job. Boring. I just don't see myself loving it," I complained.

"So you want to love your work, but you don't want to suffer for that love?" Gregory asked.

"Who loves what makes them suffer?" I asked.

"Ha! Boy, you are young and misguided," he said.

"What do you mean!?"

"What you love always makes you suffer."

"Now that is pessimistic!" I protested.

"Just as I thought you were learning something, you start screaming for helicopters, kid."

"Huh?"

"I mean you want out of life, man. You don't get it. You keep refusing a basic principle that everyone once knew."

"What? I just busted ass to stay in life!"

"Maybe, when it comes in real clear, but only when it gets simple as possible. Look at what you are saying now—you want an easy, secure way of living that don't get stifling or boring. You want excitement and love with no risk or struggle. You can't make up your mind between the two because it seems you shouldn't have to. You've missed out on same basic and critical lesson that the hard working man knows. You've been fed a lie, and you've been living like a half dead person because of it."

"What lie?"

"It's all the schooling, that's your problem."

"What lie?"

"There is a certain subtext to your education, to your indoctrination; it's been with you since you were a kid."

"I don't know what you're talking about."

"When you went to school and took math—what was your homework?"

"Math problems."

"And what were you suppose to do with those problems?"

"Solve 'em..."

"And when you went to history class, what was in the back of each chapter."

"Study questions."

"And what were you suppose to do with those questions?"

"I don't know, answer 'em."

"Exactly. And what happened if you got 'em wrong?"

"Well, duh! I'd get a bad grade."

"And the reason for that?"

"'Cause I didn't get them right!"

"And what if you didn't answer them at all?"

"Then I'd fail."

"See—all of your schooling has taught you that problems can be solved, that questions *have an answer*. So then you approach every problem— every issue of suffering—as something that must be solved, that can be solved. You see fire in the forest and you want to put it out; you see wolves – you want to kill them; you see disease and you want to cure it; you see starvation and you want to feed it. The lesson you get from all of your learning is that everything has an answer. But that just ain't the truth. Problems exist as a simple part of the ecosystem. Fire in the forest.

"Now, here you are, in a place where there is a problem, but the only answer is to accept the problem. You feel it's unfair. You feel like you deserve deliverance, a simple and certain way out. Yesterday the delusion simply wouldn't last any longer. You were put in a place where you'd either burn up or do something excruciatingly painful. Both paths were problems; none were answers. You couldn't get it. It seemed like it was unfair, because the pain was so great either way. So you kept crying for me or some goddamn helicopter to come and take you away from it, as if you were owed that much.

"The same thing is going on in your life," Gregory continued, "except you're not being forced to see it like yesterday. You got an education. You could

273

have a good, solid job, get a nice home, and eventually be all settled, fat, and happy. But you don't want to 'cause, you might get bored. Or you could take a path that is exciting, but that demands suffering and high gambles. You don't like either, because both present problems—suffering—and you feel like there must be some way out—a perfectly correct answer.

"Maybe you were just breastfed too long," Gregory added.

"Now that's personal." I responded.

"Yeah, maybe, but that don't mean it ain't true."

"Okay—maybe I'm a pussy—whatever. I've been told that one way or another the last three days constantly," I said. "But forget about me—look at the broader picture—we are solving problems. My issues aside, we have done a great many things as a species—we are solving problems—diseases, hunger, all sorts of things...the world is getting better."

"You can't solve the problem, you just move it, or put it off, or make the energy behind it build up," Gregory said. "Just like this here forest. You haven't taken fire out of it; you've just delayed it— put the fire off, so that it burns hotter—you've put the disease off so it gets more virulent."

"It sounds like you are simply denying the entire idea of progress, of science and technology. You want to go back to outdoor plumbing?"

"Hey, might lower your utility bill."

"Funny, but seriously—we've ended so much human suffering, so many problems, from tooth decay to bacterial infections."

"I don't know how to break this to you, Kid, but people still lose their teeth—it just happens at a later date, and for a longer time, 'cause they live longer."

"Pessimism to the highest rank," I said.

"Pessimism is just another insult for those who accept the world as it is. For those who don't need no leader, scientist, or politician telling them where to go. That's why they make it derogatory. You can't lead people who know the grass ain't greener."

"The grass ain't greener, man. It's burned, and we can stop it from being so, if we put our mind to it," I said.

Gregory shook his head in exasperation. "You know, out of all them books I read in the library, and the ones I read in prison, one really said it all," he continued.

"Yeah, which one?"

"Cat in the Hat Is Back."

"The Dr. Seuss book?" I asked.

"Ever read him?" Gregory said, feigning haughtiness.

"It is a classic, sir," I said returning the tone.

"Well then I suppose you get the point right?" he asked, returning to his normal cadence.

"The point? It's a kids book—not a manifesto."

"You remember the story?"

"Kinda. It's been a long time."

"There are these two kids—a boy and a girl—and they get left alone by their parents. So they take a bath—together. And when they're done there's this big old yellow ring around the tub," he said.

"I think it was orange."

"Yeah, sure—I never been great with color. Anyway, the kids freak 'cause they know when mom and dad get home they're going to know the kids were up to no good."

"So then comes this cat," Gregory continues, "and what does this cat do?" he asked, then paused.

"Yeah well—"

"What does the cat do?! You read the story!" Gregory demanded.

"He offers to get rid of it."

"That's right—says he's going to remove the stain, and that's what he does—but that's not the end of the story, is it?"

"No 'cause the stain is then all over the bathroom," I said, now remembering.

"That's right, and then it's all over the house, and then pretty soon it's all over the snow!"

"Yeah—seemed kind of gross—orange snow."

"But see the point—all these things come around and promise to get rid of the stain, but all they really do is move it somewhere else."

"Didn't Voom, or Zoom, get rid of it in the end?"

"Ever wonder where he put it? 'Cause I don't think I want to know. I think Voom is death—the only way to get rid of the stain, the only way to end suffering, is death—see 'cause suffering and life, they the same thing—like heat and friction."

"I kind of thought Voom was Jesus Christ," I said.

"Well, what do you think Christ represents!? I mean look at a crucifix with the body hanging on it! We are forgiven in death! I mean that ain't no picture of a playground boy!"

"So we are forgiven in death—that's what the book says that makes it so monumental?"

"I wasn't pointing it out for what it says about death. I was pointing it out on what it says about life. And that is, there is just a certain amount of shit—of suffering, of stain, embarrassment, that you have to endure in life—that all must endure. A collective debt. And if someone comes around thinking they can fix it, all they are really doing is putting it somewhere else, and often in a way that makes it much worse. Like turning all the pretty white snow into orange shit."

"So now you're proving your point using a Dr. Seuss book?" I asked. "I mean at least the fire metaphor didn't have cartoon characters in it."

"The fire had you in it. Damn near close," Gregory said.

"How about I draw on some creative work, like you know "Imagine." Ever hear that song, a song that promises no war, people living together in peace, harmony, all that good shit?"

"Ha. Yeah, that one. Glad you brought it up, 'cause when you sit down and really picture it, that world that is painted in that song is one thing and one thing only."

"What is that?"

"Boring."

"A world without strife," Gregory continued, "is a world without challenge. Death to the living. Living things have energy, see, and all energy creates friction, heat, conflict. It is not only in our cells, not only in our DNA but in the very molecules and atoms that make us up. The only thing at "peace" is zero kelvin. Dead space.

"Did I tell you I read *National Geographic*?" He added.

"So the whole idea of self actualization, the idea of enlightenment. You don't believe in it? And that we can do it on a grand level?"

"Ha. Grand level. I ain't seen one person walk on rice paper without leaving a mark yet, Kid.

"Have you seen anyone walk on rice paper *at all*?" I asked.

Gregory grimaced. "Okay... you got me there."

"I mean, according to your theory, maybe we should go back to sacrificing virgins at the altar," I said.

"Yeah, that doesn't sound too nice," Gregory said. "But see, even in that sacrifice, those primitive cultures were demonstrating their understanding of the world's need for pain, for suffering. They were saying, 'look, God, we get it. We must have pain in this world. We know – so if we give up this most precious thing to you, perhaps you will let our crops grow! Perhaps this will keep the precious balance!'"

"So we should reinstate human sacrifice? Is that what you're saying?"

"I'm saying you never stopped. Look at all the suffering your 'answers' have caused. Look at how much poverty, debt, state violence, and imprisonment your system demands. All in search of a final answer. A final solution."

"Well, when you put it like that..." I said diffidently.

I heard a crash outside—the whine and thunder of a falling tree. I looked outside the window of the cabin to see a giant black conifer, alive only with flames, slam into the ground, and spit dust and fire all over the grass surrounding the cabin. Immediately a wall of fire began to form in the grass, burning greedily towards the cabin, and us.

"Holy Shit! Let's get out of here!" I said, scurrying towards the door.

But Gregory just sat back down, as if resigned.

I noticed this and stopped. "What are you doing!? Let's go!" I demanded.

"No. That's not what we want to do."

"Yeah, if this is your idea of accepting suffering or some shit, this is why I think your idea is whack," I said, and headed towards the door. I reached it and turned the handle and prepared to run for my life.

Run for my life...the logic suddenly hit me. Grass burns fast, wood burns slow. I scurried back to the family room.

"What do we do?"

Gregory stood back up, now with the reserved nervousness of a man who is banking his life on his intellect despite the raging passions of his instincts. "Just remain calm. Let it pass—when you start hearing rain, you'll know it's time to go."

"Rain?"

"It means the eaves have caught fire."

The flame front surged on to the house—the window in front of us beamed heat and light so that we squinted, sweat, and covered our faces, until the glass burned black. We ran into the kitchen, grabbed some cans of food and anything else we could fit in our pockets. The fire had spread around the house, so we could see it from the three side windows—almost instantaneously the field turned into a dazzling lake of fire.

"You'd be one cooked fish by now," Gregory bellowed.

Then came the heavy rain drops—a pop and a crack which quickly morphed into the sound of a torrential downpour. It was so convincing I had to look outside to put to rest the auditory illusion.

"Let's count to ten—then bust out of here," he yelled over the cacophony.

We counted out loud. On two, smoke started to snake through the windows. By five, flames started to burst from the walls, by seven, the house was shaking from the beams succumbing to combustion. And on ten, we were running towards the front door, which was now wholly engaged with a ribbon of vibrating orange tendrils.

"Maybe there's a way out the back!" I yelled.

Without comment Gregory flung himself headlong into the door. He busted through it like a linebacker, and fell to the smoking dirt in front of it—leaving open a passage of blue sky and clear air for me to follow, which I did.

Outside we watched the building succumb to the flames. The solar panels first turned black from the heat, then fell through the caving roof. The flame lengths moved from the roof down the wood siding, like a swarm of hyper-animated insects devouring a carcass. Their long shimmering orange tails formed a pillar of fire that gushed viscous black smoke.

"Well, there goes another oasis," Gregory uttered, after the fire had passed its apex.

"What do we do now?" I asked, looking at the pile of burning rubble. I surveyed the hill, and figured it was too steep of an incline for a helicopter to land on. But there had been a crew that must have landed nearby at some point to do the initial structure protection.

"Well, we could take a look up the hill there, see what's on the other side, might be able to get a better view," Gregory suggested.

A shadow suddenly bolted through the trees in front of me. I motioned to Gregory to look. It was an animal—but I couldn't see what kind—only that it was wild and fast.

"It's a god-damn bear" Gregory exclaimed. The creature jumped into the clearing confirming Gregory's description.

I froze. "Don't run from it, whatever you do!" I blurted.

"I ain't afraid of no bear!" Gregory said, kicking up ash and waving his arms.

The bear looked to be three or four hundred pounds. Its pelt was black, but it had burn patches over much of it, especially on its legs and paws. Its ears perked up, as it moved with an alert, but erratic grace, shifting from trot to bolt, and bolt to trot, as if sick or crazy.

"That bear's not right," Gregory said, put his arms down, and stood still along side of me.

"Never met one that was," I said.

"Have you ever met one, *at all*?" Gregory joked with a nervous voice.

"You got me there."

The bear came within ten meters of us as we stood petrified. It rose up on its back legs and inhaled deeply through its nose, exposing large and swollen nipples. It let out a whine in our direction—as if demanding explanation. Something in the desperate yet commanding sound—the pure emotional resonance of it, like a baby's screech but much lower—made me stumble, flinch, and take a few steps back—I thought as if I might suddenly cry.

The bear's ears folded down and charged us. The open mouth, with its red tongue flapping over barred fangs—the immense rippling muscles of the powerful body in motion was too much—I panicked and ran from it.

"Thought you said not to run!" Gregory blurted, as he too broke into a run also. The bear was now after us both. Gregory scooped up a rock, stopped turn and blasted the bear in the face with it. But the only effect it had was that the bear now clearly targeted him. Gregory returned to a bolt and realizing he had made himself the bull's eye, headed towards the pile of burning rubble.

Seeing the bear was no longer a direct threat, I stopped and turned. "Don't run from it!" I yelled.

Gregory reached the burning debris with the bear just a few feet behind. He picked up a burning piece of wood from the pile just as the animal lunged at him. He swung the wooden beam, and it found the bear's nose, stopping the charge immediately. The bear shook its head and snorted. It stood again on its hind legs and the two beings stared at each other, facing off in a sort of probing communion. Gregory then waved the burning two by four in the animal's face and shouted at it to go. The bear got back on all fours, turned away, and walked off.

We watched in silence as it reached the charred woods. She turned towards us, rose on her hind legs, and exposed her bloated nipples, sniffed the air, then lumbered mournfully behind the trees and out of sight.

"Now that damn bear didn't look too happy," Gregory said.

"I think she's lost her cubs," I said.

The image of my mother watching the TV news report on the fire struck me—her horrified face helplessly watching the story of the burn. Right now she is probably just like that poor bear, I thought. She's calling everywhere, waiting by the phone, making blind charges at anyone who comes along her path that is of no help.

I called her the night I arrived at the fire.

"Hotshots!" She had protested. "Aren't those the ones that always burn up? Why did you agree to such dangerous work? I raised a gentleman, not a beast! You're not made for that kind of thing! How are you going to keep up?" She continued the onslaught of protests until I pointed out that she was in no way helping my already troubled morale.

"Well, I damn near lost my ass!" Gregory said with a laugh—he beamed with an even greater vitality than normal.

"Yeah, you fought her off. That's one of the craziest things I've seen. I mean, really impressive!"

"Well that's one of the craziest things I have ever done! But a man does what he has to, I guess. See it's when a man is in a tough position that he's got no choice but to accept his plight, accept his fear, suffer, and go forward through it. That's when you get to find out who you are, find your potential."

"Here we go again."

"It's true, boy! I feel great! I just fought a bear! Strange as it sounds, I just knew a moment of...presence...completeness...hell I don't know how to describe it, but it was cool! Because I was in a struggle, 'cause I was fighting!"

"Okay, okay. If this is all some tirade to get me to walk up to the top of the hill on my own, I'll do it," I said.

"Well, good, you're starting to see," Gregory said.

"I'm not saying you're right," I said.

"Before we go, drop that bucket down one more time in the well," Gregory said.

"Hey, I don't know about you but I couldn't drink one more drop," I said, rubbing my bloated belly.

"Ain't for you. It's for the bear. She'll get thirsty soon," Gregory said.

"Thought the bear was suppose to suffer, according to your philosophy," I muttered as I went to the well.

"That bear is suffering. Never said there wasn't room for a little compassion now and then. Never said that. I'm just saying that the bear will suffer, yes. I am not trying to wipe out its suffering. The only way to do that would be to kill it. See? You think all suffering should be gone, that it's a problem that must be solved. But look at that bear: she is suffering, you bet. Her cubs are gone and not coming back. But she'll continue. She'll mate again, birth again, be a mother again. All this is assured by nature, as long as she agrees to suffer!"

"Okay, sorry I brought it up," I said as I threw the bucket down the well.

We started to search for tracks leading where the people before us might have gone. We found singed firefighting equipment, but any sign in the grass was gone from the burn. Then along the forest perimeter we saw footsteps, and so we followed them up the hill along the southern side of the valley.

We made our way slowly to the top of the hill on the south side of the valley. It was not nearly as steep or as long as the others. The new vista revealed more of the same undulating geography, but there was one distinct feature that we hadn't seen in some time: living trees. The boundary between green and black was, for the most part, far off in the distance. But in bold relief, a large section of green trees jutted into the black land like a peninsula of life. It covered a conical hill that sprang dramatically from the valley directly below us. Then I saw another striking feature.

"People!" I yelled, pointing at four figures sitting on a fallen tree in the middle of the burn below. They wore the blue hard hats of my crew, and it seemed they looked familiar, but I couldn't tell for sure.

"Maybe it's your rescue team," Gregory said, peering down. "Or maybe it's just some poor fuckers that are as lost as we are."

"Maybe we can catch them!"

"You willing to try? You ain't moving too fast," Gregory said.

"Looks like they're just sitting there, and it's downhill towards them. Maybe they know something," I said.

"Well, I'm glad you are up for a challenge," Gregory noted.

∞

The four hotshots sat on a log strewn across the ashen ground. Jacobson was on the end, covered by shade produced by a standing burned up tree.

"I think I'm ready to move again," Jacobson said.

"Give it more time," Skip said.

The wind whipped up black cinders and created a slight rustle and growl as it blew gently through the moonscape. The men had fallen mostly silent as they had trudged through the burned out scenery—like astronauts on a forgotten planet – too tired and traumatized to think, let alone speak. The only time words were formed was when Skip grunted it was time to rest about every quarter hour. He kept this interval with vigilance to better the chances that Jacobson wouldn't succumb to the rising heat of the oncoming sun.

"They don't do it out of arrogance," Skip said, breaking the silence.

"What?" Marcus asked.

"What Edgar said earlier, about tragedy fires, about the finger pointing everyone does afterwards. It's not arrogance that makes them do it. It's about feeling safe," Skip said.

"Well, being safe is important, of course, learning what you can is good, but...," Edgars responded.

"I didn't say they do it to *be* safe. I said they do it to *feel* safe."

"To feel safe?" Edgar asked.

"Yeah, maybe we are brave, yeah, we are tough, but there isn't one of us that wants to die, not one of us that hasn't been scared of it, or of it happening to those that work with us or that follow our orders.

"So we analyze the past, because, when you look back on a fire, it's so much easier to see what was coming and to believe that certainly we would have done something different, that we would have made sense of the situation in time. We want to believe that we would have been smarter, quicker, that we know fire well enough to not get caught off guard by it.

"And when you look at a tragedy fire, you know what is coming. It's best to believe that since you can see it in hindsight, you would have seen it in foresight. You want to believe you would have kept your wits. You need to believe that. You need to believe that it's easy, that it's simple and knowable and that you'll be fine if you're ever caught in a similar situation. So we look at these tragedies, we rationalize, we even blame, and we do it because it helps us sleep at night; it gives us confidence in the moments when we need it the most. So when you hear about men dying, men you know or have seen, men that do the same thing you do, have the same skill set, you have to find a way to differentiate you from them, a way to know it couldn't happen to you, or to the crew you lead.

"So you make the deal. You buy into the analysis the higher ups give you—the interpretation—that they broke the rules, they broke a fire order, or didn't pay attention to a watch out—even though every one of those is up to interpretation in any situation—you buy into their lack of situational awareness, and you do it so you can get up the next day and go out there and risk it all yourself. So that you think you can get away with it, so that you can make decisions as if there is order in the world—even though like you said, at the heart of it, it is chaotic, like a hurricane or an earthquake, or the strike of lightning. But you have to believe you would know, 'cause so much is really at stake."

He took a pause, as if he was bothered by a thought he didn't know whether he should voice or not.

"I mean," Skip said, "we aren't just talking about dying ... we are talking about burning to death."

The men sat in silence for a few moments, hearing only the breeze over the destroyed land.

"Well, on that note, can we get going?" Jacobson asked.

"Yeah, it's time to get going," Marcus said. He stood up, extended his hand to Skip, who took it, and came to his feet, as did the others, and continued their march through the bone yard of a forest.

Eventually they reached the first living tree of the green finger. The cool air of darkness had robbed the fire of its ferocity the night before, so that it burned only through the underbrush and left the forest canopy intact. They rested in the thick shade it provided and leaned on the sure support of its trunk.

But after a few minutes, they returned to the march and soon were walking up the first slight incline of the conical hill. After a few more minutes, they came to a long ribbon of fire that extended as far as the eye could see on both sides of them. The flames burned sprightly between two and four feet high, causing the tree limbs above to sway gently from the thermal updrafts generated by the combustion. This was the fire's southern boundary.

The men paused in front of it.

"So who's going first?" Jacobson asked.

"Shit, that ain't nothing," Marcus said, and in the same beat charged the flames. He leapt into air as he made contact with the flames, grabbing as much sky as a his large body could muster against gravity. For an instant he appeared to be only a silhouette before disappearing behind the fire.

Evidence of his survival came from the grunts and rustle.

"It's not too bad. Come on through," he said finally.

Skip and Jacobson ran towards the flames almost simultaneously and jumped through without incident, leaving Edgar standing alone. He crouched, as if to run and even started to move his arms, but then froze solid. His heart raced and his hands sweat, and a sudden sense of panic started to make him dizzy. He turned away from the fire and tried to get his composure.

"You coming!?" Skip yelled.

"Yeah, just a second!" He yelled back.

He gripped his hands into a fist and bit down on his knuckles, as a realization hit him: he had become afraid of fire. In fact, he had always been afraid of fire, but he'd always been able to stuff that fear somewhere, and now that place was full.

"Don't fucking doddle! Get to it. It's not that bad," Skip shouted.

Edgar turned back towards the flames, felt an urge to cry or scream or puke—he couldn't tell which. He wanted to turn away, but there was simply no way around it: He had to jump through just like the others.

He felt like a kid at the high dive. He would turn around, build up his courage to charge the obstacle, but the moment he turned and faced it, his bravery withered.

"Are you rubbing one out over there? " Jacobson chided.

And how did he get over his first jump at the high dive, he asked himself. He closed his eyes. And so he closed his eyes once more, turned and faced the heat so obviously beaming on his face, and ran. With each step the temperature became more intense, until it seared into his skin like acid. He leapt into the air, felt the shriek of his skin rupturing from the energy over all exposed skin, then on his legs and genitals, so his body burst into agony. His feet hit the ground, and he jumped again, but some of the thick burning branches still maintained enough integrity that they hindered his forward progress. His flailing arms lashed about wildly to clear a path, and he busted through. The whole process took less than a second.

He got to his feet seizing in pain and stomping the ground with his thick boots as the heavy leather and socks held the heat longer than the fabric of his clothing. He growled in a few spasms until the heat dissipated.

"Fucking worse hot foot fucking ever!" he said angrily, to the men surrounding him.

Marcus put his hand on Edgar's red, slightly burned face. The hair of his long unshaven face came off as ash.

"At least you won't have to shave for a while," Marcus joked.

"Get the fuck off me!" Edgar demanded, and in a fury ripped Marcus's hand away so violently that the larger man fell to the ground.

"Easy," Jacobson said. "It'll grow back. Just next time remember to jump far, not high."

Edgar wiped crinkled hair from his face and felt a blister forming under his chin. The hair on the back of his head was burned too.

Marcus got to his feet without a word. The men recomposed themselves and began to fight their way up the hill through the immensely thick brush.

We followed the tracks in the ash, which led us to the green trees and the base of the conical hill. We reached the ribbon of flame shortly thereafter.

The bushes crackled in protest as the flames danced and devoured them. Strangely, this was the first time I actually examined fire in the forest close up. It didn't seem out of place, but it was certainly dynamic. It made the forest—a place typically associated with serenity—seem particularly vibrant and animated. The woods suddenly became a place not of peace and quiet, but of vigor and activity. The fire was an open symbol conveying the underlying truth of the constant struggle between predator and prey rarely witnessed by the humans who tramp through it. And—while I would not dare say the area it left behind was pretty—by comparing the forest of living trees cleared by fire, and the forest only steps away, which was clogged by underbrush, it was evident that the fire was doing something important.

"Only one way through, my man!" Gregory said. "You're going to have to accept it. Jump through it. Take the pain. Take the suffering."

"Oh, you and your suffering," I said. "We don't live in the dark ages any more, we live in a time of progress, *progress*, and progress will end your beloved suffering!"

"Let's just say for a minute that happens. Let's say your silly European idea of progress is true. What happens to the soul that has no suffering, of the stories it has to tell?"

"What do you mean, stories?" I asked.

"What's the best story in your life, the one that would really captivate almost any one?" Gregory asked.

"I got trapped in a wildfire with a convicted criminal after I received a third degree burn sheltering myself from a forest fire with seventy foot flames," I responded.

"Not that one, mother fucker! Before all this!"

I thought for a moment. "My high school sweetheart, who I dated for two years broke up with me and started dating a guy within one week," I said.

"Exactly," he quipped.

"What do you mean, 'exactly'?

"How often do you tell that story?" he asked.

"Well I guess I don't really. Not anymore at least."

"Yeah, and you shouldn't, 'cause it sure as hell isn't *Moby Dick*."

"Hey! It hurt!" I protested.

"Hey—I bet it did. But it didn't set you apart from anyone else who went through being nineteen. You see, up until yesterday, up until you really had suffering, you had no story. No adversity. No character. So in the end, you think something like late adolescent heartbreak is monumental, because you have nothing else. A life without suffering is a life without story. And story is the very essence of meaning. Even God has one. Even God was betrayed by his own creation. Even God had to give up his only son. Even God had to suffer."

"I guess I'd rather have my shitty little story than yours," I said, shrilly, smarting from the invalidation.

Gregory's face looked like he took a punch, but he recovered just as quick.

"You might have a point there," he said. "But I guess that is exactly what I am trying to warn you of. Get some stories. Don't be afraid of pain. Otherwise you could end up with just one terrible story—like I did. 'Cause I wanted a comfortable easy job, in a comfortable little college, and a cute, comfortable wife. I thought I was smart enough, or lucky enough to get it. Because you see, that was what made me a fool, and that is what makes you weak. Despite all our obvious differences, I was a lot like you."

A breeze blew over us and the flames picked up for a moment. I knew we should jump out of the fire while we still could.

"You see in the end this is all about you. Forget about the grand scale societal bullshit, though I think it's true. I am talking to you as an individual. People have and will try to promise you an end to your suffering. They'll do it in science; they'll do it in politics. They always have, and they always will. This is really just to get you to do what they want you to do. They will sell you on new products, new medicines, new laws, hell even with new tax schemes. Their arguments will always be based on the *theoretical*. But what I am telling you is based on the *empirical*. You have suffered in the past, and you are suffering now. And you will in the future. Always. Stop trying to avoid it. Stop buying into some illusion that promises you a life without it. And stop thinking you are entitled to a life without it. You are not. Be ready. Don't cower from suffering, and don't let avoiding it control you. It will only lead to disaster. Just as the forest evolved from fire, and now must have it, you evolved from suffering and must have it. "

Gregory then crouched as if readying himself to run towards the flames.

"Wait!" I said.

"What?"

"So if all paths lead to suffering, how do I know which one to take?"

Gregory stood back up. "Ha. I guess that is the golden question—and to tell you the truth, I don't know. But my gut tells me something," Gregory said.

"Well, what is it?"

"The path that requires the most courage, for real courage is, by its truest nature, an acceptance of suffering."

With that Gregory charged toward the fire, and with a graceful jump, disappeared behind it.

Now it was my turn. My calf ached at the thought of it. I became afraid. I sweat, and my heart raced.

Finally I mustered and ran towards the fire, felt my heart beating in the destroyed skin of my calf that was so sensitive to the oncoming heat. My legs contracted, leapt, and I sailed through the air. I collided with the vegetation, found myself in a burning web, kept moving forward, and in a moment, I was clear of the fire. I screamed from the heat but was free of the flames.

I danced about, shaking off the pain, and finally settled down. Vegetation surrounded me like dirt to a coffin. I couldn't see more than a few feet ahead as the underbrush was as tall as I was and choked my vision. I called out to Gregory but heard nothing. I probed around as best I could, continued to call out, but heard no response. I was alone.

Chapter Ten

I finally conceded that Gregory had abandoned me, which left me baffled and lonely, but I was too tired to dwell on it. I continued up the hill in hopes of finding the other firefighters. There were no longer footsteps to follow in the underbrush, only the slope, and I assumed up was where they were headed. Since the hill was conical, I would reach them once I climbed it.

But the going was excruciating. The unburned forest was choked with brush that was often over my head, so that I had to bushwhack through it with only my hands. Often my feet wouldn't even touch the ground for stretches of ten feet or more, because it was easier to step from limb to limb. It seemed I was a broken insect stuck in a three-dimensional web of overgrowth.

My health had worsened. Chills of an intense fever racked my muscles, and I constantly stopped for fear that I was about to faint. The sizzling pain in my calf radiated through my every nerve, even into the pulp of my teeth. I shrieked in agony as the branches scraped against my wound with my every step. I looked behind me to see my path marked with blood and pus.

And suddenly the shrubs and vegetation gave way to a clearing that consisted of rows of plants much smaller with no trees overhead. I stood up and examined their uniform growth and form. It was a pot patch.

I couldn't believe my luck. As if the last twenty-four hours hadn't been crazy enough—now here I was in the middle of an illicit drug operation. They were juvenile plants, not yet with buds on them, and just over thigh high. I walked up the row, noticing their green, and obviously well supervised, growth. It was a small patch, about seventy feet wide and long. Probably just small enough to not be identifiable from an airplane, unless it flew particularly low.

And as I approached its end, I heard the sound of grunting. I followed, and soon saw Gregory lying on the ground. There was blood on his leg, bright and obvious, and then I saw a hook through his foot. He'd set off what I thought at the time was an animal trap and was now stuck to it.

"Shit, dude!"

He looked at me, his eyes raging with pain.

"Fuck, so much for my mysterious exit," he said.

"What happened?"

"What does it look like? I hit something, or something hit me," he said.

I crouched down to get a better look at the situation. The large steel hook went completely through his foot so that the barb at the end glistened with red blood and steel.

"I can't pull that out! I don't know what to do!"

"Kid, that fire below is starting to gather. Just head out yourself. I'll figure something out."

"I can't do that! I owe you more than that!"

"What you owe me is getting the hell out of here!"

"Why did you leave?"

"Seemed like the right thing to do."

"The right thing to do?"

"Remember what I said. You can learn now what I did not know when I was young, "

"Really man, I can't do just that."

"That's all you can do. Don't try to overcome all things. Don't try to get around the suffering and sacrifice."

"I have to get you out of this!"

"Then do this kid—go find those folks at the top. Go see if they can help. Cause you sure as hell ain't pulling me off this!"

"Man, I can't just leave you here!"

"Oh yes you can. Easy or hard, you can. And you better. So go do it."

"Maybe I can figure..."

"Hurry!" Gregory demanded.

"Fine! I'll be back!"

I crashed into the dense vegetation at the end of the patch, charged through with as much vigor as I could muster. But the trembling in my arms was growing so strong that just reaching for branches to push or pull through became close to impossible. My peripheral vision began to fade into a yellow fog, and the weakness in my body made my lungs seem incapable of expanding.

After about thirty or forty feet of tromping and crashing through limbs, a particularly stubborn branch I was pushing on slipped from my hand and struck me in the forehead, knocking me out. In the haze of white, purple, and red blotches that burst on the screen of my closed eyelids, I saw a vision of my own body. The black crow again emerged from my calf, squawking and flapping its wings furiously trying to release itself. The pain was unbelievable, but it was not coming from my body; rather, from the crow's. The bird paused for a moment as it gathered its strength. Then in one single, graceful, and uniquely horrifying moment, the bird flapped its wings and snapped off its own leg in order to free itself from the now lifeless body. The crow swooped into the air, its torso looking like that of a man's.

The vision startled me awake. I straightened myself out of the contorted position I was in and continued the effort up the hill. And then I heard the sound of a chainsaw. It was close.

After thirty more steps, the light of the horizon opened up. I yelled out to the men I believed might be up there as I pushed myself into the clearing. I came crashing through one last thick brush and landed on the hard ground of a clear cut.

"What the fuck is that?" Edgar yelled to Jacobson as he saw me land in the clearing with a thud. The two of them ran towards me.

"It's detailer!" Jacobson blurted. The men waved to Skip to cut the saw and come over, which he did. They reached me and picked me up onto my feet.

"He looks like a fucking dying vampire," Edgar said.

"You there buddy?" Jacobson asked, looking into my vacuous eyes. I came to just as Skip approached.

"He made it! He's still here!" he barked excitedly. "He looks like shit."

"You guys ever going to stop putting me down?" I muttered.   Then I remembered my purpose. "There's a guy down there. He's stuck in a trap or something. You got to get him. The fire is about on him!"

"Huh? Who? And why aren't you with the crew?"

"He was with the con crew. He saved me—several times. You guys have got to get him. You can't let him burn down there!"

And just as my words were finished came the beat of steel blades pulsing through the air, louder and louder.

"That's our bird!" Jacobson said.

Skip ran over towards the center of the clearing and jumped up on the stump of a tree. The others followed him, propping me up and taking me along.

"That's it! That's the helicopter," Skip said.

"We can't leave!" I protested. "You have to go get him!"

Skip peered out and spotted a white helicopter moving south of the clearing. From its belly hung a black cord, and at the end of the cord was a black box.

"Oh shit!" he said. A terrible possibility suddenly bolted through Skip's mind.

"What? Is it our bird?" Edgar asked.

"Get me a flare, hurry!"

"What!"

"Do it!"

Jacobson lit a flare and handed it to Skip, who waved it through the air as vigorously as he could in hopes of signaling the pilot.

"Is it our bird? What's going on?" Jacobson demanded.

"It's a bird, but I get the feeling it's not *our* bird," Skip said. And then the terrifying possibility became a reality.

From the black box dropped a long, slender stream of fire. The flaming gelatinous substance, similar to napalm, clung to the trees and the shrubs it fell upon, immediately setting them ablaze, leaving a thin but growing orange band on them.

He waved his hands and the flare, yelling "Stop!" over and over, but to no avail. The helicopter moved east, repeating the process.

Of course, he thought, castigating himself. They are going to torch the green finger out, not line it. It was a process to save labor—it would take far fewer man-hours to simply sacrifice, or "cut off," the green finger that extended into the burn and build a line connecting the turns on both sides of it.

"What's happening?" Edgar demanded.

"They're pissing fire all over us. They're burning out the green finger."

"They're terra torching the place?" Marcus asked.

"Yes," Skip said. The situation was clear to him now. There would be fire on both sides and no way to run.

"Fuck! Do they see you?" Edgar asked.

"I fucking wish they would," Skip said in heavy breath, motioning Jacobson to give him another flare. He started to wave both around spastically

Eventually the helicopter seemed to note the signal and moved off, flying out of site, but not until three strips of fire had been laid, all of which were growing. Seeing the aircraft disappear into the air, Skip couldn't help but consider that the same thing had just happened to their whole plan and their chances for survival.

He jumped down from the stump and threw the flares onto the dirt in frustration. "I guess he finally saw me, I think..."

"What in the fuck are they doing?" Edgar demanded.

"This green finger extends almost a half mile into the fire." Skip said, "Incident Command and Operations figures it's better to burn it out, rather than line the whole thing. They don't expect us this far in the black, so it makes sense—to them."

"Yeah, to them, maybe," Edgar said.

"Looks like we're back inside. Fuck!" Marcus grumbled

"What about Gregory?" I asked.

"Who?" Skip asked.

"The guy I told you about. You have to save him!"

"Skip, we got fire closing in on both sides of us, north and south," Marcus said.

"We could run west," Edgar suggested. "Try to beat the trap door."

"We'd have to run through all that fucking brush," Marcus said, "You remember how hard it was coming up here. Who knows if we'd make it—plus we'd lose sight of the fire. At least here we can see what it's doing. We're going to have to fight our way out of here."

"What about Gregory?" I insisted.

"I'll go down and try to find him," Edgar offered.

"You'll need two people to help get him," I said.

"We can't spare it," Marcus said. "We need to start building a buffer around this clearing right now, remove the fuel, make it clean as possible. It'll take everyone."

"Go down Edgar, see what you find, and try and take a close-up look at the fire coming up from that side. See what it's doing if you can," Skip said.

I followed Edgar to the edge of the clearing and told him about the pot patch, and that he could most likely follow the path of tromped-on bushes and blood to find it.

"Perfect, and if that doesn't work I'll just follow the smell of burning weed," he said sardonically. With that he disappeared into the woods.

I then swooned and fell on my butt. The men surrounded me, dragged me to a stump, leaned me against it, and fed me some water.

"So what's the plan, Skip?" Marcus asked as the men surrounded me.

"First off, let's finishing clearing some of these smaller trees, so the helicopter can land if it comes back. I'm not sure if it saw us or not, but if it did, it might come back and get us or send another one out. That's our best hope.

"Marcus, you help me with that. Jacobson, go into the center there and find us an area you can clear of vegetation as best you can. Try to make it at least thirty feet wide—but the bigger the better. Then make us six divots about a foot deep if you can, one for each of us to lay in. You'll have to use the hand tools. I'll use the saw to clear some of the brush and trees."

With that Skip fired up the saw and started bucking a fallen tree nearby. Jacobson grabbed a Pulaski and went to work finding an opportune area to clear, one that would be relatively in the center and which already had few shrubs to remove.

And I sat on a log—lame, only able to drink water, watch the men work, and wallow in my own impotence. But after about twenty minutes of rest, some small reserve of strength returned. Coupled with the aggravation of worthlessness, it drove me to find a Pulaski and join Jacobson in the attempt to make a safety zone by scrapping out the shrubs that grow in the disturbed and compacted soil of a former logging operation. Jacobson saw me and asked if I could handle it—I said it was better than sitting while the others worked.

"Just might make a firefighter out of you yet, Taylor," he said.

311

Slowly, I swung at the small trunks of the shrubs and moved them out of our zone. I did barely one-fourth of what Jacobson was doing, and after every swing I felt my knees buckle and my head float and spin. But I continued until I heard once again the sweet sound I'd hoped for time and time again— the helicopter, and this time it was coming in close.

Skip waved at us to move off, and he started to guide the helicopter down on the path. Dust kicked high into our eyes and ears, and the thunder of the blades pummeled the atmosphere and my ear drums.

Edgar looked down at the bloody hook on the ground next to the patch of plants. He picked it up, examined the shreds of skin on it, then looked down the trail of blood leading off into the forest. He turned his attention to the fire noticing that the smoke boiled from the trees one hundred yards or so below him, and orange streaks of light occasionally dazzled through the trees. The fire was gathering steam.

He walked a few feet in the direction of the trail of blood and yelled out, "Hello?" Then he heard the hot sizzle and airy howl of a large conifer starting to torch up in flames, and turned to see the top of an old growth tree being overwhelmed by flames some one hundred yards below him on the hillside.

"Fuck!" Then he heard an even more disturbing sound—the thud of a helicopter coming in above. Realizing that it was landing on the clearing to pick up the men, he was overcome with the fear of being left behind. He ditched the trail and started back up the hill at once with push and pull, battling through the growth with all his might.

For three desperate minutes he scrambled through the vines and limbs, practically kicking and scratching to open up the way for his mad dash. His skin was quickly soaked with perspiration and his breath heaved in agony. His desperation came to a crescendo as he heard the engine rev up for takeoff.

"No! No!" he shouted out to the air, in anguish. His powerful emotion collapsed into resignation when he heard the engine slowly become faint and distant. He looked up through the trees to see the helicopter flying away, believing he was likely alone on the hill. He put his hand over his face to hide the emotion from his own solitude.

But after a few minutes he concluded there was nothing to do but to keep trudging forward and muster up some sense of hope that either another helicopter was on the way, or perhaps they had accounted for his well being in some other way.

Or maybe he was just left behind. Still, what else was there to do? Inactivity was suicide.

∞

"Get your asses in here!" the helicopter pilot demanded to the three men outside the passenger door. "This thing is taking off!"

"We got a man on his way. We have to wait," Skip said.

"Fuck that! I'm short of fuel, and not me or nobody else is going to try to land in this spot again. I'm the only show in town, anyway," the ornery man in his late fifties said. Like many helicopter pilots, he likely gained his expertise in the military and probably in combat. His ego and anger were only outmatched by his hard-won talents. It was known by all smokejumpers and hotshots that if there was one guy not to second guess, it was a helicopter pilot.

"We can't fucking leave Edgar here. No way!" Marcus demanded.

Just one minute ago Skip had been happily absorbed with bucking up a downed tree. There was an unusual bind in the trunk, which demanded much of his skill and knowledge, but like a puzzle, could clearly be resolved. Now he was faced with a decision that was much more nebulous. Save the men he could at the certain cost of one, or put everyone in jeopardy in hopes of saving them all? The small amount of leadership he had resumed since leaving the house was awkward and tentative. Now he felt like a man on a plank. Each step, each thought, each word to the other men had to be measured and confident, firm, even creative—and still it would most likely end in some loss.

"Look gentlemen," said the pilot. "If you want out of here, I'm it. I don't have time to fuck around. If that thing crowns, which it sure as hell could, you're getting fucking cooked. You want that risk? Fine. Then let me fucking know so I can get the fuck out of here, 'cause I fucking don't!"

"We have a man down there, sir!" Skip exclaimed with matched force of will.

The pilot looked exasperated, as if he wanted to spank the foreman and force him into the aircraft. But his expression softened into resignation as the pilot realized that he wasn't dealing with a boy whose head was filled with dreams of heroics, but a man whose virtue and resolve was being tested to the limit for an undisputable cause.

"I've got a Chung gun in the back and some flares, take 'em. You're going to fucking need 'em," the pilot said, with a meager ounce of empathy.

Skip reached in the back and grabbed the long, tubular apparatus and its companion tank of compressed air, then grabbed a large box of flares.

Jacobson grabbed Skip by the shoulder and shouted in his ear. "The detailer, he might as well go. He looks like shit and he's about to go tits up. He needs a hospital ASAP,"

Skip nodded. "Wait a minute! I have one man who'll go with you."

"Hurry!" the pilot demanded.

∞

The three men rushed towards me, waving for me to come towards them. I met them halfway to the helicopter.

"All right man, you're getting out of here," Skip said.

"What about Edgar – and Gregory?" I asked.

"We're going to stay behind for them and hope to hell we can fight this thing out," Skip said.

I started to follow the command and walk towards the helicopter with the men, somewhat dumbfounded, then aggravated. Here was the moment I had been waiting for, and it felt like defeat. A searing energy in the pit of my stomach suddenly turned to hot steel, and I stopped.

"No. I'm staying here," I stated with the clearest resolve I've had in my life.

"Don't be stupid. You're sick and injured. You're of little use at all," Skip said.

"Little use is better than no use. I can still do something," I said firmly.

"We don't have time to argue," Skip said.

"Then let's not."

Skip peered at me with the poker face of a professional gambler. Finally he turned towards the pilot, who threw his hands up and gestured towards his gas gauge. Skip gestured back, *Go on*. The pilot threw his hands into the air again, and shook his head as if to show exasperation for all human stupidity. He geared up his aircraft and lifted off the ground.

"I hope you know what the fuck you got yourself into," Skip said to me.

"Well, I guess were all in now," Jacobson said.

"Good! I'm sick of running from this fucking fire anyway," Marcus said.

Skip climbed back up the stump, looking down on the southern section of fire, which was now torching through an occasional tree as it headed towards them. He turned towards us.

"Jacobson, you and the Taylor keep building that area. Marcus, you and I will start thinning around the edge of the clear cut. Not the big trees, just the largest underbrush that's most likely to let the flames ladder up into the canopy. We'll do the best we can, but soon we are going to have to stop and start laying fire down. We'll try to get a buffer of black along the edge, before the flames hit. As long as it's not fully engaged in the crown when it reaches us, we can probable deny it enough fuel to keep the heat bearable."

Jacobson and I continued building the space as directed. He handed me a shovel and told me to work on the divots while he cleared the shrubs and blackberries. I threw the blade at the compacted soil, wanting to puke and pass out with every thrust, trying to ignore the sneaking suspicion that I was digging my own grave.

Skip went after only the largest brushes and he did it fast, making snap judgments as to whether one would stay or one would go and running from chosen bush to chosen bush. He would plow his blade into them with the precision of a robot, cut them into pieces, and Marcus would then scatter those pieces into the clearing. Each time he made sure not to group them together so as to not make a "jackpot"—a mound or group of woody materials that could generate intense heat, sending out embers that could cause spot fires and radiating such high temperatures that other fuel would burn around it, causing a chain reaction of sorts.

When Skip had circled half the clearing, cutting only the underbrush that might be the most obvious of problems for sending flames into the canopy during their backburn, he returned to the stump that served as his perch. To the south, the fire was well on its way to them. Individual old-growth trees were overwhelmed in flames, and he had no doubt that a full crown fire would form as the fire hit the steeper incline of the conical hill.

To the north, Skip could not see as well. The trees at the perimeter of the clearing were too close and too tall to give him much of a view, but he could see an obvious increase in the amount and viscosity of the smoke that came somewhere behind them. It was clear the fire was coming—but how far, how fast, and how big, he could only guess.

Either way, it was time to start burning. But where the fuck was Edgar? Skip jumped down from the stump, grabbed the two drip torches and ran to where Marcus was swamping the last of his own cut.

"Time to get to it. Where is Edgar?" Skip said, handing Marcus a drip torch.

"I don't know, but we can't start the burn, or he'll get trapped by it," Marcus said.

"Fuck. Well, start on the south."

"No fucking need for that!" Edgar said as he burst into the clearing, filled with obvious joy that the men were still there.

They slapped hands to the reunion.

"So what'd you find?" Skip asked.

"A bloody hook, but no man. I saw his trail, but only followed it for a minute before I heard the helicopter. Figured you guys were leaving me here to cook. Almost gave up on it all—then I heard your saw, and I knew you were still here."

"No way, man. We wouldn't leave you," Marcus said.

"Did you see what the fire is doing?" Skip asked.

"It doesn't look good," Edgar said. "It's starting to torch. I won't be surprised if it fully engages the canopy soon."

"The sun is starting to dip. It'll be dark before too long. Might bring it down," Marcus said.

"Well from what I saw, it was only getting more active. Doesn't feel like the humidity is going up either," Edgar said.

"Yeah, I got that same feeling. In fact, something in my gut tells me it's going down," Skip said.

After a heavy, silent moment, he bellowed, "Well, we're here to burn! One way or the other, God damn it! Let's get to it." He handed the drip torch to Edgar and gave the men their orders. "Here's the plan. I'm going to go keep cutting. You guys start laying fire. Now, keep it low. Don't drop too much down at all. Keep it light. We just want to burn up some of the undergrowth and hope to God that thing doesn't come at us with full steam. Take your time. I'm going to saw for a bit and see if I can get some more of this shit out of here, too. When I signal, drop your torches and come to the space that Jacobson and the detailer are clearing out. That's where we're going to hunker down and pray. "

"Work Hard, Pray Hard? That's the plan?" Edgar asked.

"Don't get biblical yet. We have a chance," Skip said.

Skip marched off towards the clearing that Jacobson and I were preparing.

"All right Edgar," Marcus said. "Skip said to keep it small. We put too much down, it'll head right into the crown and we'll get crisped by our own burnout."

"You don't have to tell me twice," Edgar said. He pulled out his pocket lighter and lit the torch. His hand was shaking so badly he spilled the diesel and gas mix over his glove while turning the torch downward to prime the wick while flicking the lighter. The flame immediately clung to his glove as well as the wick. He whipped his flaming hand through the air, cussing, and patted it out on his pants.

"Keep it cool, Edgar. It's going to be all right. It could just come at us in a series of stringers that won't blast us with too much heat," Marcus said.

"It's sweet of you to be so optimistic. I don't think I've ever seen such a sweet side of you before, Marcus," Edgar said, with a rattled voice. He took off his hot glove to expose a red hand that had small pockets of white dead skin already rising into blisters. He couldn't help but wonder if soon his whole body would look like that, or worse.

"Yeah, keep it to yourself. Now let's do it," Marcus said, lighting his own torch.

"Let's give it hell!" Edgar said with contrived bravado. The two men raised their lit drip torches and clanked them together in a toast. Then they started to burn.

∞

"What's the word?" Jacobson asked as Skip approached us.

"Looks like it's lightening up on both sides," Skip said. "We're starting the burn now."

"Where's Gregory?" I asked.

"No word. He wasn't there. Edgar said he found a bloody hook, that's it. Look, you got enough to worry about, so stay focused. And make sure to neatly place the dirt by the divots. We're going to want to push it over us as best we can once we lie down," Skip said, and with that he turned to pick up his saw.

"So, *I am* digging my own grave..."

"Look on the bright side, kid," Jacobson said.

"What's that?"

"You'll get both buried and cremated. All at once. And for no expense to your family."

"I know a deal when I see it," I said, and struck blade to ground.

Skip grabbed the saw and continued to cut brush on the north side of the clearing, swamping his cut as he went. The feel of the saw was sweet and empowering, and something about the sensation of the blade running through bark gave him momentary ease. But he couldn't help sense he was engaging in a minimally helpful activity at best, and a guilty pleasure at worst. Maybe he should be watching the fire for signs of changes, but what good would that do? They were stuck with only one strategy. Perhaps he could throw flares and help more directly with the burn, but he wanted to keep the burnout small, and two people were enough for that. Maybe he should just watch and supervise, but again, that struck him as nothing at all. So he stuck with what he knew, and kept sawing.

Edgar watched the small beads of burning gas fall on the leaves of salal, ivy, and vine maple. The first hint of sundown made the burning gas particularly colorful. The small drops of blue and yellow fell like seeds and bloomed into incandescent orange flowers that devoured the shrubs as their petals grew at dazzling speed. But the beauty filled him with unease. While most hotshots find burning out to be the acme of firefighting, Edgar had never been fond of it—and now, with this newfound phobia of fire, he found it unnerving. He could not help but grit his teeth at the sight of the fire around him that spread by his own doing.

He conceived a mental trick to ease his anxiety by pretending that the bushes represented all of the fear built up over the last day. He cast the fire down on the shrubs, making believe they were the pain, fear, frustration, and loss of the last two days—the men running down the spine, the hot anguish of the shelter, the sight of Steve during the moment of horrific realization. He tried to take delight in how the leaves crackled and shriveled to nothing, as if they were these events.

The idea took hold, and soon his whole history was involved: ex-girlfriends, unrequited love, demeaning teachers, school bullies, even his parents' divorce were all represented in the woody material in front of him, which he would now incinerate in effigy. He started to speed walk through the forest, and the strength he found from the idea soon turned to a rampage. He whipped the drip torch nozzle through the air, ruthlessly sending out shotgun sprays of lambent fuel. The power rushed through him, and his pursuit of the burn became impassioned and wild.

But his mania was cut short by a hissing yet vacuous roar, the signature sound of a mature tree torching into flames He looked behind him to see his backburn had gotten far too intense. It had moved into a series of large bushes and set a seventy-foot Douglas fir ablaze.

"Oh fuck," he muttered.

The infusion of light and heat dazzling in the dusk air immediately caught Skip's attention. He turned and looked at the torching tree and the backfire that led right to Edgar. Skip cut his saw and started to march at Edgar, waving at him to stop and yelling curse words the whole way. Skip stomped to his stump perch, climbed up, and received more bad news.

The fire to the south had now formed a blazing wall of seventy-foot flames that screamed through the canopy and moved rapidly up the conical hill towards them. And while he could not see well to the north, he could tell by the large column of smoke that glowed orange, it was just as ferocious. The two would likely hit the top at the same time, as the gigantic fires would battle each other for oxygen, creating their own wind and sucking both flame fronts together. This would spray radiant heat of two thousand degrees all over the clearing. Such intensity would ignite the few thin shrubs and brush that grew in the compacted soil of the clear-cut. The place would turn into an inferno that no living thing could survive. Even if with luck the two waves of fire hit the clearing at different times, Edgar's fire would negate the possibility of moving from one side to the other. They were doomed. And the one shred of hope, the one fighting chance they might have had was lost because of his lack of supervision, because of his incompetence, because his subordinates did not follow his orders.

The thought electrified his mind with rage and he charged off the stump, intending to punch Edgar right in the face. But the overwhelming anger pulsing through every cell also jarred dormant neurons into action. As he walked towards Edgar, shoving his finger angrily towards the torching tree, he noticed something and stopped in his tracks.

The flames of the torching tree were not standing straight up, but rather leaning heavily to the north—towards the approaching fire on that side of the hill. A vision suddenly struck him. From a bird's-eye view he saw the conical hill, surrounded by a ring of fire moving up it—but he also saw another ring, one that as yet did not exist, that was inside of the outer fire, on top of the hill. This ring on top of the hill did not move towards the clearing, as this was where it began, but away from it, downhill, towards the outer ring that was closing in on it.

Yes! That is it! Skip realized. The key was to get the backfire into a roaring storm of its own, so that it would begin to create its own demand for oxygen, its own wind. Then the two fronts would suck themselves towards each other as they fought for oxygen. They would in effect slam into each other, somewhere close to halfway down the hill, safely away from the firefighters. It was desperate, but it was possible.

He gestured and yelled at Edgar to keep going. Then he ran to Jacobson, who was still improving the safety zone.

"Jacobson!" he yelled at a run. "Grab the Chun gun and the flares and come with me." He got to the clearing as Jacobson turned his attention to him, looking for an explanation. Skip hollered, "Come on, we got to move! Now!"

"Want me to come?" I asked.

"No, you stay here and finish those divots! We're going to need them!" He ran off with Jacobson in tow.

Skip and Jacobson loaded the Chun gun, a device that consists of a long tube connected to a chamber and a compressed air tank, which it uses to shoot flares a long way and in rapid succession. He strapped the tank to Jacobson's back while Jacobson took hold of the long tube.

"We need to let this thing rip! I want you to get this south side ablaze. Fire as much and as many as you can into the underbrush. Get it going!" Skip said.

"But what the hell?"

"Just do it!" Skip stuffed a handful of flares into his own pocket. He ran through the oncoming blue of twilight, which was tinged with the orange glow of fire as embers now started to drift downward on the clearing.

∞

Skip reached Edgar in a moment.

"Look, I'm sorry, I lost—"

"Fuck that! Keep it going; let it burn. Big as possible—go! Throw it down like a madman! Go! Go!" Skip yelled, raising his hands as if to raise the fire, like a raving maestro presenting the crescendo of his final orchestra.

He then ran to Marcus and commanded him to do the same thing. Marcus looked surprised at first, but then intuited the new grand strategy. The firefight was on in earnest.

The Chun gun spit orange flares in a series of four, like a machine gun. Flares streaked through the air with a brimming glow, battling the descending darkness and setting all they touched ablaze. Pockets of fire began to rage, bathing us all in heat and light. The men's battle cries pierced the air.

Edgar continued to use his newfound mental trick. He pictured the vegetation not only to be people from his past but entire scenes and circumstances, such as the first time he asked a girl to a junior high dance.

"You! I wouldn't go with you!" she scoffed as she ran away laughing. That one was a vine maple, now drenched in fuel and fire.

The time he gave a class presentation in eighth grade with his fly down—that was a downed alder now crackling in fire and shrieking as his burn devoured it.

Then he decided to burn an entire fifteen-foot patch to junior high in effigy—all of it put up in smoke and consumed with the cleansing energy of his fire. If he wasn't going to make it out alive, then neither would his bad memories. He finally turned and looked at his work. Anywhere he had stepped was now asunder in flame. He was struck with a thought: perhaps a difficult childhood was not solely a source of burden, but also of muscle.

I managed to continue, one dig, one throw of the shovel at a time. Often a spell of dizziness would overcome me and my body would lurch in a dry heave. All muscles would threaten to slack, and I felt consciousness waiver. But the wave would pass, and I would continue. Occasionally I would look up to breathe and witness the battle around me, somewhat amazed that the possible last scene of my life was so dynamic.

Finally I finished the divots, each with the dirt I had dug neatly piled beside them. I took one last look at the massive blaze now surrounding me and the burning gas and flares flying around to make the conflagration. Then I laid myself down, and with a final, heavy breath, I prepared to die.

Skip tossed his last fuzzie into the forest as he met Edgar on the western edge of the clearing. The heat was already unbearable, but the fire still had plenty of fuel to continue to feed. About one third of the large trees were now torching, and almost all the underbrush adjacent to the clear-cut was fully engaged.

"Let's get to the safety zone!" he ordered, then bolted around to the others and gave them the same command.

They arrived in a group and found me only barely conscious.

"He finished them all, in the state he was in," Edgar said.

"Whoa, that's..." Jacobson started with hesitation.

"That's *thick*," Marcus said.

Did they just say that? I was thick!

The men jumped in their pits. Skip went around throwing the dirt on us as protection from the intense radiant heat, which already pierced our skin like needles. The fire continued to rage, and we squirmed, moving the fabric of our shirts to keep specific hot contact points from causing too much damage. The heat still seared through our clothes, maddened vibrations of infrared fervor bursting the cell walls of our skin. We groaned to vent the agony as our own fire raged down heat upon us.

But slowly a distinct change occurred in the resonance and roar of the fire—it became hollow, distant, and the intensity of the heat began to dissipate. Skip looked up and saw the flames moving downhill. The plan was working!

"It's working! It's working! It's going to work!" he yelled.

After twenty minutes the men could bear to get out of their divots and watch the flames below the hill combine. They began to laugh, dance, hoot, and pound their chests.

I could not even stand, but somehow, in that moment I knew we had pulled it off, that we had won and that I was a part of it. My soul began to fly. I felt pushed into the stratosphere with the euphoria of victory, of a hard battle long fought and finally won. It felt for one second that the stars were mine, that I was finally someone—a man, a warrior, a king. Glory passed like a breeze; infirmity and fever overtook me in the next instant. My body sunk into the earth, and I seemed to disappear into the ground around me.

∞

But I did awaken—to the sound of a helicopter beating above me. The earliest rays of dawn had arrived, and we were all alive to see it. Everyone was red from burns, even blisters on the back of our necks, and Marcus on his arms from wearing only a crew t-shirt.

The aircraft landed and the men put me on it with Jacobson. Apparently they only had room and fuel for two. The others would have to walk. The pilot dropped off some water for them, and a box of MREs. He also gave them a direction to find a road and vehicles that would be shuttling men in for the next day's attempt. Skip told them about Gregory and about Steve, and asked the pilot to relay the information to incident command. Then we lifted off, leaving the men behind.

∞

"Well, what now?" Edgar asked, seeing the helicopter ascend into the sky.

"Let's break into those boxes of food," Skip said. "Then we'll head towards the road the pilot told us about."

The men walked to the box of MRE.

"Blind grab?" Marcus said.

"Fair enough," said Edgar, closing his eyes and taking out the first brown package his hand came to. He opened his eyes and read the label.

"Ham Slice," he said with disgust.

"Sucks to be you," said Marcus, who went through the same ritual.

"Ham Slice," Marcus said dryly.

Skip then followed and came up with the same result.

"What the fuck!" Edgar demanded, and started rummaging through the box. "They're all fucking Ham Slice!" he said in disdain as he looked at the packaging.

Marcus shrugged and opened the package, which was filled with even smaller packages, the largest of which was the entre that gave it its name. He ripped that open also and watched the milky slime, made to preserve and flavor the ten year old meat, run over his gloves and expose the pork.

"Just proves that the old school is still living," he said, with a rare hint of satisfaction. He took a bit of the grayish pink meat, chewed it and then remarked, "Not bad, either, if you got no choice."

"Guess you're right," Skip said, as he opened his package and also took a bite. "Let's eat and drink and get moving."

∞

As the helicopter reached its flying altitude, I awoke. My leg was so infected, I would be surprised if it could be saved by even the best burn doctor. It bothered me, but at the same time I knew that a fundamental change would occur with the loss. Something that would make me stronger, fuller, and wiser as I entered into adulthood. My capacity to despair and persevere had both been proven and strengthened—perhaps galvanized is the word for it.

I looked out the window at the tortured forest below and thought of the man who had guided me through this most difficult lesson. Gregory had made it; I knew it somehow in my gut. His tough, tortured, bleeding, wise soul had somehow managed to set himself free—free from his past, from the hook, from the fire. At that moment he was in immense pain, but alive and fighting, struggling, suffering, surviving. He accepted that it was simply his plight, and one that he would become strong enough to live with, persevere through. Until the last beat of his heart, he would now be free and live under that animal law—that law, and no other.

Farther out, the fire was now marching wildly south, with flames that reached well above the tallest trees. In the path of the fire was a suburb of Vancouver, where people invariably fretted over the daily concerns of traffic, work, clean houses, and new cars. A world in which the most pressing problems are adolescent acne, obesity, diabetes, and ageing—and other issues which manifest from "too much good stuff." And now comes the fire, which certainly they feel entitled to be spared from, which they demand to be spared from. But their demands are just denial—denial of the pain that is embedded in us all, and always will be. With the fire comes a brutal lesson that a society so placated would be outraged to learn, but would learn all the same.

Afterword

I fought to save my lower leg, but the doctors finally deemed it was time to remove it or the infection would likely spread above the knee. This could result in me loosing the joint and limiting my mobility even more. They cut off my foot and sliced away my calf. This condition caused me much grief, as one might imagine. Indeed during my twenties I encountered a decent amount of ostracizing from my more able bodied peers, and the joy of women's company was harder to come by. However, I took to heart certain things I learned from my short-time companion and the experience in general. I kept myself in shape, worked, and sweat to overcome my inability and strived not to fall into the trap of self pity by understanding that the suffering I incurred now, was at its heart, natural, and perhaps needed.

Strangely, because of this, at the time of this writing, now that I am in my forties, I find myself much more able than many my age. With the help of prosthetics and regular exercise, I find I am able to run faster than most of my sedentary peers and am generally more fit. Sometimes I even show up the hefty mechanics that put together the water slides at the family fun park where I now work as an engineer.

The hotshots I struggled with all returned to fire and finished the season on their respected crew. Skip continued fighting with hotshots until he was thirty five and now is a fire manager at a park. Joe Jacobson eventually got a desk job with the California

Department of Fire and is still married to his wife. Edgar fought fire for another two years before going to law school and now maintains a thriving practice in San Francisco. Marcus stayed on the fire line until last year, when he became eligible for twenty year retirement.

Gregory's body was never found. He was presumed dead. He received a pardon from the Governor of Washington, along with all the other fallen convict firefighters. However, I doubt to my core that he was lost during the fire. I'd like to believe he is on some beach in Mexico, enjoying himself, but it is just as likely, in fact far more likely, that he is working as a dishwasher somewhere completely off the radar, trying to "accept the suffering" of life, like he so desperately tried to teach me. Perhaps somehow he has managed to get both. After all, oases are only found in deserts.

This is a self published work, currently available only on the Amazon platform. Any honest review would be sincerely appreciated.

Bill Morris spent three seasons on the fire line, his last of which was with the Arrowhead Hotshots. He currently lives in Portland, Oregon, where he teaches history at a nearby community college. He enjoys gardening. This is his first novel.

Join in the discussion of *Inside The Fire* at:

Insidethefire.net

facebook.com/groups/insidethefirenovel